SIDEWINDERS: TEXAS BLOODSHED

SIDEWINDERS: TEXAS BLOODSHED

William W. Johnstone
with J. A. Johnstone

PINNACLE BOOKS
Kensington Publishing Corp.
www.kensingtonbooks.com

PINNACLE BOOKS are published by

Kensington Publishing Corp.
119 West 40th Street
New York, NY 10018

PUBLISHER'S NOTE
Following the death of William W. Johnstone, the Johnstone family is working with a carefully selected writer to organize and complete Mr. Johnstone's outlines and many unfinished manuscripts to create additional novels in all of his series like The Last Gunfighter, Mountain Man, and Eagles, among others. This novel was inspired by Mr. Johnstone's superb storytelling.

ISBN-13: 978-0-7860-2806-1
ISBN-10: 0-7860-2806-8

First printing: June 2012

10 9 8 7 6 5 4 3 2 1

Printed in the United States of America

Do not search for trouble,
lest it find you.
—Ling Yuan

We don't go lookin' for trouble—
It's usually there when we
wake up in the morning.
—Scratch Morton

CHAPTER 1

Scratch Morton peered up at the gallows and said, "I'd just as soon go somewheres else, Bo. This place surely does give me the fantods."

"You don't have anything to worry about," Bo Creel told his old friend, "if you haven't done anything to give Judge Parker cause to order you hanged."

Scratch frowned and shook his head. "I dunno. They don't call that fella the Hangin' Judge for no reason. He can come up with cause if he wants to."

Bo laughed and said, "Come on. We don't have any business with the judge, hanging or otherwise."

The gallows they'd been looking at was no ordinary affair. It stood off to one side of the big, red-brick federal courthouse in Fort Smith, Arkansas, and had eight trapdoors built into it. When huge crowds gathered on the broad courthouse lawn to watch convicted criminals put to death, it was quite a spectacle at times. It wasn't that unusual to see eight men kicking out their lives at once at the end of those hang ropes.

As Scratch had said, Judge Isaac Parker wasn't known as the Hanging Judge for no reason.

The Texans continued strolling past the courthouse. It was a crisp, cold, late winter day, and large white clouds floated in the deep blue sky above Fort Smith. Off to their right, bluffs dropped steeply to the Arkansas River where it curved past the city, forming the border between Arkansas and Indian Territory.

Bo and Scratch had been to Fort Smith before—they had been almost everywhere west of the Mississippi in their decades of wandering—but it had been a while, and after stabling their horses, they had decided to stroll around town and have a look at the place to see how much it had changed.

They probably should have started somewhere besides the courthouse and its adjacent gallows, Bo mused. His old friend Scratch was generally a law-abiding sort, as was Bo himself, but they had wound up on the wrong side of iron bars a few times in their adventurous lives, albeit briefly and usually because of some sort of mistake.

Both men were about the same height. Age had turned Scratch's hair pure silver and put streaks of gray in Bo's dark brown hair, but the years hadn't bent their rugged bodies. Bo was dressed in a sober black suit and hat that made him look a little like a hellfire-and-brimstone preacher, while Scratch was the dandy of the pair in high-topped boots, whipcord trousers, a fringed buckskin jacket over a white shirt, and a cream-colored Stetson with a fancy band.

Scratch's fondness for the flashy extended to his

guns, a pair of long-barreled, ivory-handled Remington revolvers that rode comfortably in cut-down holsters. Bo, on the other hand, as befitted the conservative nature of the rest of his attire, carried a single Colt .45 with plain walnut grips.

The similarity between them was that both Texans were fast on the draw and deadly accurate with their shots when they had to be, although they preferred to avoid trouble if that was at all possible.

Trouble usually had other ideas where they were concerned, though.

In fact, one ruckus or another had been dogging their heels ever since they had met as boys in Texas, during the infamous Runaway Scrape when the Mexican dictator Santa Anna and his army chased the rebellious Texicans almost clear to Louisiana. However, General Sam Houston had known what he was doing all along, and when the time finally came to make a stand, the Texicans lit into Santa Anna's men in the grassy, bayou-bordered fields near San Jacinto and won independence for their land and people.

Despite their youth at the time, Bo and Scratch had been smack-dab in the middle of that epic battle, and each had saved the other's life that day. That was the first time, but hardly the last.

They probably would have been fast friends for life anyway, even if they had settled down to lives as farmers and ranchers as they had intended. But Fate, in the form of a fever, had come along and taken Bo's wife and children from him after several years of that peaceful existence, and rather than stay where those bitter memories would have haunted him, he rode away and set out on the drift.

He hadn't gone alone. Scratch had ridden with him, and the two of them had seldom been apart for very long since. They had wandered all over the frontier, taking jobs as ranch hands or shotgun guards or scouts when they needed to. Bo was a more than fair hand with a deck of cards and kept money in their pockets most of the time just by sitting in a poker game now and then. His preacherlike appearance didn't hurt. Because of it, folks tended to underestimate his poker-playing ability.

As they passed some steps leading down to the courthouse basement, Scratch shivered, but not from the chilly temperature.

"Hell on the Border," he said. "I've heard about that jail Parker's got down there in the basement. Sounds like a doggone dungeon if you ask me."

"I'd just as soon not find out firsthand," Bo said.

The creaking of wagon wheels made him look to his right. A wagon with an enclosed back was approaching along the drive that ran in front of the courthouse. One man perched on the high driver's seat, handling the reins hitched to the four-horse team. He wasn't all that big, but he had broad shoulders, a prominent nose, and a drooping black mustache. He looked plenty tough and was well armed with two pistols worn butt-forward and an old Henry rifle laying on the wagon seat next to him.

Pinned to the man's coat was a deputy U.S. marshal's badge, Bo noted.

He and Scratch walked on past the entrance to the jail as the wagon rolled up behind them. The deputy hollered at his team as he hauled back on the reins and brought the vehicle to a halt. Bo glanced curiously over his shoulder and saw the lawman climbing down from the seat.

The deputy was probably either delivering or picking up some prisoners, Bo thought. Either way, it was none of his or Scratch's business. He heard a lock rattle, then the deputy called out, "All right, climb down outta there, you—"

That was as far as he got before he let out a startled yell. A second later, a gun went off with a boom that rolled across the broad courthouse lawn.

"What in tarnation?!" Scratch exclaimed as he whirled around.

Somehow, Bo wasn't surprised that trouble had erupted right behind their backs.

CHAPTER 2

Bo turned quickly, too, his hand going to his gun as he did so. He saw the deputy marshal who'd been driving the wagon wrestling with a burly, unshaven man as they fought over possession of the deputy's rifle.

Another man and a woman were dashing away across the courthouse lawn.

"Those prisoners are escaping!" Bo snapped. "Come on, Scratch!"

It never occurred to him to just stand there and watch the drama unfolding, which is what most people would have done. In fact, there were already a number of bystanders gawking at the struggle behind the wagon or at the fugitives running past them.

The Texans started running, too. Luckily, the direction in which the escaping prisoners had fled sent them on a course that Bo and Scratch could intersect at an angle. If that hadn't happened, they probably wouldn't have had a chance to catch up, because the prisoners were younger and faster.

The woman was especially swift. She'd hiked up her long skirt, and her bare calves flashed in the winter sunlight as she sprinted for freedom. Long, curly blond hair bounced on her shoulders and back as she ran. Scratch, who was a little faster on his feet than Bo, went after her, while Bo targeted the tall, skinny hombre with long black hair.

Bo's pulse was pounding hard after only a few feet. He knew he couldn't hope to win a distance race with this long-legged gent, so he took a chance and launched himself off his feet in a diving tackle at the man's legs.

He almost fell short, but he was able to get a hand on one of the man's ankles. The fugitive let out a startled yell as he pitched forward out of control. The yell turned into a pained grunt as his face plowed into the grass and dirt of the lawn.

The impact of Bo's own landing on the ground knocked the breath out of him and stunned him for a second. He knew, though, that he didn't have time to lie there and recover. He scrambled onto his hands and knees and lunged toward the man he had tripped up.

The fugitive rolled over and brought a mallet-like fist swinging up at Bo's head. Bo twisted so that the blow landed on his left shoulder instead.

The punch packed enough power that it made his arm go numb all the way down. He dropped on top of the man, driving his right elbow into the fugitive's belly as he did so. Sour breath gusted from the man's mouth into Bo's face.

Years of finding himself in such rough-and-tumble

brawls had given Bo plenty of experience. He considered himself an honorable man, but when you were fighting for your life, no holds were barred and no blows were too low. He aimed a knee at his opponent's groin. That was usually the quickest way of ending a fight.

It probably would have been in this case if the knee had landed. But the man blocked the blow with a thigh and slammed clubbed fists into Bo's jaw. The brutal wallop sent Bo rolling across the lawn.

The man lunged up into a stumbling run and scrambled after him. He bent, reaching for the Colt in Bo's holster.

Bo had no idea who the man was or why that deputy marshal had arrested him and brought him here to Fort Smith, but he knew it wouldn't be a good idea to let an escaping prisoner get his hands on a gun. Bo jerked his right leg up at the last minute and planted the toe of his boot in the man's belly.

The man's own momentum, along with a heave from Bo's leg, sent him flying through the air above the Texan. He crashed down hard, and this time the soft lawn didn't cushion his fall. He landed on one of the flagstone walks instead.

Bo rolled over, came up on a knee, and drew his gun. He leveled the Colt at the fugitive, who was also gasping for breath now as he lay on the ground.

"Don't move . . . mister," Bo warned as he tried to catch his own breath. "I'll blow one of your knees apart if you do, and you'll never walk right again."

The man's face contorted in a snarl. He started to

push himself up and said, "I'll never walk again after they hang me, anyway!"

That made sense. He didn't have anything to lose. Bo's finger tightened on the trigger.

Meanwhile, Scratch had given chase to the blonde. She must have heard him coming after her, because she glanced over her shoulder at him with wide blue eyes. Seeing him closing in on her, she increased her speed.

Scratch didn't have enough breath left to curse, or he would have. Instead he just tried to run a little harder.

The woman had almost reached the streets that ran through Fort Smith's business district. If she made it into that maze of hills and buildings and people, she would stand a good chance of getting away. Scratch knew that. If he drew one of his Remingtons and took a shot at her, he could probably bring her down, even on the run like this.

But he had never liked the idea of shooting at a woman, even one who must have broken the law. Nor did he know what crimes this particular gal was charged with. Gunplay didn't seem called for.

And he couldn't close the gap, so it was starting to look like she was going to escape.

She likely would have, too, if a man leading a team of mules hadn't emerged from the mouth of an alley just as the woman rounded a corner and started along the street. She let out a startled cry and had to come to a sudden stop to avoid running into them.

Scratch saw that and poured on the last of the speed he had in reserve. He reached out and grabbed the collar of the blonde's dress as she tried to dart around the mules and their startled owner.

With a loud rip, the garment tore, splitting down the back and exposing a considerable expanse of smooth, creamy skin. Scratch bunched his fingers in the fabric and didn't let go. He tried to haul the woman closer so he could get hold of her.

"Help!" she screamed. "This crazy old coot's trying to rape me!"

Well, shoot! Scratch thought. That was a smart move on her part. They had gone around a corner and were out of sight of the courthouse now, and the folks who'd been walking along this street had no earthly idea what was going on. Naturally, they believed the woman's apparently terrified claim that she was the victim here.

The man with the mules let go of the reins and came toward Scratch.

"Let go of her, you varmint!" he yelled.

A woman cried, "Somebody fetch the law!"

More men shouted threatening curses as they closed in around Scratch. He couldn't fight all of them, and he sure couldn't hang on to the blonde if they jumped him.

So he did the only thing he could. He pulled the woman closer to him with his left land, drew his right-hand Remington, and bellowed, "Everybody back off, dadblast it!"

From the corner of his eye, he saw the woman's hand come up. Sunlight flashed on something she was holding. He jerked his head back, and it was a good thing he did, otherwise the small straight razor she had flicked open would have cut his throat neatly from ear to ear.

She grunted in fury as she twisted in his grip. The dress ripped even more. She slashed down at his arm with the razor, and he had to let go of her and yank his arm back to avoid being cut. As it was, the blade sliced through the sleeve of his buckskin jacket.

She could have run again then, but rage made her come after Scratch instead. She swiped the razor back and forth at his face, forcing him to give ground. Scratch was more tempted now to shoot her, but if he did that, some of the bystanders might open fire on him.

Somebody grabbed him from behind, wrapping strong arms around him and saying, "I got him, ma'am! He won't hurt you now!"

The same couldn't be said of the blonde. With her face twisted in lines of hate, she kept coming, obviously intent on carving Scratch's rugged face into bloody ribbons.

Back on the courthouse lawn, Bo was about to fire at the prisoner he'd been battling when somebody suddenly stepped past him and swung a leg in a well-aimed kick. The man's boot crashed into the fugitive's jaw and laid him out again. The newcomer moved in and brought the butt of his rifle crashing down on the back of the man's neck.

Bo recognized the rugged-looking deputy marshal who had driven the wagon up to the courthouse. More law officers swarmed past him and grabbed the unconscious fugitive.

The deputy swung his rifle toward Bo and snapped, "Put that gun down, mister. Better yet, holster it. You're makin' me nervous."

Bo pouched the iron as he came to his feet. Obviously, the deputy had overcome the man he'd been fighting with at the wagon, maybe with help from other deputies who'd come running out of the courthouse.

"Did you see which way that yellow-haired gal went?" the lawman went on.

"She was headed that way," Bo said as he pointed toward the downtown area. "My partner was after her."

"Come on, then. She's the most loco one in the whole bunch!"

Bo and the deputy ran toward Fort Smith's business district. They heard a lot of yelling, and as they rounded a corner they saw a group of people in the street. Through gaps in the crowd, Bo caught a glimpse of Scratch being held from behind, his arms pinned by a burly townsman.

The blonde that Scratch had pursued was coming at him, a razor in her uplifted hand.

The deputy skidded to a halt and fired three shots into the air, cranking off the rounds as fast as he could work the Henry's lever. The roar of the shots made people in the crowd gasp, curse, and fall back.

They also made the woman hesitate, and Scratch took advantage of the opportunity to lift his left leg in a kick that caught her wrist and sent the razor flying from her fingers.

Disarmed, the woman whirled around to flee again. The deputy snapped the rifle to his shoulder and fired again, this time through a narrow gap in the crowd. The bullet smacked into the paving stones at the woman's feet.

The deputy worked the Henry's lever and called, "Next one goes in your back, Cara! You know I ain't foolin'!"

The mob that had surrounded Scratch and the woman was vanishing rapidly as people scrambled for cover. There was nothing like a few gunshots for clearing a street in a hurry. The deputy had an unobstructed aim now as he settled the rifle's sights on the woman's back.

She must have known he would kill her rather than let her get away, because she stopped and raised her hands. The torn dress hung open almost indecently, revealing her smooth back down to the curve of her hips.

"Marshal, that woman needs something to wear," Bo said, his chivalrous instincts coming into play even in this situation.

"Don't worry about that murderous whore," the lawman muttered.

More deputies who had come running from the courthouse closed in around the blonde. They jerked her arms behind her back and clapped handcuffs around her wrists. Only when she was securely manacled did one of the men take off his coat and drape it around her shoulders where the mutilated dress was threatening to slip down and expose even more of her.

The lawman who stood next to Bo and Scratch finally lowered his rifle and stepped aside to let the other deputies lead the prisoner past them.

"Lock her up, boys, but don't put her in with Lowe and Elam," he ordered. He turned to the Texans and looked like he was about to say something else, but a stentorian shout interrupted him.

"Brubaker!"

"Aw, hell," the deputy muttered. "Here comes Parker."

CHAPTER 3

It was the famous Hanging Judge stalking along the street toward them, all right. Bo had seen photographs of Isaac Parker before, although he had never met the man and certainly never appeared before him in court.

Parker didn't cut that impressive of a figure at first glance. He was a medium-size man with dark hair and a Van Dyke beard, dressed in a brown tweed suit.

You had to get close to him to see the unquenchable fire for justice that burned in his eyes.

As judge for the western district of Arkansas, which included Indian Territory, he rode herd on one of the wildest areas in the country. The tribes who had been settled on reservations in the Territory several decades earlier were peaceful for the most part, but they had their share of criminals and troublemakers just like any group will.

For the most part it was white owlhoots who made Indian Territory such a lawless, untamed region. Smugglers, bootleggers, rustlers, bank robbers, thieves, road agents, and murderers of all stripes viewed the Territory as a refuge beyond the reach of the law.

That wasn't strictly true. The various tribes had their own police forces, such as the Cherokee Lighthorse, but those officers dealt only with Indian matters. Judge Parker employed a force of tough deputy marshals to patrol the Territory and bring in lawbreakers, but they were spread pretty thin.

Bo had heard it said that a lot of Parker's deputies were little better than outlaws themselves, and for all he knew, that might be true. The one called Brubaker certainly looked mean enough to have broken a few laws in his time.

Parker strode up to them and said in his powerful, commanding voice, "I'm told that three prisoners in your custody have escaped, Brubaker. Is this true?"

"No, sir, it's a dadblamed lie," the deputy responded without hesitation. "They gave me a mite of trouble, but they're all locked up now, Your Honor, or they will be as soon as the boys get Cara LaChance behind bars."

Parker's eyes flashed with interest. "You arrested the LaChance woman?" he asked.

"Yes, sir, along with Dayton Lowe and Jim Elam. The rest of Gentry's bunch gave me the slip, but as soon as I provision up again, I'll be headed out on their trail."

"Not so fast," Parker said. "I may have another job for you." He looked over at Bo and Scratch and frowned. "Who are these men?"

Brubaker scowled and said, "They, uh, gave me a hand corralin' them prisoners."

"Gave you a hand?" Scratched repeated incredulously. "Why, if we hadn't pitched in, two of 'em would've got away, and you durned well know it, mister."

Brubaker was about to frame an angry response when Parker stopped him with an upraised hand. The judge looked at Scratch and asked, "Is that a Texas accent I hear?"

"Texan born, bred, and forever," Scratch answered without any attempt to keep the pride out of his voice. Despite their years of wandering elsewhere, he and Bo had never lost the drawl that was part of their Lone Star heritage.

"I'm Bo Creel, Your Honor," Bo introduced himself. "My pard here is Scratch Morton."

Parker nodded and said, "I'm pleased to meet you, gentlemen, and you have my sincere thanks for your assistance in this matter." He glanced at Brubaker, whose face was flushed with anger. "Those prisoners never should have gotten loose in the first place. How did they manage that, Brubaker? Why weren't they shackled in the back of that wagon?"

"They were, Judge," Brubaker replied. "I put the irons on 'em myself. There ain't no doubt about it. But when I swung open the door on the back of the wagon, Lowe jumped me and tried to get my rifle away from me. While I was tusslin' with him, the other two jumped out and lit a shuck. They got loose somehow, but durned if I know how."

"Did you search them before you locked them up?" Bo asked. "Some people are real good at picking locks if they've got a little steel bar."

"Are you tryin' to tell me how to do my job, mister?" Brubaker shot back hotly. "Of course I searched 'em! What kind of blasted fool do you take me for?"

"Nevertheless, the prisoners were loose when you got here and unlocked the door," Parker pointed out.

Brubaker looked angry and miserable at the same time.

"The girl must'a had somethin' hidden somewhere on her," he admitted. "I ain't gonna speculate on where, because I searched her so blamed good I was embarrassed about it for fifty miles! But if any of that bunch is tricky enough to pick some locks, it'd be Cara LaChance."

"I agree," Parker said with a nod. "But at least they're still in custody. We're fortunate about that." He looked at Bo and Scratch again. "I repeat, we're obliged to you gentlemen for your help. I'd offer you a reward, but the federal government doesn't provide me with an abundance of cash to operate my court."

"That's all right, Your Honor," Bo said. "We were glad to pitch in."

"Yeah," Scratch added. "Even if that blond hellion almost did cut me up with a razor."

Parker's rather bushy eyebrows rose.

"A razor?" he said. "I hadn't heard about that. So she had a razor hidden on her person, too, eh?"

A muscle in Brubaker's jaw jumped a little as he gritted his teeth and growled.

"I'll make the whore talk," he said.

"You've delivered the prisoners," Parker said. "Your job is done."

Brubaker looked like he wanted to argue, but he didn't say anything.

Parker nodded to Bo and Scratch, said, "Good day, gentlemen," and turned to walk back to the courthouse.

"I hope you don't plan on standin' around waitin' for me to thank you," Brubaker told the Texans.

"We didn't do it for thanks or a reward," Bo said. "Just didn't want any outlaws getting loose to raise more hell."

"We ain't overfond of outlaws," Scratch put in.

Brubaker snorted and stomped after Parker.

"Well, I reckon we can go get us a drink now," Scratch went on. "That's what I had in mind to start with. I remember a certain tavern on one of these hilly streets from the last time we passed through here."

"I do, too," Bo replied. "Why don't we go see if we can find it?"

They found the tavern without much trouble and were glad it was still in business. The place was a dim, cavelike room in a stone building with very thick walls, built into the side of a hill. Warm in the winter, cool in the summer, it was run by a burly, redheaded Irishman named Michael Corrigan, who pointed a blunt finger at Bo and Scratch from behind the bar as they came in and declared in a loud voice, "I remember the two o' ye! Start any more trouble and this time I'll bust yer heads open with me trusty bungstarter!"

"We didn't start the trouble last time, dadgum it!" Scratch protested.

"And that was years ago," Bo added. "How do you even remember it?"

Corrigan scowled darkly at them.

"Some things ye don't forget, boyo," he said. "It took me nearly a week to clean up all the damage from that ruckus!"

"We're peaceable men," Bo insisted as the Texans came up to the bar. "All we want are a couple of mugs of beer."

"That I can do ye for," Corrigan said.

"And maybe some coffee later on," Scratch said.

"Aye, that, too."

Corrigan drew the beers and slid the mugs across the hardwood. Bo paid for the drinks, and he and Scratch carried them to a table in one of the rear corners of the tavern. The place wasn't very busy at this hour, so it was no problem finding a place to sit.

"This is more like it," Scratch said after he'd leaned back in his chair and taken a long swallow of the beer. "Nobody tryin' to wallop us, stab us, or shoot us."

"Better not get used to it," Bo replied with a chuckle.

"Oh, I ain't gonna. It don't seem to matter how hard

we try to steer clear of trouble, it finds us. I'm just hopin' that little fracas was our share of it for this trip."

Bo shared that hope, but like his old friend, he wasn't going to count on it.

"Did you get a look at that gal I was scufflin' with?" Scratch asked after a moment.

"I did," Bo replied. "She was pretty good looking."

Scratch snorted.

"Too good lookin' to be an outlaw gal, if you ask me," he said. "But she cussed like a bullwhacker, and she sure went after me with that razor. Reckon that just goes to show you, you can't always tell what somebody's like by lookin' at 'em."

"You should've figured that out a long time ago," Bo said.

"Oh, I did. I ain't no babe in the woods, as you well know. But when you see a gal like that . . . Oh, shoot, you know what I mean."

Bo knew what his friend meant, all right. Scratch had an eye for a pretty girl and had always been that way. He thought they all ought to be as nice and sweet as he wanted them to be.

Unfortunately, that wasn't always the case, and sometimes Scratch had to pay a price for his idealism and romantic nature.

From time to time, Bo had been fooled by women himself, although with his practical nature that was more difficult. He had an instinctive wariness Scratch lacked.

But Scratch's more reckless personality had gotten them out of plenty of scrapes in the past, too. They made a good team, which was one reason they were still riding together after all these years.

After a while, Corrigan brought cups of coffee over to them. As he set the cups on the table, the tavern keeper said, "I've got some stew in the pot. Would ye like some?"

"That sounds mighty fine, Mike," Bo told him. "Thanks."

Corrigan nodded and started to turn back toward the bar. He paused as the door opened and a man came inside. The newcomer closed the door behind him a little harder than was necessary.

"What's got yer dander up, Forty-two?" Corrigan asked.

Deputy Marshal Brubaker ignored the question and strode up to the table. He glared at Bo and Scratch.

"I've been lookin' for you two," he said. "Somebody told me they'd seen a couple of Texans come in here. Let's go."

"Go where?" Bo asked.

"We ain't under arrest, are we?" Scratch added.

"No, you ain't under arrest, but we're goin' to the courthouse," Brubaker said. "The judge wants to see you, and I mean right now."

CHAPTER 4

Bo and Scratch sat there looking at the deputy in surprised silence for several seconds before Bo asked, "What does Judge Parker want with us?"

"Maybe he's gonna give us a ree-ward after all," Scratch suggested.

Brubaker snorted disdainfully. "Don't hold your breath waitin' for that," he said.

Scratch's eyes narrowed.

"He ain't come up with some excuse for hangin' us, has he?"

The deputy marshal sighed in exasperation and said, "Just come on, will you?"

Bo took a sip of his coffee.

"Mike here was about to get us some bowls of Irish stew," he said. "I'm a little hungry. I hate to miss out on that."

Brubaker wheeled around and glared at the tavern keeper, who raised his hands in surrender.

"Don't be givin' me that evil eye, Forty-two," Corrigan said. He looked at Bo and Scratch and added,

"I'll keep the pot warm for ye, lads. Ye can have some o' my fine stew later."

"We'll hold you to that deal, Mike," Scratch said as he got to his feet. He noisily slurped down some of the coffee from his cup.

Bo took another sip of his and stood up as well. He said, "All right, Marshal, lead the way."

Muttering under his breath, Brubaker stalked out of the tavern with the Texans behind him.

As they walked up the hill toward the large level bluff where the courthouse was located, Bo asked, "What's that forty-two business? Mike was calling you that like it's your name."

"That's what some of my friends call me," Brubaker admitted with obvious reluctance.

"That how old you are?" Scratch asked. "They gonna start callin' you Forty-three next year?"

"No, blast it, that's not how old I am! I'm thirty-six."

"Then how come folks don't call you Thirty-six?" Scratch persisted.

Brubaker yanked his hat off, dragged his fingers through his hair, and then wearily scrubbed his hand over his face before he put the hat back on.

"They call me Forty-two," he said with forced patience, "because I like to play dominoes, and Forty-two is my favorite game."

A big grin split Scratch's face.

"Well, why in tarnation didn't you say so? Bo and me been playin' Forty-two for years and years, ain't that right, Bo?"

"Nothing I like better than a good game of Forty-two," Bo said. "Maybe if we can find a fourth man, we can play sometime, Deputy."

"You don't reckon His Honor would be up for a game, do you?" Scratch asked.

"I wouldn't bring it up if I was you," Brubaker said. "He's already in a pretty foul mood."

"Because of those prisoners escaping?" Bo asked.

"They didn't escape! They're locked up right now. Lowe and Elam are down in the basement, and that she-devil's in one of the women's cells."

"Well, almost escaping, then," Bo said.

Brubaker blew out his breath so hard it made his drooping mustache flutter slightly.

"Do you two ever shut up? My God, every Texan I ever met just loved to flap his jaw!"

"I might take that as an insult," Scratch said, "if I didn't know you liked to play Forty-two. Shoot, you can't get mad at a fella who likes to play Forty-two. Now, Moon is a different story. I never liked that game near as much."

Brubaker went back to muttering under his breath and moved a couple of steps ahead of them. He was shorter, so he had to hurry to stay ahead of their long-legged strides.

Behind his back, Bo and Scratch grinned at each other. It probably wasn't the smartest thing in the world, hoorawing a lawman like that, but the deadly serious, short-tempered Brubaker made such a tempting target.

When they reached the courthouse, the deputy escorted them not to Parker's courtroom but to an office adjacent to it. Parker was waiting there behind a big desk covered with papers. Despite the number of documents, there was nothing messy or littered about the desktop. The papers were in neat stacks, and a person could tell just by looking at them that everything was in its proper place.

Parker greeted them by getting to his feet and saying, "Come in, gentlemen, come in. I'm afraid I can't offer you drinks or cigars. The decorum of the court, you know."

"That's fine, Your Honor," Bo said. He and Scratch had both removed their hats when they came into the courthouse. Knowing Parker's fearsome reputation, they didn't want to do anything to show disrespect toward him.

Parker waved them into a pair of chairs covered with Morocco leather that were placed in front of the desk.

"Have a seat," he instructed. "I hope Marshal Brubaker didn't interrupt you in the middle of anything important."

"We were about to have some Irish stew at Corrigan's place," Scratch said as he sat down and balanced his cream-colored Stetson on his knee.

A faint smile tugged briefly at Parker's mouth for a second. He resumed his seat behind the desk and faced the Texans. Brubaker sat in a straight-backed chair off to one side that didn't look nearly as comfortable.

The judge got right down to business by asking, "Do you know anything about those prisoners you helped to apprehend while they were trying to escape?"

"We've heard their names spoken, but that's about all we know," Bo said.

"That and the fact that the blond gal's a holy terror," Scratch added.

"That's a good description of Cara LaChance," Parker agreed. "She's the inamorata of an outlaw named Hank Gentry."

"Inam-what?" Scratch asked.

"The judge means that Miss LaChance and this Gentry hombre are sweethearts," Bo explained.

"Oh. Well, she's right pretty, no doubt about that, but she didn't strike me as the cuddlesome sort. Leastways, not unless you like to cuddle up with a rattlesnake."

"Hush up and let the judge talk," Brubaker snapped.

Parker lifted a hand and said, "That's all right, Marshal. I want to make certain that Mr. Creel and Mr. Morton are clear about everything that's involved before I make my proposition to them."

"You've got a proposition for us, Your Honor?" Bo asked with a surprised frown.

"That's right, but first you should know that the LaChance woman, along with the other two prisoners, Dayton Lowe and Jim Elam, are all members of what is without a doubt the most vicious outlaw gang operating in the Territory at this moment. Marshal Brubaker was able to arrest the three of them, but there are at least a dozen more of the desperadoes still at large."

Scratch looked at Brubaker and asked with newfound respect in his voice, "You went after fifteen of the varmints by yourself?"

"I never figured on being able to capture all of them at once," Brubaker explained stiffly. "But I thought if I was smart enough, I might be able to whittle 'em down a few at a time."

"Marshal Brubaker is extremely intelligent," Parker said, "and one of the toughest officers I know. His only flaw is an occasional tendency toward over-confidence."

"Guilty as charged, Your Honor," Brubaker said, looking straight ahead.

"The point of what I just told you, gentlemen," Parker went on to Bo and Scratch, "is that not only are these three prisoners quite dangerous in their own right, they have friends still at large who represent a grave threat."

"You said there are a dozen more in the gang, Judge?" Bo asked.

"That's right."

Bo shook his head and said, "I don't think even that many men would dare to attack the courthouse right here in Fort Smith, if you're worried about them trying to break those three out of jail."

Parker leaned back in his chair.

"I agree with you, Mr. Creel, but that's not what I'm worried about. You see, the State of Texas has a prior claim on the prisoners. Before the Gentry gang fled northward into the Territory, they operated quite successfully south of the Red River, holding up numerous trains and banks in Texas and murdering a considerable number of innocent people."

Bo said, "I figured a federal court would trump a state court when it came to such things, Your Honor."

"It's actually a federal court that wants them, the one that covers the eastern district of Texas," Parker explained. "Gentry and his gang looted the mail bags in the express cars of those trains they held up, which makes their crimes fall under federal jurisdiction. Because those offenses were committed before their crimes in the Territory and elsewhere were carried out, it's the federal court in Texas that has first claim on them." A faint tone of dislike came into Parker's voice as he added, "Judge Josiah Southwick."

"Bigfoot Southwick's a federal judge now?" Scratch exclaimed in astonishment.

Parker's eyebrows rose. "You're acquainted with Judge Southwick?"

"We knew him in our younger days," Bo said. "He was a lawyer then."

"Part lawyer, part snake oil salesman," Scratch added. "Mostly snake oil salesman."

Brubaker snapped, "Keep a civil tongue in your head. That's a federal judge you're talkin' about."

"I'm sure I've been called worse than a snake oil salesman," Parker said. "At any rate, Judge Southwick has requested that any members of Gentry's gang who are captured be transferred to his jurisdiction for trial, and a short time ago I received a telegram from the Justice Department directing me to comply with that request."

"You've got to send the prisoners to Texas," Bo said.

Parker nodded. "To Tyler, to be precise. Judge Southwick's court is located there."

"That's a shame," Scratch said. "You were probably lookin' forward to droppin' 'em through the traps out yonder on that big gallows o' yours."

"I don't look forward to men being hanged," Parker said with a frown. "But I am dedicated to seeing justice carried out. In this case, that justice will have to be dispensed in another court. The matter was decided in Washington and is out of my hands. My responsibility is to see to it that the prisoners are safely transported to their destination. To that end, I've charged Marshal Brubaker with delivering them. Despite what happened earlier, I remain convinced that he's the best man for the job."

"I expect you'll be sending a number of deputies with him," Bo said. "You have to be concerned that the rest of the gang will try to rescue those three."

Parker laced his fingers together on the desk and nodded gravely.

"That's exactly what I'm worried about," he said. "Unfortunately, you overestimate the manpower I have available to me at the moment, Mr. Creel. All my deputies are engaged on other chores."

Bo was good at reading sign, and he had already figured out where this trail was leading. But he wasn't going to make it easy for Parker.

"What's that got to do with us, Your Honor?" he asked the judge.

"I think you know very well what I'm getting at,

Mr. Creel. I can't afford to hire more full-time deputies, but I do have a small amount of funds that can be used at my discretion. I want to hire you and Mr. Morton temporarily to help Marshal Brubaker take those prisoners to Tyler. What do you say? How would the two of you like to go home to Texas?"

CHAPTER 5

Bo and Scratch looked at each other. It wasn't that they were opposed to returning to their home state. They had been back to Texas a number of times over the years, most recently to El Paso before a dangerous sojourn down into Mexico, to a place called Cutthroat Canyon. They had even returned to the area where they had grown up on a few occasions, but the last time had been about a decade earlier.

"Been a while since we've been home," Scratch commented. "If we was to go to Tyler, it wouldn't be that hard to drift on down to Victoria."

"It's still quite a ways," Bo pointed out.

"Yeah, but we'd be closer than we are now."

Bo shrugged in acknowledgment of that undeniable fact.

Brubaker said, "I want you to know, I didn't ask the judge to hire you fellas. I figure I can deliver those prisoners to Judge Southwick without any help."

"That's certainly a possibility," Parker said, "especially if Gentry doesn't get wind that we're moving them until it's too late to go after them. But I don't think we can count on that, Jake. Gentry has a number of friends among the criminal element here in Fort Smith."

Brubaker shrugged and said, "I'll go along with whatever you decide, Your Honor."

His tone made it clear that he might not like or agree with the decision, though.

"It's not my decision to make," Parker said. He nodded across the desk toward Bo and Scratch. "That lies in the hands of these gentlemen."

"How much money are we talkin' about, Judge?" Scratch asked.

"Forty dollars apiece, plus ten cents per mile. One way, of course. Where you go after you reach Tyler with the prisoners is your own affair."

"That's as good as we could make cowboyin'," Scratch said to his old friend.

"Probably a little better, once you throw in the mileage," Bo said. "How do you intend to pay us, Your Honor?"

"I'll give you the forty dollars when you're ready to ride out with Marshal Brubaker," Parker replied.

Scratch grinned. "Afraid to give us the dinero ahead of time because we might take it and run off or fritter it away on whiskey and wild women, eh?" he asked.

"A federal judge must be prudent," Parker said.

"What about the mileage?" Bo asked.

"Judge Southwick will pay you that portion of your fee when you deliver the prisoners to his court.'

"Does Bigfoot . . . I mean His Honor Judge Southwick . . . know about that?"

"I'll send him a telegram advising him of our arrangement, once we've actually reached agreement on the particulars."

Scratch grimaced and shook his head.

"So he's liable to tell us to go climb a stump and suck eggs instead of givin' us the money," he said.

Parker clenched one hand into a fist that he thumped on the desk.

"Blast it! I'll guarantee the payment out of my own pocket if Judge Southwick refuses to abide by the terms I've laid out."

"Well, I suppose that's fair," Bo said. He'd had a strong hunch all along that he and Scratch would agree to go with Brubaker, but it never hurt to jaw a little first. "I'll say yes. How about you, Scratch?"

"Reckon I'll go along with the deal, too," the silver-haired Texan drawled. "Be mighty good to see some of the Lone Star State again."

"Then we have an agreement," Parker said with an emphatic nod. He came to his feet. "Shake on it?"

"Sure thing," Bo said as he stood and reached across the desk to shake hands with Parker. Scratch did likewise.

"Marshal Brubaker will give you all the details," Parker went on. "I'll just say good luck, gentlemen."

"You reckon we're gonna need it?" Scratch asked with a grin.

Parker's expression was solemn as he nodded

and said, "Knowing Hank Gentry's reputation, I'm absolutely certain that you will."

After leaving Parker's office, the three men paused just outside the courthouse.

"I'll say again, this wasn't my idea," Brubaker told the Texans. "And not to mince words about it, I don't appreciate the judge saddlin' me with a couple of amateurs."

"You'd rather go it alone, is that it?" Bo asked.

"I'll have enough to do just keepin' up with those prisoners, without havin' to look after a couple of old pelicans like you two."

"Old pelicans, are we?" Scratch asked hotly. "Let me tell you, sonny boy—"

"Don't make the marshal's case for him, Scratch," Bo said. "And as for you, Marshal, Scratch and I may not be young anymore, but trust me, we've still got some bark on us. You won't have to look after us. You just worry about the prisoners."

Brubaker snorted and said, "Fine by me. You're on your own, then if there's trouble. My only concern is gettin' those three varmints to Tyler."

Bo nodded. "That's a deal. When are we leaving?"

"First thing tomorrow mornin'. I want to be on the road by sunup."

"That's fine. You plan to carry them in the same wagon you used to bring them here?"

"I figured I would," Brubaker said. "You got any objection to that?"

"Not at all. It looked pretty sturdy. What about supplies?"

"There's a boot under the driver's seat we can fill up with provisions. If we run low, there are settlements between here and there where we can buy what we need."

"Are you taking along a saddle horse?"

Brubaker frowned and asked, "What business is that of yours?"

"Just curious," Bo said with a shrug.

"Yeah, I'm takin' a horse. I'll tie it on behind the wagon. Do the two of you have good mounts?"

"We do. We won't have any trouble keeping up."

"Well, good," Brubaker said, although he didn't sound all that pleased by the prospect. "You can meet me here at the courthouse at . . . let's call it six o'clock tomorrow mornin'. Be ready to ride."

"We will be," Bo promised.

Brubaker gave them a curt nod and stalked off toward the stairs that led down to the basement jail. From the looks of it, he intended to pay a visit to the prisoners.

"That little banty rooster don't like us," Scratch said as he watched Brubaker walk away.

"He doesn't appear to like much of anybody," Bo said. "I wonder why not." He shook his head and clapped a hand on Scratch's shoulder. "Let's go see if Corrigan kept that stew warm for us like he said he would."

* * *

The tavern keeper had kept his promise. He set steaming bowls of Irish stew in front of the Texans, along with fresh cups of coffee. Then he surprised them by pulling out a chair and sitting down at the table with them.

"Why don't you join us?" Bo asked dryly.

"Don't mind if I do, seein' as 'tis my place and all," Corrigan said, grinning under his red mustache. "What did Forty-two Brubaker want with you?"

"It wasn't Brubaker who wanted us," Scratch said. "It was that durned judge."

Bo considered how much they ought to tell Corrigan, then decided that the Irishman could be trusted. Corrigan had been running this tavern for a long time and had a good reputation.

"You heard about the ruckus with the prisoners who tried to escape earlier, I suppose," Bo said.

Corrigan nodded. "Aye. Some of my customers have been talkin' about it. Quite a brouhaha from the sound of it."

"We kept a couple of them from getting away, and that brought us to Judge Parker's attention. He wanted to hire us as temporary deputy marshals."

"He's sendin' ye into the Territory after badmen, then?"

Bo shook his head.

"We're going to Texas with Marshal Brubaker. He has to deliver the prisoners he brought in today to another federal judge down in Tyler."

Corrigan let out a surprised whistle.

"I'm bettin' Parker don't care much for that," he said.

"Once he gets a lawbreaker in that Hell on the Border jail o' his, most of 'em don't come out again unless it's to make the acquaintance of George Maledon."

Bo knew that was the name of the hangman who conducted the executions for Parker.

"In this case, the judge didn't have any choice. He got a telegram from Washington telling him to go along with what the judge down in Texas wants."

"Bigfoot Southwick," Scratch muttered. "I still can't believe that galoot and those big clodhoppers of his wound up bein' a federal judge. When we knowed him, I always figured he was more likely to wind up behind bars his own self."

"And that'd be a good place for a bunch o' them judges, if ye ask me," Corrigan declared.

Bo was enjoying the stew. After he washed down another mouthful with a sip of coffee, he asked, "How well do you know Brubaker, Mike?"

"Tolerably well," the tavern keeper replied. "We've been acquainted for four or five years, I'd say."

Scratch commented, "He's sure got a burr up his backside, don't he?"

"He's not a man who's easy to warm up to, I'll admit," Corrigan said. "Ye can't question his dedication to the law, though. It cost him his marriage."

"How's that?" Bo asked.

"Well, it cost him his engagement, I should say. He never did make it to the altar. But he'd be married to a mighty pretty girl with a rich daddy by now if he'd agreed to give up packin' a badge. She and her da wanted him to go to work for the old man in his lumber business. The way I heard the story, Forty-two agreed, but then he changed his mind. I reckon he just couldn't bear the thought o' sleepin' in a nice warm bed with a nice warm wife and collectin' wages for a cushy job, instead of spendin' his days blisterin' under a hot sun and freezin' in a cold rain and gettin' shot at by some o' the worst rapscallions west of the Mississippi. The man's daft, if ye ask me, but don't ever question how he feels about doin' his job."

Bo nodded slowly and said, "That's good to know, since we'll be traveling with him for a while."

"Well, there's dedication, and then there's sheer pigheadedness, and Forty-two's capable of that, too," Corrigan said. "Have a care, lads, that he don't get both of ye killed."

CHAPTER 6

Bo and Scratch were sitting on their horses in front of the courthouse the next morning when Brubaker drove up in the wagon. The air was cold enough that the breath of men and horses alike turned into plumes of steam.

The Texans' saddlebags were full. Despite what Brubaker had said about taking along plenty of supplies, the Texans had decided that it wouldn't hurt anything to bring extra provisions.

The sun had not yet peeked over the horizon, but it would be doing so soon. The heavens to the east were full of yellow, gold, and red light, and that brilliance turned the fleecy clouds floating in the sky pastel shades of those same colors, creating a spectacular view.

It was a view those locked up in the basement jail couldn't see, except maybe for tiny bits visible through the small, ground-level, iron-barred holes used for ventilation. For the most part, Hell on the Border would be dark, cold, and clammy.

All the more reason not to behave like an owlhoot and get locked up, Bo thought as he shifted and eased his weight in his saddle.

He knew that not everybody who wound up behind bars had only themselves to blame for it. Genuine mix-ups could occur, and some of the things that had happened to him and Scratch were proof of that. But most people who wound up in jail or prison were there because they had it coming for something they had done.

From the sound of it, Cara LaChance, Dayton Lowe, and Jim Elam deserved to be right where they were, locked up so they couldn't hurt anybody else.

Brubaker brought the wagon to a halt and looped the reins around the brake lever.

"I wasn't sure you fellas would be here this mornin'," he said. "I thought you might've decided to back out."

"Once we've shook on somethin', we don't back out," Scratch said.

"And you're not going to get rid of us that easily, Marshal," Bo added.

Brubaker climbed down from the wagon seat.

"Wait here," he said. "I'll go get the prisoners. The jailers are supposed to have them ready to travel."

He went down the stairs to the basement. While Bo and Scratch waited for him to return, they rubbed their gloved hands together for warmth.

A few minutes later, a whole mob of people came up the stairs, led by Brubaker, who had his revolver in his hand. Behind him came a couple of guards carrying shotguns as they backed up the steps so they could point the Greeners down into the dark basement.

Jim Elam, the skinny hombre with long black hair who Bo had scuffled with the day before, emerged next, wincing at the light. He shuffled along carefully because his hands were cuffed behind his back and a chain ran from those manacles down to the shackles on his ankles. Those shackles had just enough play in them to allow him to move up the steps.

Burly, bearded, glowering Dayton Lowe was next. He was chained up the same way. He resembled a bear, and Bo wouldn't have been surprised to hear him growl.

That left Cara LaChance. She came up the stairs last, chained and shackled like the others, wearing a fresh dress and a shawl draped around her shoulders that left her head uncovered. Bo was struck once again by just how pretty she was. At first glance she looked like she ought to be somebody's bride, setting out on a new course in life.

Then when he looked closer, he could see the loco fires burning in her eyes, and he had no trouble remembering that she'd been ready to carve up Scratch the day before. She would carve up anybody who got in her way, Bo thought.

Several more shotgun-toting guards followed the

prisoners up from the basement and then spread out to surround them as they hobbled toward the back of the wagon, where Brubaker opened the door.

"You first, Elam," he ordered. "Get in there and sit on that bench."

"Ain't you gonna chain our hands in front of us?" Elam asked with a whining note in his voice. "It's gonna be mighty uncomfortable ridin' with our arms pulled behind us this-a-way."

"You should've thought of that before you went around robbin' and killin' folks all over creation," Brubaker snapped. He prodded Elam in the back with the barrel of his revolver. "Now get in there, and don't make me tell you again."

Grumbling, Elam awkwardly climbed into the wagon and moved along the bench that ran down its center. Following Brubaker's orders, he sat down at the far end. Brubaker crouched inside the enclosed wagonbed, covering Elam as one of the other deputies climbed in and looped another chain around Elam's waist. That one led down to a sturdy iron ring bolted into the floor of the wagon bed, where it was fastened with a massive padlock.

Lowe was next, chained into place on the middle of the bench. He didn't say anything, but his expression made it clear that he would have been glad to tear all the guards limb from limb with his bare hands.

While Lowe was being put into the wagon, Cara LaChance looked up at the Texans where they sat on their horses. Her baleful gaze fastened on Scratch. She said, "I should've cut you when I had the chance."

"It weren't for lack of tryin' on your part, miss," Scratch pointed out.

"Shut up," Brubaker told Cara. "Prisoners don't talk."

"Go to hell!" she spat at him.

Brubaker looked like he wanted to slap her. Bo was glad when he didn't. He didn't hold with hitting women, even murderous hellcats like Cara LaChance, unless it was absolutely necessary. He knew from Scratch's frown that his old friend felt the same way, despite what Cara had tried to do to him.

When the time came for Cara to climb into the wagon, she refused to do it. A couple of guards moved in to take hold of her and lift her into the vehicle. She fought furiously against them, despite the irons on her. She screamed, cursed, spat, and writhed like a snake. Curses as colorful and vile as anything a teamster or bullwhacker could come up with spilled from her mouth in a steady stream.

"Lord, it's like she's got a devil inside her," Scratch muttered as he and Bo watched the spectacle. "Say, I've heard stories about folks bein', what do you call it, possessed like that. You don't think—"

"No, I don't," Bo said. "That's not possession we're seeing, it's pure meanness."

The officers finally got Cara inside the wagon and locked down. By then her loud, profane carrying-on had drawn the attention of quite a crowd. Bo looked over the citizens of Fort Smith who had gathered in front of the courthouse to watch the outlaws being loaded into the wagon, and he wondered if any of them were connected to Hank Gentry, Cara's lover and the leader of the owlhoot band to which she and the other two prisoners belonged.

It would have been smarter to sneak the prisoners out in the dead of night, Bo thought, and keep their destination a secret. That way there would have been a better chance of getting them to Tyler without Gentry coming after them.

That wasn't the way Parker had handled the matter, though, and Bo speculated that some of that could have been because of the judge's dissatisfaction with the situation. Parker would have preferred to put the outlaws on trial here and carry out the inevitable sentence on his own gallows. But that wasn't what was going to happen.

Brubaker checked the irons on all three prisoners, then climbed out of the wagon, slammed the door closed, and fastened it with another massive padlock.

"Satisfied?" Bo asked.

"They're not gettin' loose this time," Brubaker said. "And that's for certain sure. All three of 'em got stripped down to the skin and searched this mornin', and they're chained up in there so good they couldn't get to anything to help 'em get loose, even if they had it."

"What about when the gal has to tend to her private needs?" Scratch asked.

"She'll have to take care of that with one of us holdin' a gun on her." Brubaker held up a hand to forestall any protests. "I don't like it any better than you gents do, so don't try pullin' any of that Texas gallantry on me. I'm takin' no chances, and if you don't like it, you're free to go on your way since you ain't taken the judge's money yet."

"We'll stick," Bo told him. "This isn't a one-man job, Marshal."

Brubaker glanced at the sky and frowned.

"I figured we'd be on the road by now," he said. "Wait here. I'll let the judge know we're ready to pull out."

A few minutes later, Parker came out of the courthouse, followed by Brubaker. The judge looked at the wagon and nodded as if he could see through the sides and approved of how the prisoners were chained up. Cara must have gotten tired or lost her voice, because she had finally stopped screaming obscenities.

Parker came over to Bo and Scratch.

"Gentlemen, I believe I promised you forty dollars apiece," he said. "I'll pay you as soon as you've been sworn in."

"Do we have to wear badges?" Scratch asked. "We don't much cotton to wearin' badges. Every time we've helped out the law, we've done it sort of unofficial-like."

"No badges," Parker said, "but if you want the two double eagles I have for each of you, you'll have to be sworn in and sign a receipt."

"Let's get on with it, Your Honor," Bo suggested. "I think Marshal Brubaker wants to get started."

Brubaker just snorted and didn't say anything.

The formalities were soon over with, and two double eagles apiece rested in the Texans' pockets.

"You're now legally appointed representatives of the United States government, gentlemen," Parker told them. "Conduct yourselves accordingly."

"We'll bear that in mind, Your Honor," Bo said.

"And we'll try not to be an embarrassment to the gov'ment," Scratch added.

Brubaker climbed to the wagon seat and unwrapped the reins from the brake lever.

"Are we ready now?" he asked impatiently. "The sun's comin' up. We're burnin' daylight."

Bo nodded and said, "Ready whenever you are, Marshal."

Brubaker slapped the reins against the backs of the mules hitched to the wagon. He backed and turned the team and started away from the courthouse. Bo and Scratch fell in behind the vehicle.

Behind them, Judge Parker called, "Good luck, gentlemen!"

"He's sayin' something under his breath about how we're gonna need it, ain't he?" Scratch asked quietly as they rode along the flagstone drive behind the wagon.

"More than likely," Bo agreed.

CHAPTER 7

They took the road south out of Fort Smith, which followed the boundary between Arkansas and Indian Territory fairly closely. Bo rode up alongside the wagon seat and asked Brubaker, "How long do you think it'll take to get to Tyler?"

"Five or six days, I expect," the deputy marshal replied. "If we don't run into any trouble."

Scratch had come up to flank the wagon on the other side. He grinned and said, "If that's true, then the dinero we're gettin' paid works out to be better than the wages we could make cowboyin'."

Brubaker grunted.

"You'll earn every penny of it if Gentry and his bunch come after us," he warned.

The thick wooden walls around the wagon bed had a few small, slitlike windows set high in them to let in some light and air. Obviously those openings permitted the prisoners to hear some of the conversation that was going on outside, too, because Cara LaChance yelled, "You just wait, you damn lawdog!

Hank's coming after you, all right! When he catches up to you, you'll wish you'd never been born! He'll take his skinnin' knife to you, and you'll be screaming and begging for him to kill you before he's through with you!"

Cara went on explaining in gory, graphic detail just what Hank Gentry would do with his knife. Brubaker sighed and shook his head.

"Lord, we're gonna have to listen to that all the way to Texas," he muttered.

"Maybe you could gag her," Scratch suggested.

"And take a chance on her bitin' me?" Brubaker shook his head again. "That'd be a good way to get hydrophobia."

"She's like one of those kid's toys that you wind up," Bo said. "She'll run down after a while."

His prediction proved to be accurate. A short time later, Cara fell silent for a few miles.

But then the cursing and haranguing started again. Brubaker finally lost his temper and turned to yell through the narrow openings, "Shut up in there! The judge said I had to deliver you to Tyler. He didn't say that you still had to have a tongue in your head when I got you there!"

Scratch looked at the deputy in horror.

"You wouldn't really cut her tongue out, would you?" he asked.

Brubaker shook his head, but he said in a loud, clear voice, "I damn sure might!"

That shut Cara up again. Bo didn't have any real hope that it would last, but he would take all the peace and quiet he could get, even if it was only temporary.

The town had fallen well behind, leaving them to travel through rolling, thickly wooded hills broken up by grassy meadows, plowed fields that were bare of crops at this time of year, and the occasional rocky ridge. From time to time they passed a log cabin with smoke curling from its chimney into the morning air. Droopy-eared hounds bayed at them, and the commotion drew farmers and their families from the cabins to watch the wagon and the two riders go past.

"If anybody's coming after us, they won't have any trouble following our trail," Bo said.

Brubaker didn't look over at him.

"I know."

Bo exchanged a glance with Scratch over the top of the enclosed wagon. It seemed to him that Brubaker was being awfully nonchalant about the prospect of a bloodthirsty outlaw gang pursuing them, and Scratch's frown told Bo that his old friend shared that concern.

Brubaker was the boss, though, and since the Texans had taken money to back his play, there was no doubt that they would do so.

It just seemed like they might be riding straight into trouble with their eyes wide open, and Bo didn't cotton to that feeling.

The day warmed as the sun rose higher in the sky, but the air still held a slight chill, even at midday as the wagon approached a low, rambling wooden building beside the road.

A buggy and a farm wagon were parked in front of the building, and several saddle horses were tied up at the hitch racks. Thick billows of white smoke came from the stone chimney.

"Clark's Trading Post," Brubaker announced. "We'll stop here and let the horses rest for a spell. We'll take the prisoners out one at a time and let 'em go out back to the privy, too."

He brought the wagon to a stop at the side of the building. Bo and Scratch reined in and dismounted while Brubaker climbed down from the high seat. The Texans drew their Winchesters from saddle sheaths.

"I reckon we'll cover them while you turn them loose?" Bo said.

"I'm not turnin' 'em loose," Brubaker snapped.

Bo shrugged. "Bad choice of words. While you unlock the chains holding them to the floor."

"Right." Brubaker reached into his pocket and brought out the big key that would unfasten the padlocks. "The girl's comin' out first."

Bo and Scratch worked the levers on their rifles. They stood back, one on each side of the door in the back of the wagon. Brubaker unlocked the padlock on the door and took it off. Then he stepped back quickly and dropped his hand to the butt of his gun, just in case the prisoners had gotten loose somehow and were about to try busting out.

Nothing happened, except that Jim Elam's whiny voice asked, "Where are we? Why have we stopped?"

"We're at Clark's," Brubaker replied. "I'm gonna take you out one at a time, let you tend to your business, give you some food and somethin' to drink. If you don't give me any trouble, it'll go a hell of a lot easier."

Cara laughed. "Easier for you, maybe."

"Easier for you, too," Brubaker told her. "Unless you enjoy goin' all day with nothin' to eat or drink and like pissin' in your pants."

She cursed at him. The deputy sighed and said to Bo and Scratch, "This is gonna get mighty old."

He reached forward, grasped the handle on the door, and pulled it open. All three prisoners flinched away from the midday light that spilled through the door. It had to be painfully bright to their eyes after spending the morning inside the dim, shadowy wagon bed.

"You first, Cara," Brubaker said.

"Why, ain't you the little gentleman?" She screeched with laughter. "And I do mean little."

Lowe joined in with some rumbling laughter of his own, and Elam snickered. Brubaker ignored them. He stood on the steps leading up to the open door and reached in to unlock the padlock holding Cara's chains to the ring on the floor. Then he backed off and drew his gun.

"You're not gonna take any of these other chains off me?"

"Not hardly."

"I need my hands free. I can't take care of my business with my arms chained behind my back!"

"You'll just have to make do," Brubaker told her stubbornly.

"Why, damn you—"

"Shut up now, or you can just stay in the wagon."

Bo could see the hatred seething inside Cara. It seemed to light her up, like she was on fire inside. But she didn't say anything else.

Instead she climbed awkwardly out of the wagon with the chain that had fastened her to the floor now dangling awkwardly from her other chains, weighing her down. Between that and the shackles on her ankles, there was no way she could run. She could barely shuffle along.

"Creel, you come with me," Brubaker said. "Morton, stay here and keep an eye on the other two. If either of them does anything suspicious . . . shoot him."

Scratch said, "I reckon ol' Bigfoot Southwick wouldn't like it if he didn't get to hang all three of 'em."

"I don't care what Judge Southwick likes or doesn't like. I'd rather bury a prisoner than have one escape." Brubaker jerked his head at Bo. "Come on, Creel."

Bo and the deputy followed Cara as she inched her way along the side of the building. An outhouse sat behind the trading post, at the edge of some trees. That was their destination. It took quite a while to reach it.

When they did, Cara said again, "I tell you, I got to have my hands loose. I got to pull my dress up. My God, Brubaker, ain't you got no decency to you at all?"

"You're a fine one to talk about decency," Brubaker said. "I seem to remember Gentry and his gang burnin' down a farmhouse with the family that lived there still inside it. You were there."

Cara giggled. "One time when we passed through those parts before, that damn Cherokee sodbuster sent word to the law. He tried to turn us in. We barely got away. Hank swore then that the redskin would pay, him and his squaw and all their brats."

"Go on and get in there, if you're goin' to," Brubaker ordered.

Cara shuffled into the two-holer.

"Ain't you even gonna close the door and give a lady some privacy?" she demanded.

"I would if there was a lady here."

"I can't . . . Son of a . . . Brubaker, this ain't gonna work!"

The deputy heaved a sigh.

"Creel, use the barrel of your rifle to lift her skirt some," he said.

Bo was too old to be easily embarrassed, but he felt his face warming now. He said, "I'll give you the rifle, and I'll cover her with my Colt."

"All right, blast it." Brubaker holstered his revolver and practically snatched the Winchester from Bo's hands. Bo moved back a step and drew his Colt.

Brubaker reached into the outhouse and used the

rifle barrel to hoist Cara's dress enough that she could sit down on one of the holes. Bo wanted to avert his eyes, but he didn't. Maybe he and Scratch should have thought about Judge Parker's offer a little longer before they agreed to help Brubaker deliver the prisoners, he told himself. He was about as uncomfortable as he had been in a long time.

After a while Cara said, "All right, I'm done."

"Stand up and come on out, then," Brubaker told her.

"You're a miserable excuse for a human bein'."

"Leastways I never killed any innocent folks, like you and your butcherin' crew."

She laughed again as she stood up and started to come out of the privy.

"Hank and the boys will butcher you, all right," she said. "Lay you wide open and show you your own innards. How's that gonna feel to you, lawman?"

"If I was you," Brubaker said, "I'd worry more about what it's gonna feel like when that trapdoor drops out from under you and that hang rope tightens around your neck—"

"Marshal," Bo said. He didn't want to listen to the two of them fussing at each other anymore.

Besides, three men had just stepped out the back door of the trading post, and every instinct in Bo's body was suddenly warning him that they were trouble.

CHAPTER 8

Out in front of the trading post, Scratch stood alertly, holding his Winchester and watching the two men inside the wagon.

"It just ain't fair, the way you fellas are treatin' us," Jim Elam complained.

Scratch said, "From what I've heard of your checkered career, son, bein' fair ain't something you've ever worried about much. It ain't fair to rob people of money and property they've worked hard for."

"Hell, the gub'mint does it all the time, don't they?"

"That don't make it right," Scratch said.

In his rumbling voice, Dayton Lowe said, "If you ain't tough enough to hang on to what you got, you don't deserve to have it."

"Well, there might be somethin' to that, but this here is what you call a civilized society. We ain't barbarians."

Lowe glared at him and said, "A man's either a barbarian inside . . . or he's fodder for them that are."

Scratch sighed. Danged if he knew why he was

standing around arguing philosophy with a couple of outlaws and mad dog killers. He didn't say anything else, and after a few minutes, Elam said, "I wish them other two would hurry up and get back with Cara. I need to visit that outhouse."

"They'll be here when they can," Scratch said. Voices drew his attention. He stepped back and saw that a couple of roughly dressed men armed with six-shooters had come out of the trading post. They stood on the front porch, talking.

Scratch tensed. He didn't know Hank Gentry or any of the other members of Gentry's gang by sight. It was possible these were two of the owlhoots, and they might be planning on trying to free Elam and Lowe.

Instead, one of them took a silver flask from under his jacket and unscrewed the cap. He lifted it to his lips and took a healthy swig of whatever was inside, then offered the flask to his companion.

"Whoo-eee," the first man said. He wiped the back of his free hand across his mouth. "That'll sure warm you up on a cold day. Try it, cuz."

Scratch could see a faint resemblance between the men now, so he could believe that they were cousins. Not that it was any of his business, he reminded himself, as long as they didn't bother him or the prisoners.

The second man took a long drink from the flask, belched, and handed it back to the first man.

"You're right, that's prime corn," he said.

The first man nipped at the flask again, then capped it and put it away. The two of them came down the steps, a little unsteady on their feet.

Just a pair of country boys who were drunk already, even though the sun was directly overhead, Scratch thought.

But at the same time, he continued to be wary. They could be putting on an act. They headed toward a couple of horses tied at the hitch rack, and Scratch hoped they would just mount up and ride away.

Instead, the first man hesitated and looked over at him. He nudged his companion with an elbow, then came toward Scratch with a leering grin on his face.

"You belong to a medicine show, old man?" he asked.

"What makes you say that?" Scratch said.

"Them fancy clothes you got on. Or is there a circus comin' and I just ain't heard about it yet?"

"You boys better just move on," Scratch advised.

The second man stumbled after the first. He waved a hand toward the wagon and asked, "What's in there that you're guardin'? You got a bear or somethin' locked up in that wagon?"

"I'll bet it's one o' them tigers," the first man said.

"Or maybe some whores," the second man suggested. "Fella dressed that fancy could be a whoremonger."

Scratch was getting annoyed by these fools.

"Go finish gettin' snockered somewheres else," he told them. "Leave a man to do his job, why don't you?"

Suddenly, from inside the wagon, Jim Elam cried, "Help us, boys! Get us loose! Kill this old man and we'll make it worth your while!"

Alarm bells had never stopped going off inside Scratch's head, so he wasn't surprised when the two strangers dropped the pretense of being drunk and swept back their coats to claw at the holstered revolvers on their hips.

Bo barely had time to exclaim, "Brubaker, look out!" before three men on the back porch had their guns drawn. He didn't know who they were—members of Hank Gentry's gang, come to rescue their friends, more than likely—but it didn't matter.

Any time a man slapped leather, Bo left off wondering and commenced shooting instead.

The man on the end at Bo's right was the fastest of the three. He had his gun out of its holster, and flame was spitting from its muzzle by the time Bo brought his rifle to his shoulder and pulled the trigger.

The Winchester cracked. The slug that flew from its barrel punched into the gunman's chest and flung him back against the wall behind him. Before the man could even fall, Bo had already worked the rifle's lever and swung the barrel toward the second man.

He had heard that first bullet whistle past his head and thud into the outhouse wall behind him, and he didn't want to give the other two a chance to have better aim. He fired again before the second man could get off a shot and drilled him cleanly through the body.

But before Bo could fire again, Cara LaChance

managed to throw herself forward, despite the chains burdening her. She rammed a shoulder into Brubaker's back. The deputy had whirled around to meet the threat of the three gunmen, and turning his back on her was a mistake.

The impact sent Brubaker stumbling into Bo just as the Texan squeezed the Winchester's trigger a third time. Being jostled like that threw off his aim. His shot went over the head of the third man, who sprayed lead at them as fast as he could jerk the trigger of his revolver.

Bo flung himself forward on the ground as slugs whipped through the air above him. From the corner of his left eye, he saw that Cara had bellied down, too, to make herself a smaller target while the bullets flew. Brubaker had dropped to his knees. Bo spotted blood on the deputy's face.

There was no time to see how badly Brubaker was hurt. Bo heard shots blasting in front of the trading post, too, and knew that Scratch was probably in danger, but he couldn't go to his trail partner's aid right now, either.

The third gunman back here still had to be dealt with. From his prone position, Bo fired again. Not surprisingly, the shot went a little low. It clipped the third man's thigh. Blood flew, and the slug's impact was enough to spin the man halfway around and drop him to one knee as the wounded leg went out from under him. He dropped the gun he had emptied by now and used that hand to grab a porch post and steady himself while he yanked another pistol from behind his belt.

He and Bo fired at the same time. The gunman's bullet smacked into the ground about five feet in front of the Texan, kicking dirt into his face and momentarily blinding him.

Bo had already sent a slug ripping through the gunman's neck, though. The man rocked back as crimson gore fountained from his ruined throat. His gun roared again, but it had sagged toward the ground right in front of the rear porch. His fingers slipped off the porch post, and he pitched forward to land on the ground, where the blood welling from his throat quickly formed a dark red puddle in the dirt.

Blinking rapidly to clear his vision, Bo shoved himself to his feet and levered another round into the Winchester's chamber. He was fairly confident that all three gunmen were dead, but he kept them covered anyway as he glanced over toward Brubaker. The deputy had collapsed, and he was either dead or passed out.

And Cara LaChance was trying to crawl away, dragging her chains after her.

The two men in front of the trading post had made a mistake by getting as close to Scratch as they had. As they went for their guns, the silver-haired Texan lunged forward and rammed his Winchester's barrel into the belly of the nearest man as hard as he could.

That brutal blow made the man double over, retching, and he forgot all about trying to draw his gun. The next instant, the butt of Scratch's rifle slammed into the side of his head and sent him sprawling on the ground at his companion's feet.

The second man had to dart aside to avoid tripping over the man Scratch had knocked down, and that slowed his draw by a split second. That was long enough for Scratch to swing the Winchester toward him and fire.

The heavy bullet smashed into the man's chest and knocked him backward. His finger jerked the trigger of his gun just as he cleared leather. The shot tore downward through his own boot, probably blowing off a toe or two.

That injury was the least of the man's concerns. He pressed his free hand to his chest as he tried to stay on his feet and struggled to lift his gun. Blood bubbled over and between his fingers. His eyes rolled up in their sockets, and he went down in a slow, twisting collapse.

The first man had regained his senses enough to draw his gun and fire up from the ground at Scratch, who jerked aside just in time to avoid the two slugs as the man triggered twice. Both shots went through the open door of the wagon and drew frightened shouts from Elam and Lowe.

Scratch hoped the stray bullets hadn't hit either of the prisoners, but he didn't have time to worry about them. He swung his leg in a kick that sent the gun spinning from the hand of the man who had just tried to kill him.

Scratch stepped back quickly and leveled the rifle at the man on the ground.

"All right, mister, get up," he ordered. "But don't try anything else or I'll ventilate you."

The man was still pale from the pain and shock of being hit in the belly by Scratch's rifle and then getting clouted on the head. He groaned and then gasped, "You . . . you killed Cousin Bob!"

"You're lucky you ain't dead, too," Scratch told him. "Now get up."

During the ruckus, he had heard shots coming from behind the trading post, quite a few of them, in fact, and he was worried about Bo. Obviously the two who had played drunk and tried to get the drop on him that way hadn't been acting alone. Their partners had gone after Bo and Brubaker.

The shooting had stopped now, and Scratch wanted to go see if his old friend was all right. First, though, he had to do something with this varmint.

A horrified cry erupted from inside the wagon. Jim Elam screamed, "Oh, my God! Dayton's hit! There's blood all over the place! Somebody help him!"

Instinctively, Scratch turned in that direction, just for the barest instant.

That was long enough for the man on the ground to surge to his feet and lunge at Scratch, the midday sunlight winking off the long, heavy blade of a Bowie knife he had drawn from under his shirt. He swung the knife up, aiming to plant the cold steel in Scratch's belly.

CHAPTER 9

Bo stepped over to Cara and reached down to grab hold of the trailing chain.

"Hold it," he told her. "You're not going anywhere."

She rolled onto her side and started cursing him. He ignored her and used the chain to drag her back the few feet she had managed to cover. That made her howl even more obscenities. He knelt beside Brubaker and took the padlock from the deputy's coat pocket.

While he was this close, he rested a hand on Brubaker's back and felt it rising and falling. Brubaker had passed out, but he wasn't dead. That was a relief, but Bo was still considerably worried about Scratch.

He used the padlock to fasten Cara's chain to the handle of the outhouse door. She might be able to pull the handle off the door or the door off its hinges, but that would take quite a bit of time and Bo intended to have things squared away by then.

He set his rifle well out of Cara's reach—not that she could do much with it while her hands were chained behind her back—and grasped Brubaker under the arms. Bo dragged the deputy out of Cara's reach as well.

He had already figured out it was best not to take any chances with her.

Then he picked up his Winchester and loped toward the front of the trading post.

He heard Jim Elam yelling something about blood inside the wagon. As he swung around the vehicle, Bo's keen eyes spotted a man leaping toward Scratch with a knife in his hand. There wasn't much room to get a shot off without risking hitting his friend, but Bo didn't have a choice. Another second and that varmint would bury the blade in Scratch's body.

Bo lifted the rifle and fired, letting instinct and experience guide his aim.

The slug shattered the man's shoulder and drove him off his feet. He dropped the knife and rolled on the ground, screeching in agony. Scratch kicked him in the head to stun him and shut him up, then looked over at Bo and nodded.

"Much obliged," he said. "I might've been able to get out of the way of that Bowie, but it would've been close. Where's Forty-two?"

"He was hit when they jumped us back there by the outhouse," Bo said. "Don't know how bad he's hurt. How about you?"

"I'm fine," Scratch assured him. "Not so sure about the prisoners. Where's the gal?"

"Chained to the outhouse."

Scratch grinned for a second.

"Seems fittin', considerin' the filth that comes outta her mouth." He turned toward the wagon and covered the two men inside. Elam had stopped yelling. "Anybody really hurt in there, or were you just tryin' to distract me?"

Neither of the prisoners answered.

"All right, go ahead and bleed to death," Scratch said. He slammed the door closed. "We got work to do out here."

The man he'd kicked in the head was still unconscious. Scratch checked the one he'd shot and grunted.

"Dead, all right. How about the ones out back?"

"Pretty sure they're dead," Bo said.

"You didn't find out?"

"I came to see if your mangy old hide had any holes in it."

Scratch grinned again.

"And I appreciate that," he said. "But you better go make certain-sure the others are buzzard bait."

Bo kept one eye on the trading post as he hurried behind the building again. The five men who had jumped him and Scratch accounted for the saddle horses tied up outside, but the buggy and the farm wagon told him that at least a few other folks were still inside. They might not represent any threat, but he didn't want to take a chance on that.

He knew the man he'd shot in the throat was dead. Nobody could lose that much blood and survive. Quickly, he checked the other two men and found that one of them had crossed the divide, as well. The third man was still breathing, but as Bo bent over him, a breath rattled grotesquely in the man's throat and then his chest ceased its movement. He was dead now, too, without ever regaining consciousness after Bo shot him.

Brubaker groaned. Bo trotted over to him as the deputy struggled to sit up. Bo grasped his arm and helped him. He saw an ugly red welt on the side of Brubaker's head. Blood had leaked from it and run down the deputy's weathered face.

"Wha . . . what happened?" Brubaker asked.

"Looks like a bullet creased you and knocked you out," Bo told him. "How do you feel?"

"Head hurts like blazes," Brubaker snapped. "How the hell do you think I feel?" His eyes widened as he looked around frantically. "The prisoners—!"

"They're all accounted for. Miss LaChance is all right. I don't know about Lowe and Elam, but I have a hunch they are, too."

"Help me up," Brubaker muttered. "I gotta go check on 'em. They're my responsibility."

Bo assisted the deputy in getting to his feet. Brubaker was a little unsteady when he started off, but his steps strengthened. As he passed the bodies of the three dead gunmen, he looked down at them impassively.

"Recognize any of them?" Bo asked. "I thought they might be members of Gentry's gang."

Brubaker started to shake his head, then winced as the motion must have made throbbing pain shoot through his skull.

"I never saw any of 'em before," he said. "They're not part of Gentry's bunch."

In that case, Bo wasn't sure why the men had jumped them, but unless the man he'd shot in the shoulder had bled to death, they had a prisoner they could ask about it.

When Brubaker reached the wagon, he drew his revolver and jerked the door open.

"Either of you make a funny move, and I'll smoke you both down," he threatened as he climbed onto the step. "Are you hit, either of you?"

"We're all right," Lowe answered with obvious reluctance. "Except I don't think Jim here needs to visit the outhouse anymore. Havin' bullets flyin' around sort of took care of that for him."

"Shut up," Elam muttered.

"I didn't think they were hit," Scratch said, "but I wasn't sure."

Brubaker backed off the steps and closed the door.

"Is that the only one still alive?" he asked as he nodded toward the man with the bullet-busted shoulder.

"Appears to be," Bo said.

"Morton, keep an eye on him. Creel, come with me. I want to get the gal back in the wagon before we do anything else."

A man in overalls appeared on the trading post's front porch, edging tentatively through the door. Scratch told him, "Better stay right there, mister, unless you're lookin' for trouble."

The man gulped, making his prominent Adam's apple jump up and down.

"No, sir," he told Scratch. "I'm sure not lookin' for trouble. Just seein' if all the shootin' was over."

"It is," Scratch said. "For now, anyway."

A short, portly, white-haired man in a dark suit and hat emerged from the trading post as well, followed by a bald, lanky individual in an apron. Scratch figured the gent in the suit went with the buggy, while the apron-wearer was probably the proprietor of the trading post.

"What is all this?" the man in the suit demanded. The blustering tone of his voice told Scratch that the fella was a pompous windbag. "Someone could have been killed!"

"Somebody was," Scratch said, nodding toward the dead man on the ground. "More than one somebody, in fact." Something occurred to him. "Any of you happen to know these hombres who jumped us?"

The man in the apron pointed to the other man lying near Scratch.

"The one with the busted shoulder is Jink Staley. Other fella is his cousin Bob Staley."

"They from around here?" Scratch asked.

The storekeeper nodded.

"Born and raised in these parts, both of 'em," he said. "And never any good, them or their relatives."

Knowing that the attack on him and the one on Bo and Brubaker had to be connected, Scratch asked, "Who else was in the tradin' post with them?"

The proprietor hesitated, as if worried that if he answered he might wind up on somebody's bad side, but after a moment he said, "Jink's brother Mort was in there, along with a couple of friends of theirs, Goose Tatum and Bridger Horn."

"And the three of them went out the back while Jink and Bob came out front, am I right?" Scratch guessed.

The storekeeper shrugged and nodded.

"Yeah, I reckon so. That's what happened."

"And then the shootin' started," the man wearing overalls put in. "What happened, mister? Are you the law?"

"That should be my question to ask," the suit-wearing windbag objected. "I'm Judge Hopper," he told Scratch. "Justice of the Peace in these parts."

"Well, things are plumb peaceful now, Judge," Scratch told him, "so I reckon you don't have to worry. They got quieted down with Winchesters. Works better than a gavel most of the time . . . just don't ever tell the Hangin' Judge I said that."

"Parker?" the local JP asked, sounding impressed. "You work for Judge Isaac Parker?"

"Right now I do," Scratch confirmed. "My partner and I are temporary deputies, helpin' out one of Parker's more permanent star packers." He nodded toward the rear of the building, where Cara was back on her feet and shuffling along with Bo and Brubaker behind her. "Here they come now."

Cara was quiet for a change, but the usual murderous fury burned in her eyes. Her expression softened slightly, though, as she looked at Scratch.

"Were you hurt, mister?" she asked, surprising him.

"Uh . . . no, I'm fine, I reckon," Scratch said. Given

the way she'd acted so far, he never would have expected the blond hellcat to inquire as to his health.

"Good. You seem to be about the closest thing to a gentleman in this bunch."

She cast scathing glares toward Bo and Brubaker.

The deputy swung the wagon door open.

"Get in there," he told Cara.

"What about us?" Dayton Lowe asked. "Don't we get to come out?"

"In a few minutes," Brubaker said. "I want to find out who these blasted troublemakers were."

"I can tell you that," Scratch said. "I've been talkin' to the fellas on the porch. These gunnies are local boys."

"Is that so?" Brubaker asked with a frown.

The justice of the peace spoke up.

"I'm Judge Theodore Hopper, Marshal," he said. "You're one of Judge Parker's men?"

"I am."

"Well, then, I extend my apologies for this unpleasant incident. I had no idea what those Staley boys and their no-account friends were planning to do . . . or why, for that matter."

"I've got a pretty good idea as to why," Brubaker said. He toed the wounded shoulder of the unconscious Jink Staley. "Wake up, you polecat."

Jink winced and groaned. His eyes fluttered open.

"Don't . . . don't do that," he begged. "I'm hurt awful bad."

"You'll feel worse in a minute if you don't tell me what I want to know." To reinforce his words,

Brubaker rested the sole of his boot on Jink's shoulder. The marshal didn't put any weight on it, but the threat was unmistakable.

"Marshal . . ." Bo began.

"Stay out of it, Creel," Brubaker snapped. "I'm handlin' this my way." To Jink, he went on, "Why'd you fellas try to jump us?"

"We . . . we heard about those prisoners . . . you're takin' to Texas." Jink had to force the words out through pale, tightly clenched lips. "We've always wanted to . . . ride with somebody like Hank Gentry. Figured that if we . . . turned these three loose . . . Hank would have to . . . let us in the gang."

Bo and Scratch glanced at each other. The wounded man's words held the ring of truth as far as the Texans were concerned.

Brubaker seemed to agree. He nodded and said, "All right. Can't say as I'm surprised." He looked up at the men on the porch. "Is there a doctor around here? Anywhere closer than Fort Smith?"

"There's a midwife who does a fair job of patchin' up bullet wounds," the storekeeper said.

"Good. Somebody can fetch her for this boy. And you can either plant the dead ones or throw 'em in a hog pen somewhere, it don't make no never mind to me which way you do it."

Brubaker looked down at Jink and leaned a little on the young man. Jink screamed at the pressure on his shattered shoulder.

"Got your attention?" Brubaker asked. "Listen to me, Staley. I ought to arrest you, but I've got places to go and things to take care of, so here's what I'm gonna do. I'm gonna let you go. But if I ever see you again, around here or up in Fort Smith or over in the Territory, I'm not gonna ask what you're doin' there. I'm not gonna even speak to you. I'm just gonna shoot you dead right then and there, you understand?"

Jink whimpered but didn't answer. Brubaker bore down with his boot again.

"I understand!" Jink screamed. "I understand! You won't n-never see me again, Marshal, I swear it."

"Good." Brubaker looked up at the storekeeper. "Got any hot food in there?"

"Yes, sir, we sure do," the man answered nervously. "Some nice roast beef."

"Bread?"

"Yes, sir."

"Slap some beef between bread, then, enough for the three of us. We'll get it when we're ready to pull out again."

Bo asked, "What about the prisoners?"

Grudgingly, Brubaker nodded and told the man in the apron, "Enough for them, too, I suppose. And some coffee, if you've got it. I promised 'em something to eat and drink. Now let's all get busy. The sooner we're back on the road again, the better, as far as I'm concerned."

CHAPTER 10

It took a while to get Lowe and Elam in and out of the privy. By that time the storekeeper had made the sandwiches. Bo, Scratch, and Brubaker ate first, then Scratch and the deputy covered the prisoners while Bo fed them and gave them sips of coffee from a wide-mouthed jug. The three outlaws were cooperative for a change, and Cara didn't even cuss at any of her captors.

Bo figured that hunger and thirst had gotten the best of their natural-born orneriness.

Finally Brubaker climbed to the seat and unwrapped the reins from the brake lever. He had his black hat resting on the back of his head so that it wouldn't rub against the welt where the bullet had grazed him. He had refused medical attention for the injury, insisting that it would be fine.

"If that slug had been a few inches to one side, it would've blown my brains out," he said. "But it didn't, so that tells me I ain't fated to die from it."

That seemed like pretty shaky reasoning to Bo, but Brubaker was in charge, so he didn't argue.

The wagon continued rolling southward all afternoon, with occasional stops so the team of horses pulling it could rest. Late in the day, which ended fairly early at this time of year, Bo asked Brubaker, "Are we going to try to find a settlement with a jail so we can lock up those three for the night?"

Brubaker shook his head.

"This wagon is sturdier than any back-country jail we're liable to find. They can stretch out on the floor to sleep. Judge Parker just said to get 'em there. He didn't say anything about keepin' 'em comfortable along the way."

"You're a pretty hard-nosed hombre, aren't you, Marshal?"

Brubaker snorted. "Try keepin' the peace in Indian Territory for a while," he suggested. "You'll learn right quick that gettin' sentimental is a good way of windin' up dead."

Bo couldn't dispute that. He had seen firsthand evidence of it over the years. There were plenty of bad men in the West who would stop at nothing, including cold-blooded murder, to get what they wanted. If you misjudged the wrong man, it usually meant a bullet. It was a hard land, and it took hard men to live in it, and trust was a rare commodity.

As they set up camp in a clearing where Brubaker had pulled off the road, Bo said to the deputy, "We'll be taking turns standing guard?"

"That's right," Brubaker said. "Think you can stay awake and alert enough to handle it?"

"We've stood many a night watch," Scratch said. "You can depend on us."

"Good. Because it's your lives at stake, too, not just mine. Hank Gentry and his men would kill you without ever blinkin' an eye."

Bo didn't doubt it. He had seen the sort of men who rode with Gentry.

And the sort of woman.

There was no outhouse around here, of course, so before it got dark, Bo and Brubaker took Cara into the bushes near the camp and let her tend to her business. Brubaker warned her to stay where he could see her head, and he kept his Colt trained on her the whole time.

When they got back to the wagon, Cara pouted and said, "Why can't Mr. Morton take me when I have to go? He's nicer than you two."

"He'd keep you covered just like I do," Brubaker said. "At least he would if he's got any sense."

"Yeah, but I'll bet he wouldn't leer at me."

"Dadgum it, I didn't leer—" The deputy stopped short for a second, then went on, "You're just tryin' to put a burr under my saddle. It's not gonna work."

Cara laughed. Bo figured she already had a burr under the deputy's saddle, and she knew it, too.

Scratch volunteered to do the cooking. He fried some bacon and cooked cornbread and beans to go with it. The meal was simple but good. After everyone had eaten and Bo and Scratch had checked on the horses one more time, Brubaker said, "I'll take the first watch. You fellas get some sleep."

It was going to be a cold night, but these were piney woods and the Texans had made comfortable beds by spreading their bedrolls on pine boughs. Brubaker tossed some blankets into the back of the wagon that the prisoners could use for warmth.

The deputy sat on a log near the fire as it burned down, and Bo and Scratch rolled up in their blankets and dropped right off to sleep with the innate ability of frontiersmen to grab some shut-eye whenever they had a chance. After a few hours Brubaker would wake up one of them to take his place.

Bo didn't know how much time had passed when an unearthly shriek jolted him out of his slumber. He sat up sharply with his gun in his hand, unaware that he had even drawn it from the holster and coiled shell belt beside him.

A few yards away, Scratch was awake and sitting up, too, both hands filled with his Remingtons.

"Take it easy, you two," Brubaker said from the log where he sat. The fire was just embers now, but their faint orange glow was enough for the Texans to see him. "That was just a big cat prowlin' around somewhere."

"Got panthers in these parts, do you?" Scratch asked.

"That's right. He's probably hungry. This time of year, the huntin's not too good. A lot of the smaller animals are denned up for the winter."

"Well, as long as he don't try to feast on us . . ."

Scratch said. He slid one of the long-barreled Remingtons back into its holster, then the other.

Bo still sat there holding his Colt. He frowned as he looked toward the area where the horses were picketed. Something was wrong, and after a second he figured out what it was.

When another panther screech ripped through the night, he was even more convinced. The sounds came from the north, and so did the wind.

That meant the scent of the panthers should have been carrying to the horses, and there was nothing like the smell of big cat to spook a bunch of horses.

The team and the saddle mounts all stood quietly with their heads down, though.

"That's not a panther," Bo said quietly. "Those are signals, and I reckon they mean somebody's in position."

"Son of a—" Brubaker burst out. "You're right! Everybody take—"

Before he could finish the order, shots blasted out of the darkness and tongues of orange muzzle flame ripped through the curtain of shadows.

CHAPTER 11

The walls that enclosed the back of the wagon were thick enough to stop a bullet, so the prisoners probably were safe in there. The narrow ventilation openings were set high in the walls so that even if a stray slug went through one of them, it wasn't likely to hit Cara, Lowe, or Elam.

Bo, Scratch, and Brubaker were in much more danger because they were out in the open. Brubaker flung himself from the log in a dive that carried him close to the wagon. He scrambled underneath so that the wheels would give him some cover.

The Texans were on the other side of the fire from the wagon, so they couldn't find protection there. Their only chance was to get into the trees.

Bo rolled out of his blankets, came up on one knee, and triggered three fast shots at the muzzle flashes. Then he leaped to his feet and dashed into the pines. Bullets thudded into tree trunks and whipped through the branches around him.

Scratch's twin Remingtons boomed as he retreated

into the trees as well. Brubaker's Winchester cracked from underneath the wagon. The bushwhackers continued firing, too, and for several moments the racket was deafening as shot after shot blasted out from several different directions. Muzzle flashes tore holes in the darkness and lit up the night with their eerie, flickering glow, like bolts of hellish lightning.

Bo pressed his back to the trunk of a pine and thumbed fresh cartridges into his Colt's cylinder, filling all six chambers. He knew that Brubaker was in a bad place. The wagon wheels didn't provide enough cover to keep the deputy safe for very long. At any moment a lucky shot from the bushwhackers might zip between the spokes and find him.

"Scratch!" Bo called. "Can you hear me?"

"Yeah," the reply came from the silver-haired Texan. "You all right, Bo?"

"So far," Bo said. "We need to circle. You go right, I'll go left."

"Keno!"

The shadows under the trees were thick. Bo slid to his left. With the uproar of all the shooting going on, stealth wasn't as important as it might have been otherwise, but he tried not to make a lot of noise anyway. No point in giving away his position if he didn't have to.

As far as he could tell, the bushwhackers were all to the north of the camp. From the sound of the shots and the muzzle flashes he had seen, he estimated there were at least five of them. If he and Scratch could flank the attackers and take them by surprise, the two Texans had a chance to fight off this terrifying assault.

If they couldn't . . . Well, he wasn't going to think too much about that, Bo told himself.

Moving by feel as much as anything else, he made his way through the trees. Brubaker kept shooting, and so did the bushwhackers. Shouted curses came from the prisoners inside the wagon. They could keep that up as far as Bo was concerned. The commotion helped cover up any sounds that he made.

His hand tightened on the butt of his Colt when he judged that he was getting close to the area where the riflemen were hidden. He peered through the shadows, spotted a muzzle flash, and worked his way closer to it. The next time the rifle cracked, the sudden spurt of flame from its barrel was bright enough to reveal a man crouched behind a big, fallen pine tree.

Bo drew a bead and could have gunned the man then and there, but he held off on the trigger. If the attackers were Gentry's men, as seemed likely, they were wanted, too. If they could be taken alive, Bo, Scratch, and Brubaker could deliver them to Judge Southwick in Tyler along with Cara, Lowe, and Elam.

Dropping to hands and knees, Bo crawled closer until he was only a few feet away from the rifleman, who had paused in his attack to reload. The man seemed completely unaware of Bo's presence.

Bo waited until the bushwhacker thrust the barrel of his rifle over the log again, then struck with swift, brutal force. He reversed the Colt and brought the butt down on the man's head. The smashing impact was enough to make the man drop his rifle and slump forward over the deadfall.

Bo hit him again, just to make sure he was out cold, then tossed the man's rifle away into the brush. The bushwhacker wore a holstered revolver, too, Bo discovered as he ran a hand over the man's body. He took that gun and threw it into the brush as well after emptying the bullets from it.

Bo ripped strips from the unconscious man's shirt and used them to tie his hands and feet. That was the best he could do for now. He started stalking the next bushwhacker, sparing a thought for Scratch and a hope that his old friend was all right.

Scratch had understood what Bo meant by circling. They had done things like this many times in the past, splitting up so they could come at the enemy from two different directions. He just hoped they could deal with those bushwhackers before one of them ventilated Brubaker. The deputy had done the only thing he could when the shooting started, but now he was pinned down in a precarious position.

Scratch had holstered his left-hand Remington after reloading it. His right hand still clutched the ivory handle of the other revolver.

As he slipped through the shadows, he remembered a night more than four decades earlier when he and some other young Texicans had snuck into a camp of Santa Anna's scouts while the vast Mexican army wasn't far off. They were after supplies that night, since Sam Houston's forces were half-starved by that point, and it would have been fine with Scratch if they could have gotten into the Mexican camp and back out again without being discovered.

Things hadn't worked out that way. One of the other fellas had done something to alert the enemy—after all these years, Scratch couldn't even remember what it was—and suddenly muskets and flintlock pistols had been roaring and some of the Mexican soldiers lunged at the intruders with their bayonets.

Scratch had barely avoided getting skewered that night. He had grabbed a Mexican officer's saber and done a little skewering of his own before he and his companions lit a shuck out of there with some bags of beans they had managed to snag. But ever since then, Scratch hadn't been too fond of creeping around in the dark.

At least in the dead of winter like this, he didn't have to worry about stepping on a snake. Timber rattlers were plentiful in these Arkansas hills at other times of year.

Scratch crouched lower as muzzle flame bloomed in the darkness only a few yards from him. He was closing in on one of the bushwhackers. He didn't want to alert the others that they had intruders among them, so he waited until a whole flurry of shots rang out before leveling the Remington and squeezing off two swift shots. As the echoes of the blasts faded, he heard something crash in the brush and hoped that it was his quarry collapsing with some good Texan lead in him.

Scratch figured he would move on to the next bushwhacker he could find, but he had gone only a few feet when somebody exploded out of the shadows and crashed into him, fighting like a wildcat. A fist smashed into Scratch's jaw. The punch landing so cleanly had to be pure luck. It was too dark under these trees for anybody to see where he was aiming his blows.

But luck or not, the punch packed enough power to stun Scratch for a moment and send him stumbling back into a rough-barked pine trunk.

He didn't drop his gun. As more blows pounded his body, he slashed out with the Remington and felt it strike something with a glancing blow. That gave his attacker pause and provided a chance for Scratch to hook his left fist out in a blind punch.

His fist sunk in something soft. A man's sour breath gusted in Scratch's face. Knowing the man was close to him, he lowered his head and butted hard in front of him. He felt the hot spurt of blood across his forehead as his opponent's nose flattened under the impact.

Scratch swung the Remington again, and this time the revolver's barrel landed solidly. A heavy weight sagged against the Texan. Scratch shoved it aside. The man landed with a thump at his feet.

That made two of the varmints accounted for, he thought . . . unless this fella who had jumped him was the same one he'd shot a few moments earlier. He couldn't rule out that possibility. The bushwhacker might have been wounded, but not enough to put him out of the fight.

Scratch ran his fingers along the barrel of his revolver to make sure it hadn't bent when he walloped the hombre with it. If you were going to hit a man with a gun, it was better to use the butt, but he hadn't had time to turn the weapon around.

The Remington seemed to be all right. Scratch started working his way through the darkness again. It seemed like there weren't as many shots coming from the trees now, and he wondered if Bo had already taken care of one or two of the varmints.

Crouched in the darkness, Bo waited for a muzzle flash to pinpoint the location of another rifleman. As slugs zinged through the trees around him, he smiled grimly as he wondered if some of the bullets came from Deputy Marshal Brubaker's gun. Brubaker didn't know what he and Scratch were trying to do. As far as he would be able to tell, huddled there underneath the wagon, the Texans might as well have deserted him.

Bo was willing to take his chances. He didn't have any other choice.

Flame licked from the muzzle of a rifle in some

brush about twenty feet to his right. He shifted in that direction.

And then suddenly there was nothing under his feet but empty air. He lost his balance and fell forward, crashing down on a steep slope. Branches clawed at him as he continued rolling, unable to stop his plunge. In some part of his mind, he knew that he had fallen into a gully or a ravine that he had never seen in the darkness. And he had no way of knowing how deep it was . . .

CHAPTER 12

He found out a couple of seconds later when he crashed into something solid with such force that it left him stunned, breathless, and unable to move. He was on the bottom of the ravine.

Dirt and pine needles rained down on him from above, pelting his face and causing him to jerk his head to the side even though the rest of his body still wouldn't respond to him. Bo knew what the little avalanche meant. Somebody was sliding down the other side of the ravine, coming down after him, and he was sure they didn't mean him any good.

He willed his muscles to move, to send him scrambling away, but they were stubbornly unwilling for several seconds. He finally rolled onto his belly and with an effort pushed himself to his hands and knees.

Before he could start crawling, a great weight landed on his back, knocking the breath out of him again. An arm looped around his neck and jerked tight, cutting off his air as a knee pinned him to the ground.

"Thought I heard somebody fall down in this

gulch," a man's gravelly voice said. "Thought ye could sneak up on me, did ye? You son of a bitch! I'll choke the life out o' ye!"

The man was doing a pretty fair job of it, too. The brawny arm across Bo's throat threatened to crush his windpipe. The knee in his back bent his spine painfully. His lungs cried out desperately for air.

And he had dropped his gun when he plummeted into the ravine, so he didn't even have a weapon.

His hands moved over the ground around him in the dark, searching for something, anything. His fingers brushed against a rough surface, lost it for a second, then found it again. He closed his hand on a piece of broken pine branch slightly bigger around than his wrist. He didn't know how long it was, but when he lifted it, it felt heavy enough to work as a weapon.

A red haze from lack of breath began to settle over his brain. Knowing that he could pass out at any second, Bo struck upward and back with the makeshift club.

The blow landed with enough power to make the would-be killer grunt in pain. The pressure on Bo's throat lessened but didn't go away completely. He struck again with the branch.

This time the man's grip slipped enough that Bo was able to writhe free. He drove an elbow up and back into the man's midsection, even as he gasped and dragged air into his lungs. Twisting around, he held the club in both hands and swung it as hard as he could.

When the blow landed he heard something crack.

At first he didn't know if it was the pine branch or one of his opponent's bones. But the howl of pain the man let out told Bo it was probably a bone. Bo swung again but didn't hit anything this time.

He heard a scrambling sound, and more dirt cascaded down around him. The man was fleeing, climbing up the side of the ravine. That was confirmed when Bo heard him yell in a voice like ten miles of bad road, "Come on, boys! Let's get outta here!"

A few shots still rang out, but the sounds of battle began to fade quickly. Bo braced himself with a hand against the steeply sloping side of the narrow ravine and heaved to his feet. He didn't have his gun, so he continued gripping the pine branch in case he was attacked again.

That seemed unlikely, though, he thought as a swift rataplan of hoofbeats drifted through the chilly night air and began to fade. It sounded like the bushwhackers were taking off for the tall and uncut, all right.

Bo stood there, his chest rising and falling rapidly as he tried to catch his breath. When he thought he was up to the task, he started trying to climb out of the ravine.

It was tough going. The slope was steep enough that he had to catch hold of roots that stuck out of the ground to pull himself up.

He was still climbing when Scratch called softly from somewhere above him, "Bo! Bo, are you around here?"

"Down here!" he replied. "Better stop moving

around, Scratch, or you're liable to fall in this ravine like I did. I never saw it in the dark."

"Son of a gun! Are you hurt?"

"Shaken up a little, and some bumps and bruises, that's all," Bo told his old friend. "Plus one of those hombres tried to strangle me. Reckon I'll live, though."

"Can you get out? Do I need to fetch a rope?"

"I think I can make it. Hold on."

A couple of minutes later, Bo reached the top and rolled over it onto level ground. The exertion of the climb had made him sweat despite the cold. A shiver went through him as the night breezes hit his damp face and made him even chillier.

He sat up and said, "All right. I'm out of that blasted hole in the ground."

Scratch followed his voice and came over to him. "Are you sure you're not hurt?"

"Yeah, but I lost my gun when I fell, and I'm not very happy about that."

"Maybe we can find it later. Let me give you a hand. We better get back to camp and make sure ol' Forty-two's all right."

"And the prisoners," Bo added as Scratch bent, took hold of his arm, and hauled him to his feet.

Scratch snorted in response to his old friend's comment.

"I ain't worried overmuch about those three," he said. "But I expect they're fine, locked up in that box like they are."

"Did you swap lead with any of those bushwhackers?" Bo asked as they tried to find their way back to the camp in the thick darkness. The fact that both Texans possessed superb senses of direction came in handy.

"I shot one of 'em and walloped another," Scratch replied. "Or maybe it was the same one, I ain't sure about that. We'll have to get a torch and check."

"I knocked one out and tied him up," Bo said. "If he's one of Gentry's men, Deputy Brubaker will have himself another prisoner to deliver."

"Heck, it might be Gentry his own self," Scratch said. "Wouldn't that be somethin'?"

It would indeed, but Bo wasn't going to count on that. The man he'd tussled with at the bottom of the ravine had sounded like the leader of the bunch, and that gent had gotten away.

"Creel! Morton!" That was Brubaker, calling from the camp. "Are you out there?"

"We're here!" Bo replied. "And we're coming in!"

They followed the sound of Brubaker's voice and a moment later came out into the clearing where the wagon was parked. The deputy hunkered on his heels next to the fire, stirring up the ashes and adding twigs and dried pine needles until flames began to leap up again and cast a circle of faint light around the camp.

"Where did you two go?" Brubaker asked as he straightened and looked at the Texans.

"Why, we're just fine, thank you most to death," Scratch said. "Appreciate you inquirin' about our health."

"I can tell you're both up and walkin' around, so I know you ain't dead," Brubaker snapped.

"We circled around and flanked those bushwhackers," Bo explained. "We were able to drive them off."

"Kill any of 'em?"

"We don't know yet. We'll have to get a torch and go have a look. How about you, Marshal? Are you hurt?"

"No, they made it pretty hot under that wagon for me, but I wasn't hit."

"Have you checked on the prisoners?"

"They all called out and said they were all right when I asked them," Brubaker said. "If you're asking if I unlocked that door to take a look at them, hell, no."

"I imagine they're fine," Bo said.

The fire was burning strongly now, so he found a branch that was thinner and lighter than the one he had used as a club and set it on fire. That would make a good enough torch for him and Scratch to find their way around in the woods.

"We're going to take a look around," he said as he held the torch in his left hand and used his right to pull his Winchester from its sheath.

It was difficult to tell exactly where they had fought their battles a short time earlier. Everything looked different in the flickering light of the torch. After a few minutes, though, Bo was convinced he'd found the log where he had knocked out the ambusher. He could see the scuff marks of their struggle on the ground beside the fallen tree.

But the man was gone, and Bo was forced to come

to the conclusion that one of his friends had found him and turned him loose.

They were luckier when it came to the man Scratch had shot. That hombre lay on his side in a pool of blood, dead.

"We'll take him back to camp so Deputy Brubaker can look at him. If he's one of Gentry's gang, Brubaker ought to be able to identify him."

Scratch bent and grasped the corpse's ankles. He dragged the body roughly through the woods, not being disposed to worry about being gentle with the carcass of a man who'd just tried to kill him.

Bo had thought there was something oddly familiar about the man's face, and once they reached the camp and he was able to study it in the better light from the fire, he was sure of it.

"I don't know him," Brubaker declared. "To the best of my recollection, I've never seen him before. That doesn't rule him out completely from being a member of Gentry's gang, but it's pretty unlikely."

"I'd say you're right," Bo agreed, "because I think there's a definite family resemblance between this man and those Staleys who jumped us back at the trading post."

Brubaker leaned closer to the dead man and frowned in concentration. After a moment he said, "By God, I think you're right, Creel. This is another one of that bunch."

Scratch said, "You reckon the rest of the family found out what happened at Clark's, and they came after us with vengeance in mind?"

"That seems mighty likely to me," Brubaker said. "Blood feuds are common in this part of the country."

"They're common just about everywhere," Bo pointed out, while Scratch made a disgusted sound. In their drifting, they had run across several "to the last man" feuds, and such conflicts were usually bloody and senseless.

"That's just what we need," the silver-haired Texan said. "Not only do we have to worry about a bunch of bloodthirsty desperadoes wantin' us dead, but now we've got a whole clan of ridge-runnin' hillbillies after us!"

"Not everybody in Arkansas is a hillbilly, Tex," Brubaker shot back at him.

"No matter what you call them, they're trouble," Bo said. "And that's one thing we already had plenty of without this."

Brubaker nodded as he looked down at the dead man.

"You're right about that, Creel," he said. "And come mornin', I know damn well what I'm gonna do about it!"

CHAPTER 13

"What do you mean, we're gonna cut west into Indian Territory?" Scratch asked Brubaker as he and Bo rode alongside the wagon the next morning. "Ain't it even more uncivilized and lawless than Arkansas?"

The rest of the night had passed peacefully. In the gray light of dawn, while Brubaker was hitching up the team, Bo and Scratch had carried the dead man's body back to the ravine and dumped it in the deep gulch. Bo shoved some loose brush down on top of it. That was all the burial they could be bothered with for a no-good bushwhacker.

While they were doing that, they also searched the ravine until Bo found the revolver he had dropped the night before. It needed to be cleaned, but other than that it was none the worse for wear.

By the time they got back to the camp, Brubaker had the wagon ready to go. No one had had any breakfast yet, and Jim Elam had called from inside the wagon, "Hey! Ain't you gonna feed us?"

"Later," Brubaker had replied. "Right now I want to put some distance between us and this place."

He had done so, keeping the team moving at a good clip as the sun climbed over the eastern horizon and then rose through the sky. An hour or so had passed before the deputy marshal abruptly swung the wagon off the road and onto a narrow, rutted trail that meandered off to the west.

Bo had asked him where he was going, and Brubaker had replied that they were cutting west into Indian Territory, prompting Scratch's question. Now, in reply to the silver-haired Texan, Brubaker said, "Yeah, the Territory may be lawless and uncivilized, but I know just about every square foot of it, and travelin' along that main road makes us sittin' ducks for anybody who's on our trail."

"I can't argue with that, Marshal," Bo said, "but doesn't Gentry know this part of the country pretty well, too?"

Brubaker shrugged. "Sure, I suppose he does. And he's got friends among the tribes, too, hard though that may be to believe about such a bloody-handed scoundrel. But I'm bettin' those blasted Staleys won't know all the little trails and the cut-offs as well as I do, so maybe we can shake them off our trail, anyway."

"Can you get the wagon through?" Scratch asked. "It's pretty rugged over there."

"Sure I can," Brubaker replied with conviction. "It'll be rougher going, but we can make it through. We'll head west a ways, cut down to one of the Red

River crossings, and then swing back east to Tyler." He paused for a moment, then went on, "Might add as much as a week to our trip, but we'll stand a better chance of gettin' there safe with the prisoners."

Scratch scowled and said, "Addin' a week makes our wages not quite as good."

"You're gettin' paid by the mile, too, remember," Brubaker reminded him.

"Yeah, but if I know ol' Bigfoot Southwick, and I do, he'll try to say he'll only pay us for what would've been the shortest route. He'll claim goin' the long way around was our decision and his court oughtn't to be out any dinero because of it."

"If he does, I'll . . . I'll . . ." Brubaker didn't finish his sentence.

"Yeah, that's what I thought," Scratch said. "Who among us is gonna argue with a federal judge and come out a winner?"

"Let's just worry about that when the time comes," Bo suggested. "Right now, it seems like Deputy Brubaker's idea is a pretty good one."

Brubaker made a growling sound in his throat.

"You might as well call me Forty-two," he told Bo. "If we're gonna be travelin' together for nigh on to two weeks, there ain't no point to bein' formal."

Bo smiled and nodded.

"I'll be glad to, Forty-two. And you can call me Bo."

Brubaker just made that noise in his throat again, as if being friendly pained him.

He followed the narrow trail for several miles

before hauling back on the reins and bringing the team to a halt.

"I reckon we can stop here long enough to rustle up some grub," he said.

"Sounds mighty good to me," Scratch agreed with a nod. He swung down from the saddle. "I'll get a fire going and put the coffee on to boil."

The prisoners had been quiet this morning. Bo figured they hadn't been able to sleep much on the floor of the wagon the night before and were tired. Regardless of the reason, the lack of cussing and yelling from the back of the wagon made for a much more pleasant journey.

After bacon, biscuits, and coffee, Cara asked—in a polite tone of voice, no less—if she could visit the bushes again. Brubaker agreed, then said, "Hell, you go with her this time, Morton. She seems to like you."

Scratch frowned as he thumbed back his cream-colored Stetson.

"I ain't sure I'm comfortable—" he began.

"You ain't bein' paid to be comfortable," Brubaker told him. "There's nothin' comfortable about this whole blasted trip."

Scratch shrugged and said, "I reckon you're right about that. You gonna unlock that chain from the floor for her?"

"Keep all three of 'em covered," Brubaker said as he took the key from his pocket.

As he had done before, he let the heavy chain dangle after he'd unlocked it from the ring set in the floor. He climbed out of the wagon and moved back, drawing his gun as he did so. He stood directly behind the wagon, with Bo to the right and Scratch to the left, each of them holding a Winchester.

"All right, climb out," Brubaker told Cara.

She started down the steps hesitantly. As she did, the hanging chain swung between her ankles, and she swayed suddenly as it caused her to lose her balance. A frightened cry burst from her lips. With her hands fastened behind her back, she couldn't do anything to catch her balance or stop herself from plowing face-first into the ground when she fell.

As she toppled off the steps, Scratch jumped forward to catch her.

"Morton, no!" Brubaker yelled, but he was too late. Scratch already had his right arm around Cara as she fell against him. He held the Winchester in his left hand. He had to take a quick step back and plant his right foot solidly on the ground to keep from losing his own balance.

Brubaker whipped up his gun and pointed it at the young woman.

"Step away from her, Morton!" he ordered. "I'll shoot her if she tries anything!"

"Settle down, dadgummit," Scratch told the deputy. "She ain't tryin' anything. She just fell, that's all."

"You can't trust her, not for a second," Brubaker warned, "and you can't give her a damn inch!"

Cara ignored Brubaker. She looked up at Scratch, smiled, and said, "Thank you, Deputy."

"Oh, you don't have to call me deputy, miss,"

Scratch said. "It's just a temporary job. My name's Scratch."

"I know," Cara said.

"All right, that's enough, blast it," Brubaker said. He grabbed the chain that linked Cara's hands together behind her back and jerked her away from Scratch, causing her to let out a little cry of pain. "We all know what you're tryin' to do, and it ain't gonna work. Come on, you, if you really got business you need to tend to."

Cara objected, "But you said Scratch could—"

"Changed my mind," Brubaker snapped.

He pulled and shoved her into the brush. When they were gone, Bo said to Scratch, "You know she fell into your arms on purpose, don't you?"

"Well, she might've," Scratch admitted, "but it's hard to be sure. Havin' a chain floppin' around your feet really could trip a person up, I'd think."

"I suppose," Bo said. "But she's got it in her head she can play up to you, no doubt about that."

A grin stretched across Scratch's rugged face.

"It won't do her any good," he declared, "but I guess she's welcome to try."

Bo tried not to let the worry he felt show on his face. Scratch had always had an eye for a pretty girl, and sometimes his feelings could make him do reckless things. True, Cara LaChance was young enough to be his daughter, and his taste usually ran to women closer to his own age, but that wasn't always the case. More than once some young saloon girl had led him on and caused trouble.

More than likely none of those saloon girls were as dangerous as Cara LaChance, though, Bo thought.

"Don't forget that a couple of days ago she tried to cut you wide open with a razor," he reminded Scratch.

"Aw, shoot, that was before she knew me as well as she does now." Scratch chuckled, then added, "Don't worry, Bo. I ain't some moonstruck kid."

That was true, but Bo figured that a moonstruck old codger might be just as dangerous . . . if not more so!

They moved on a short time later, and Brubaker pushed the horses fairly hard all day. Everybody was tired by the time the deputy called a halt to make camp late that afternoon. They were in more rugged country now, as Scratch had predicted. The hills were steep, rather than rolling, and a number of rocky bluffs cut across the landscape.

They made camp where one of those bluffs dropped off sharply into a thickly wooded valley. A little creek flowed up to and over the edge of the bluff, forming a waterfall. Bo looked over the brink and saw spray rising up from the pool that the waterfall formed at the bottom.

"This is a pretty nice place, in a wild sort of way," he commented.

"Yeah," Brubaker agreed. "I've watered my horse down there at that pool more than once, and I expect every owlhoot in these parts has, too. We'll fill our water barrels from the creek before we pull out in the morning."

Cara didn't ask for Scratch to accompany her this time when she tended to her needs. He was busy fixing supper, anyway. But he saw her looking at him while Brubaker was leading her back and forth, and he smiled as he lowered his head toward the skillet full of bacon on the fire.

Sure, she was loco and as dangerous as a bag full of wildcats, but she was also mighty nice looking, and Scratch had never minded the attention of a good-lookin' woman.

That was all it would ever amount to, of course. She was on her way to Texas to hang for her crimes, and from what he knew of her, Scratch figured it was a well-deserved fate. But it was sad, too. She had gone wrong somewhere in her life, bad wrong, and that was just a pure-dee shame.

Bo's voice broke into his thoughts just then, saying with a note of urgency, "Riders coming."

CHAPTER 14

Scratch straightened and stepped away from the fire, as he did so picking up the rifle he had laid aside when he started to prepare supper. Bo held his Winchester, too, and Brubaker snatched his Henry from the driver's seat of the wagon. The deputy had just put Cara back into the vehicle and locked the door.

The hoofbeats grew louder as the riders approached. At first Bo hadn't heard them very well because of the noise of the waterfall, and it occurred to him that maybe this wasn't a very good place to camp after all.

From the sound of the horses, at least three or four riders were coming toward the camp, maybe more. Brubaker took cover behind the wagon and motioned for the Texans to do likewise.

The hoofbeats stopped as the three men waited tensely. A moment of silence went by before a voice called, "Hello, the camp! We're friendly! All right to come in?"

"Do it slow and easy, with your hands in plain

sight!" Brubaker shouted back. "You've got a dozen rifles pointed at you!"

With a steady *clip-clop* of hooves on the ground, four riders moved up into the circle of light cast by the fire. They wore slouch hats and long dusters. Bo saw gun belts under the coats, and each man had the butt of a rifle sticking up from a saddle boot. As Brubaker had ordered, they had their hands half-lifted and well away from the weapons.

Even though the strangers were dressed like white men, their faces had a ruddy glow that didn't come completely from the firelight, although the flames might have exaggerated the effect. Their skin color and their high cheekbones made it obvious these men were Indians.

Brubaker suddenly asked, "Charley Graywolf, is that you?"

One of the men grinned.

"I thought I recognized that growl of yours, Forty-two. All right if we put our hands down now?"

Brubaker glanced over at Bo and Scratch and nodded to indicate that these newcomers weren't a threat. He said, "Yeah, put 'em down."

He lowered his rifle and came out from behind the wagon. Bo and Scratch followed suit.

"This is an old friend of mine, Charley Graywolf," Brubaker said. "I don't know the other fellas, but I'd wager that they're members of the Cherokee Lighthorse, too."

"That's right," the man called Charley Graywolf

said. He jerked a thumb toward his companions. "This is Duck Forbes, Walt Moon, and Joe Reeder."

Brubaker inclined his head toward the Texans.

"Bo Creel and Scratch Morton," he introduced them. "A couple of temporary deputies. What brings you boys out here?"

Graywolf didn't answer right away. Instead he said, "I could ask the same thing of you, Forty-two."

Brubaker slapped a hand against the side of the wagon.

"Transportin' some prisoners down to Texas. They're goin' to Judge Southwick's court in Tyler."

"Kind of off the main road, aren't you?" Graywolf asked with a puzzled frown.

"Yeah, and for good reason," Brubaker replied. "We've got trouble doggin' us, and we're tryin' to shake loose from it."

"This is good country to throw somebody off your trail, all right," Graywolf said with a nod. "All right if we get down and share your fire?"

Brubaker gestured toward the flames and said, "Sure. You're welcome to coffee, too."

Graywolf grinned as he swung down from the saddle.

"Only if you'll let us throw in some provisions for supper," he said.

"Not necessary," Brubaker told him. "I know when you boys are out on the scout, you travel light."

Graywolf shrugged. "That's true. How'd you know we're looking for somebody?"

"The Lighthorse don't send out Charley Graywolf

unless there's a mighty good reason, and those fellas with you look like they've got plenty of bark on their hides, too."

"It's true," Graywolf said with a grim nod. "We're looking for some men who raided a farm north of here. Slaughtered the whole family who lived there and looted the place, not that there was much to steal."

Brubaker grunted and said, "Sounds like Hank Gentry's bunch. I've got three of 'em locked up in here."

He nodded toward the wagon.

"No, these were redskinned scoundrels," Graywolf said as he shook his head. "One of the victims managed to write the name 'Kinlock' in his own blood. Nat Kinlock's a Cherokee. We've suspected for a while that he and some of his friends were behind a string of robberies over around Checotah. Now we're sure of it, and we're going to bring him in." Graywolf paused. "Or plant him and his boys."

"Well, I wish you luck," Brubaker said. "We'll share our camp tonight and go separate ways in the morning."

"Sounds good," Graywolf agreed.

The Cherokee lawmen began unsaddling their horses. Bo had heard of the Cherokee Lighthorse, but as far as he recalled he had never met any of them. They looked like tough, competent men. The Cherokee had their own towns and government, and as one of the so-called Five Civilized Tribes, they lived more like white men than did their nomadic cousins to the north and west. They were lawyers, doctors, teachers, farmers, and businessmen . . . but the Cherokee Nation had outlaws among its members, too, and that was the reason the Lighthorse existed.

There was a friendly camaraderie between Brubaker and the Indian lawmen, and Bo and Scratch liked them as well. Tonight they could sleep a little easier, Bo mused. It was unlikely anybody would attack such a large, well-armed group. Although Hank Gentry's gang was supposed to be even larger, he reminded himself, so it would still be necessary to remain alert and stand guard all night.

When they had finished eating, Brubaker told Bo and Scratch, "All right, we'll feed the prisoners now."

"Who do you have in custody?" Charley Graywolf asked.

"Cara LaChance, Jim Elam, and Dayton Lowe."

Graywolf's hard-planed face grew even more grim.

"That LaChance woman is said to be full of evil spirits," he said. "And the other two aren't much better. Gentry's gang have robbed and killed a number of Cherokees."

"I know," Brubaker said, "and Judge Parker would like nothin' more than to hang 'em for it. But the authorities down in Texas have first claim on them because of all the hell they raised down there before coming up here to the Nations. Don't worry, they'll get what's comin' to 'em."

"As long as justice is done, that's all that matters, I suppose," Graywolf agreed. "I wish we could escort you all the way to the Red River to make sure you reach Texas safely, Forty-two, but we have a job of our own to do."

Brubaker nodded. "I understand. I'm glad we ran into you, anyway. It'll be nice not havin' to worry as much about somebody jumpin' us tonight."

After the prisoners were fed and taken out of the wagon one by one to take care of their needs, the camp settled down for the night. Bo had the first watch, and Charley Graywolf told Duck Forbes to take his turn then, as well.

Bo didn't mind having the company. It was easier to stay awake and alert if there was someone to talk to, and Duck proved to be a pleasant companion. He was short and stocky, with a round face that creased easily in a grin. He had been a member of the Cherokee Lighthorse for a couple of years, he explained to Bo as the two of them sat on rocks just outside the circle of light from the campfire.

"My father's a teacher," Duck said, "and he always figured I would be, too, but I just couldn't see sitting in a classroom all day. I always liked to be out doing things."

Bo knew that the Cherokee were maybe the only Indian tribe with a written language. The Cherokee Nation even had its own newspaper. As a people, they valued education.

But a society needed lawmen, too, so Bo thought Duck's decision was a good one.

They sat and chatted for a while before settling down to pass the time in companionable silence. Other than a couple of trips to Fort Smith, Duck had never been anywhere except Indian Territory, so he was especially interested in hearing about all the places where the Texans' wanderings had taken them.

"One of these days I'll see all that for myself," he said. "Especially the ocean. Wouldn't it be somethin' to stand there and look out over all that water, just goin' on and on like it was never gonna end."

Scratch took the second turn on guard, joined by lean, taciturn Jim Reeder. Bo said good night to Duck and rolled up in his blankets to get a few hours of sleep, knowing that Brubaker would want to be on the move again by dawn.

Dayton Lowe was in a bad mood when Brubaker awoke the prisoners while the sky was just turning gray in the east. While Lowe was out of the wagon, he glared at Charley Graywolf and the other members of the Cherokee Lighthorse.

"Filthy redskins," the burly Lowe muttered. "I could barely sleep last night because the stink of Indians was so strong around here."

"Keep a civil tongue in your head," Brubaker told the prisoner.

"Why? I ain't worried about hurtin' some damn buck's feelin's. The savages probably don't even understand what I'm sayin'."

Graywolf and the other men ignored Lowe. They'd probably had to put up with ignorant insults like that from whites many times over the years, Bo thought.

"Are you planning to cut through Massasauga Valley?" Graywolf asked Brubaker as they were all getting ready to leave.

"That's right," the deputy replied.

"That's the way the trail we've been following leads. Nat Kinlock has some family over that way. We think he may be figuring on hiding out with them. Since we're going in the same direction anyway . . ."

"I'd be pleased to have you ride along with us for a while," Brubaker answered without hesitation.

That was all right with Bo and Scratch, too, although they would have gone along with whatever Brubaker decided, since he was in charge. After a quick breakfast of pan bread and coffee, the group started in a generally westward direction along the winding trail. The sun hadn't quite risen above the eastern horizon yet, although it was already painting the sky with red and gold light. The air was still and cold, and frost lay heavy on the grass, glittering as the light grew stronger.

By midmorning the frost had melted and dried, and the sun was warmer as it washed over the rugged landscape. The going was rather slow because the trail had to twist and turn so much to avoid ridges, deep gullies, and impassible cliffs. In many places the trees crowded in close to the sides of the trail, which was barely wide enough to allow the wagon to pass. Bo, Scratch, Charley Graywolf, and Duck Forbes rode in front of the vehicle while the other Cherokee Lighthorsemen brought up the rear. There wasn't room for them to flank the wagon.

After several miles the trees thinned somewhat and the trail widened. Up ahead to the left of the trail loomed a rocky bluff. Out of habit, Bo studied it closely, searching for the glint of sunlight on metal that would tell him someone was up there. Beside him, Duck was saying, "Something else I'd like to see one of these days is a desert. Growin' up here in the Nations where there are trees and bushes everywhere you look, I can't imagine a place where there's nothin' but sand. You and Scratch ever been to a desert, Bo?"

"Death Valley, out in California," Bo said. "That's about as barren a place as you'd ever want to see. And White Sands, over in New Mexico Territory. Miles and miles of sand so white and bright it'll just about blind you when the sun shines on it."

"That would sure be somethin' to see, all right," Duck agreed. "I'm gonna save my money, and after I put in a few more years in the Lighthorse, I'll—"

Bo straightened in the saddle as he spotted the glint of sunlight reflecting off something on top of that bluff, which was now only about a hundred yards away. He opened his mouth to interrupt Duck, but before he could say anything, the flat crack of a rifle shot split the morning air.

And beside Bo, Duck Forbes grunted in pain and rocked back in his saddle.

CHAPTER 15

Bo caught a glimpse of the puff of powder smoke from the top of the bluff, but he was already turning to look at Duck. The stocky Cherokee, his eyes wide with pain, swayed back and forth in the saddle as he pressed a hand to his chest. Blood welled between his splayed-out fingers, telling Bo that Duck was badly wounded.

Everybody in the group had heard the shot and knew they were under attack. Brubaker yanked back on the team's reins, bringing the wagon to a halt as he shouted, "Everybody spread out!"

At the same time, Charley Graywolf yelled, "Take cover!"

Both of those commands sent the riders scattering for the closest rocks or trees.

Bo leaned over and grabbed the reins of Duck's horse. The tribal policeman had dropped them when he was shot. Clinging tightly to the reins, Bo led Duck's mount behind him as he galloped toward a cluster of boulders. He hoped Duck could manage to stay in the saddle.

More shots came from the bluff. Bo didn't know where the bullets went, but he reached the rocks without being hit. When he was safely behind the boulders, he dismounted almost before his horse stopped moving and sprang to the side of Duck's horse just as the young Cherokee toppled off the animal. Bo caught him and eased him to the ground.

Duck's mouth opened and closed several times as he looked up at Bo. He seemed to be struggling to say something. He couldn't get the words out, though. The only sound that came from him was a cross between a wheeze and a whistle . . . and that came from the hole in his chest.

Bo knew that sound meant the bullet had penetrated one of Duck's lungs. He ripped Duck's shirt open and saw the bullet hole still welling bright, frothy blood. Tearing off a piece of Duck's shirt, he wadded it up and shoved it into the opening as hard as he could. That would serve two purposes. It would slow down the bleeding and also close the wound temporarily, which would help Duck breathe.

Duck's distress seemed to ease slightly, but he still couldn't say anything.

"Take it easy," Bo told him. "Try not to move around any. You'll see those oceans and deserts yet, Duck."

Bo wasn't sure of that at all, but he wanted to give Duck some hope to hold on to. When a man was badly wounded, despair was often fatal, but stubborn determination and a fighting spirit could bring him back from the brink of death.

Bo ran to his horse and pulled his Winchester from its sheath. The shooting still continued, and he could tell now that the members of Charley Graywolf's posse were returning the ambusher's fire. He figured Scratch and Brubaker were getting in on the action, too. He crawled up a huge, slanting slab of rock so he could get a look at the trail and the bluff where the hidden rifleman was located.

Several shots from a clump of trees on the other side of the trail drew his attention. He caught a glimpse of what looked like Scratch's cream-colored Stetson and watched until he got a better look at his old friend. Scratch poked the barrel of his rifle around a tree trunk and squeezed off a shot. When he drew back, Bo called, "Scratch!"

The silver-haired Texan looked over, grinned, and waved. Bo returned the wave. Confident now that they were both all right, he turned his attention to the man on top of the bluff.

Large boulders lined the edge of that outcropping. The rifleman was probably firing through a narrow gap between a couple of the rocks, which meant it would be almost impossible for their return fire to hit him. He could sit up there and keep them pinned down all day.

Evidently that wasn't his goal, because he shifted his aim to the wagon and started peppering it with slugs. Cara screamed and Lowe and Elam bellowed curses, making Bo wonder if some of the bullets had gone through the ventilation slits and whipped around the heads of the prisoners. That was possible, considering the angle from which the ambusher was firing.

Scratch must have been worried about the same thing, because he yelled at the wagon, "Cara! You and those boys get down as low as you can!"

The fact that the prisoners were being endangered probably meant that the man on the bluff wasn't trying to free them. Indeed, he didn't seem to care if he killed them. That ruled out Hank Gentry and his gang.

The most likely possibility was that the men being pursued by the Cherokee Lighthorse had left someone behind to slow them down. In that case, the man wouldn't know who Bo, Scratch, and Brubaker were, nor why the wagon was traveling with Charley Graywolf and the others. But to him, they would all be enemies, anyway.

The bullets were coming too close to the team. The normally stolid draft horses finally spooked and lunged forward against their harness, desperate to be out of the line of fire. They bolted, taking off along the trail and pulling the wagon behind them. The prisoners inside the vehicle howled even louder.

Jake Brubaker yelled in alarm and broke out of the trees where he had taken cover. He ran after the wagon, ignoring Scratch's shout of warning.

"Forty-two, no!"

"Let them go, Marshal!" Bo shouted from the other side of the trail.

Brubaker's hat suddenly flew off his head, plucked

from it by a bullet. Even more than the shouts from the Texans, that had to make him realize that he was out in the open . . . and that was a bad spot to be in right now. Another bullet kicked up dirt at his feet as he whirled toward the side of the trail and threw himself behind a log that was lying there. Chucks of bark and splinters of wood flew in the air as slugs chewed into the fallen tree.

Bo opened fire on the bluff as the rest of the group resumed shooting. Brubaker was still in a bad spot. If they could keep the bushwhacker occupied for a few moments, it might give the deputy time to reach some better cover.

Brubaker surged up into a run. He made it behind some trees and rocks, where he slid to the ground. Bo watched him lie there panting heavily. As far as Bo could tell, the lawman wasn't hurt.

The wagon careened around a bend in the trail and vanished from sight.

Bo wasn't worried about the prisoners getting away. The runaway horses would slow down and stop as their panic wore off. The prisoners' chains and the lock on the door were secure. The biggest problem was that the wagon might overturn and crash before the team came to a stop. If that happened, the prisoners might be injured, or even killed in the wreck.

Bo wondered if there was any way to reach that bluff, work his way up to the top, and take the ambusher by surprise. Even as he considered the idea, he saw that it wouldn't work. The bluff commanded too broad a field of fire.

Knowing that his rifle wasn't going to make a difference in the fight, he slid back down to the bottom of the rock and hurried to the spot where Duck Forbes lay. Dropping to a knee beside the wounded man, Bo leaned over to check on his condition.

The Texan's face took on a hard, grim cast as he saw the way Duck's eyes were staring sightlessly into the blue sky. He rested a hand on Duck's chest to make sure and found that it was motionless. While Bo was up in the rocks trading shots with the man on the bluff, the young Cherokee Lighthorseman had crossed the divide.

"I'm sorry, Duck," Bo said quietly. "If I can, I'll settle the score for you. You have my word on that."

For all the good it did now. Bo couldn't stop that bitter thought from edging into his mind. Whoever was up there on the bluff had chosen the perfect spot for an ambush. He could keep them pinned down until dark . . .

But why just keep your enemies pinned down, Bo suddenly asked himself, when you could close the jaws of a trap on them? Scratch and the others were all concentrating on the danger in front of them, when something even worse could be coming up from behind.

That thought had just gone through Bo's head when a bullet whistled past his head, struck one of the boulders, and ricocheted off with a whine like the wail of an evil banshee.

CHAPTER 16

Bo whirled around as another slug smacked into the rock nearby, flattening this time instead of glancing off. The attackers were in the trees behind the group of lawmen. Bo flung himself aside as he heard the wind-rip of yet another bullet past his ear. He wedged his body into a gap between boulders.

The killers couldn't draw a bead on him, but from where he was, he couldn't get a shot at them, either. The futility of that stand-off, along with the anger he felt at Duck's death, gnawed at him. He suppressed the urge to lunge out into the open and start blazing away at the trees. That would just get him killed in a hurry and wouldn't help the others at all.

Now it sounded more than ever like a small war was going on, as shot after shot rang out from all directions. Bullets whined and zipped menacingly. Clouds of powder smoke rolled through the air and stung men's eyes and noses.

The stony gap in which Bo had taken cover was narrow enough that he thought he might be able to work his way upward between the two slabs of rock. He braced his back against one side, his feet against the other. When he shoved himself upward, his progress was maddeningly slow, but eventually he was high enough that he was able to pull himself on top of one of the slabs.

From here he could fire at the trees where the attackers were hidden, but his position also left him exposed to the man on top of the bluff. He rolled to his left as a bullet spanked off the rock only a few feet away from him. That put him behind a hardy bush that had forced its way through a crack in the rock in its eternal quest for sunlight.

The bush didn't offer much real cover, but at least the man on top of the bluff couldn't see him as easily now. Bo stayed as low as he could and took advantage of the respite to study his situation.

He seemed to be the only one on this side of the trail. Scratch and the others had taken cover in a small stand of trees to the left of the path. The gunmen who had come up from the rear were in some other trees on the same side of the trail as Bo. The bluff was on the opposite side.

So he was directly between the two forces, he realized, on an imaginary line that cut across the trail at an angle. Scratch, Brubaker, and the Cherokee Lighthorsemen were slightly off to one side but still effectively caught between two fires.

If there was some way for him to eliminate the man on the bluff, Bo speculated, then Scratch and the others could turn all their attention to the threat from the rear and would have a better chance of fighting them off. Bo parted the branches a little and squinted toward the bluff.

There was no way of knowing how long the boulders along the edge of the bluff had been perched there. Probably quite a while, Bo thought, judging by the way the earth was undercut beneath them, worn away by the elements. Sooner or later some of those big rocks would topple.

Why not today?

The odds of him being able to accomplish that were slim, he knew, but he couldn't see any other options. If things continued like they were, eventually the attackers would pick off him and all of his friends.

He thrust the Winchester's barrel through the brush and waited for the man on top of the bluff to fire again. Bo wanted to pinpoint the ambusher's location.

After a few seconds he spotted another jet of powder smoke from up there. The bullet rattled through the branches above his head, but he ignored that. Marking the exact site of the smoke, he was able to tell which boulder the rifleman was using for most of his cover.

Bo drew a bead on the bluff at the base of that rock and squeezed off a shot.

Dirt flew in the air as his bullet smacked into its target. The would-be killer probably believed Bo had just missed badly. He was probably smirking up there, Bo thought, or maybe even laughing.

Bo worked the rifle's lever as fast as he could and sent shot after shot into the same place. He emptied the Winchester in what must have sounded like a futile expression of the frustration he felt.

He expected that when he paused to reload, the ambusher would take some more potshots at him. Instead, the man seemed to be concentrating his fire on the trees where Scratch and the other men had taken cover. He must have decided that Bo wasn't a threat to be bothered with anymore.

Bo could only hope that the varmint was making a bad mistake about that.

The Winchester held fifteen rounds. Without rushing, Bo made sure of his aim and sent all fifteen shots, one after the other, into the same spot at the base of the boulder. He waited to see if it was going to move.

The big rock didn't budge.

Bo had never been the sort of hombre to give up. If he had been, despair might have welled up inside him at that moment. He was convinced that his idea was a good one and would show some results sooner or later . . . but would he have to lie here and keep shooting all day, firing off hundreds of bullets, before they did any good?

By that time, he and the others would probably all be dead.

He didn't let that knowledge stop him. Instead he reloaded, reminding himself that while he had several boxes of cartridges in his saddlebags, he would have only a few more rounds in his pocket after he emptied the Winchester this time. That fact right there was enough to emphasize that he was running out of time.

They all were, he told himself grimly.

He aimed the Winchester at the bluff and started firing again. His shoulder was starting to get a little sore from the rifle's recoil. He ignored that and continued shooting.

The boulder shifted. At first he didn't notice and even squeezed off another shot before he saw what was happening. The big rock tilted forward, and once its mass shifted, that was all it took. Bo's slugs had dug out enough dirt underneath it to destroy its balance.

The boulder toppled off the edge of the bluff, fell twenty feet or so to the slope, landed with a crash, and started to roll, taking brush, dirt, and smaller rocks along with it.

Bo didn't pay any attention to the rock slide he had caused. Swiftly now, he centered the Winchester's sights on the surprised man who suddenly was exposed as he knelt there where the boulder had been.

Bo triggered three more shots as fast as he could work the Winchester's lever.

His aim was as deadly as ever. The slugs ripped through the ambusher's body. He jerked to his feet, lurched to one side, and dropped his rifle as he clapped his hands to his bullet-riddled torso. For a second longer, he swayed there at the edge, and then he pitched forward and followed in the wake of the rock slide, bouncing and flopping like a rag doll as he tumbled down the face of the bluff.

From the trees on the other side of the trail came an unmistakably Texan whoop. Scratch must have seen the man on the bluff fall.

The attackers must have seen that, too, and now that their quarry was no longer pinned down, the odds appeared to have shifted. Bo swung around. He still had some shots left in his rifle, so he started spraying the trees where the men were hidden. That turned the tables even more.

When Bo ceased fire, he heard pounding hoof-beats. They were headed west, paralleling the trail but keeping the screen of trees between them and the lawmen.

Bo cupped his hands around his mouth and shouted, "Hold your fire! They're lighting out!"

The shots died away. After a moment, Scratch called, "You all right up there, Bo?"

"Yeah, I'm fine. How about you fellas?"

"Couple of nicks, but nothin' to speak of."

Brubaker emerged from the trees carrying his rifle. "Blast it, we've got to get after that wagon! Creel, where's your horse?"

Bo wasn't just about to turn over his horse to Brubaker. He said, "Hold on!" and slid down the rock to the ground.

He cast a regretful look at Duck Forbes's corpse, then caught his horse's dangling reins and swung up into the saddle. Duck's mount still stood there, too, so Bo led it out of the rocks and handed the reins to the eager Brubaker.

The deputy had the decency to ask, "What happened to the fella who was ridin' this animal?"

"He was the first one hit," Bo said. "He didn't make it."

"Duck Forbes, right? Damn it, I liked that boy, what little I knew of him." Brubaker hauled the horse's head around. "Come on!"

He galloped along the trail with Bo close behind him. They raced past the bluff where the ambusher had lurked, then rounded a couple of bends before abruptly reining to a halt.

The wagon was stopped as the team cropped grass at the side of the trail. As Bo had expected, the horses had run for a short distance and then forgotten to be scared anymore. All of them appeared to be unharmed, including Brubaker's saddle mount that was still tied to the back of the vehicle.

"Well, it didn't wreck, anyway," Brubaker said. "That's something to be thankful for." He drew his gun. "Be careful, Creel."

Bo could see that the door at the rear of the wagon was still fastened with the big padlock.

"They can't have gone anywhere," he told Brubaker.

"No, I reckon not, but I still don't trust 'em."

Bo didn't, either, but he didn't see any way the prisoners could have gotten free. He drew his Colt, too, as he approached the wagon alongside Brubaker.

"Hey, in there!" the deputy yelled. "Sing out and let me know you're all right!"

"You don't care whether we're all right!" Cara replied through the ventilation slits. The thick walls of the enclosure muffled her voice a little. "You want us all dead!"

"I want you all to hang after a legal trial," Brubaker replied. "There's a big difference."

"Not to us, you no-good, stinking—"

She continued with a vile tirade directed at Brubaker, his ancestors, and anybody he had ever known. Brubaker looked over at Bo and shrugged.

"Well, she sounds like she's all right, anyway," he said. He dismounted and approached the wagon. Reversing his gun, he rapped on the wall with the revolver's butt and bellowed, "Shut up in there, woman! I want to know if Lowe and Elam are all right, too."

"You damn near got us killed!" That was Elam's familiar whine.

"Who was doin' all that shootin'?" Lowe asked in his rumbling voice. "Couldn't have been Hank and the rest of the boys."

Brubaker gave Bo a nod, indicating that he was satisfied all three prisoners were alive. He didn't answer Lowe's question. Instead he handed the reins of Duck's horse to Bo and said, "You can lead this one back to the others."

He holstered his Colt and climbed to the driver's seat to swing the wagon around. That wasn't an easy job in the narrow trail, but Brubaker managed.

Bo led the extra horse, and Brubaker followed with

the wagon. By the time they reached the scene of the ambush, Scratch and the Cherokee Lighthorsemen had emerged from the trees.

Some of the men had fetched Duck's body from the rocks. It was laid out now at the side of the trail. The young man's face was oddly peaceful.

"That had to be Nat Kinlock and his bunch who jumped us," Charley Graywolf said. His face was darker than ever with fury. "Stinking murderers."

Bo said, "You told us Kinlock has relatives in this area, so you must have a pretty good idea where to find him."

Graywolf nodded. "That's right. And he knows it, too. That's why he set this trap for us. He figured he had to stop us. But if we move fast enough, we might be able to corner him and the others at his grandfather's farm."

"Then mount up and go on," Bo said.

Graywolf shook his head.

"We have to bury Duck."

"We'll take care of that," Scratch said. "Then we'll catch up with you fellas and see if we can give you a hand."

"I was just thinking the same thing," Bo added.

Brubaker scowled. "Wait just a chicken-scratchin' minute," he said. "We got our own job to do. I reckon we can take the time to lay this poor young fella to rest, but after that—"

Bo interrupted by asking Charley Graywolf, "Where's this farm you mentioned?"

"About five miles west of here," the Cherokee lawman replied. "In a valley between a couple of ridges that run east and west. Massasauga Valley, the one I mentioned earlier." He nodded toward Brubaker. "Forty-two knows where it is."

"Pretty much the way we were already goin', sounds like," Scratch said.

Graywolf shrugged and nodded.

"Now, listen here—" Brubaker began again.

"Marshal, we promised to help you deliver those prisoners, and we will," Bo declared. "But giving Charley and Walt and Joe a hand isn't going to delay us very much, especially since we're already headed in that direction."

"We're wasting time," Graywolf said. "We're much obliged to you for taking care of Duck, but we've got to be riding. Come after us or don't, it's up to you."

With that, he and his men swung up into their saddles and galloped off along the trail. They paused at the foot of the bluff long enough to take a look at the man Bo had shot. Graywolf turned in the saddle and shouted, "It's one of Kinlock's men, all right!"

Bo waved a hand in acknowledgment.

Brubaker let out an exasperated sigh.

"All right," he said. "There's a shovel in the possum belly under the wagon. Let's get that grave dug."

"You're gonna help Charley and those other fellas?" Scratch asked.

"Might as well. I'm a lawman, too, and I hate

murderin' outlaws worse than anything." Brubaker paused. "Just don't let Judge Parker hear about this."

"No need to say anything to the judge," Bo replied. He glanced at Duck's body lying beside the trail. "Anyway, this job's not really official."

"Nope," Scratch agreed. "It's personal now."

CHAPTER 17

The Texans found a suitable spot not far from the trail and took turns digging the grave while Brubaker wrapped Duck's body in a blanket. After they had lowered the young lawman into the ground and covered up the grave, they stood beside the mound of freshly turned dirt with their hats in their hands.

"I've had to bury quite a few fellas who got cut down before their time," Brubaker said. "So unless one of you wants to say a few words . . ."

"Go ahead," Bo told him.

Brubaker nodded, lowered his head, and closed his eyes. Bo and Scratch followed suit.

"Lord, we ask that You show Your infinite mercy to this young man who was foully murdered by owlhoots. His name was Duck Forbes, or at least that's the only name we know him by. I reckon You know all there is to know about him. He should still be here with his friends and family, but since he ain't, please forgive him any sins he might've done and accept him into Your kingdom with Your blessin's. Amen."

"Amen," Bo and Scratch echoed.

Brubaker clapped his hat on his head, wincing slightly at the pain from the bullet graze he had suffered during the shoot-out at the trading post with Jink Staley and the rest of that bunch.

"All right, let's go get the skunks that done this," he grated.

"Charley, Walt, and Joe may have taken care of them by the time we catch up," Bo pointed out.

"Well, if they have then we can help with the buryin' there, too," Brubaker said.

He climbed onto the wagon seat while Bo and Scratch mounted up. All of them moved off along the trail at a rapid clip, with the Texans leading the way.

They couldn't afford to forget about the continuing threats from Hank Gentry's gang and the rest of the Staley clan, Bo reminded himself. Because of that, he and Scratch kept their eyes open, scanning the countryside in front of them and to the sides, as well as checking their backtrail frequently.

The ambush had taken place at midmorning. The sun was almost directly overhead by the time Bo and Scratch heard the distant pop of gunshots ahead of them.

The Texans reined in, and Scratch said over his shoulder to Brubaker, "Sounds like Charley and his pards done opened the ball without us."

"I ain't surprised," Brubaker replied. "They were rarin' to settle the score with that bunch."

"Does this trail go through that valley where Kinlock's grandfather has his farm?" Bo asked.

Brubaker nodded. "It does, so we shouldn't have any trouble findin' the place. Come on!"

He flapped the reins against the backs of the team and got the horses moving again.

The shots grew louder and began to echo as the trail twisted through some hills. After several minutes of that, it emerged into a broad valley that stretched out for probably ten miles between two rugged ridges. In summer, this would be a green, lovely place, Bo thought, but in the middle of winter it was gray and forbidding. The continuing sound of shots just made it seem more so.

The valley floor wasn't completely flat. Some knolls and brushy knobs were scattered across it. The shots guided Bo, Scratch, and Brubaker to one of those knobs. Three horses were tied at the bottom of the slope. Bo recognized them as the mounts the Cherokee Lighthorsemen had been riding.

So did Scratch, saying, "Charley and those other two fellas must be on top of this hill. Wonder what's on the other side?"

"Old man Kinlock's farm, I'll bet," Bo said. "Those outlaws are probably forted up inside the old man's cabin."

"Let's go see," Brubaker suggested as he climbed down from the wagon seat. He brought his Henry rifle with him.

The Texans dismounted and tied their horses to saplings. The three men started climbing the slope, which was covered with brush and small trees. It was slow going, but a narrow game trail made the climb a little easier.

Before they reached the top, Brubaker called, "Charley! Hey, Charley! We're comin' up behind you, so don't get trigger-happy!"

"Come on up, Forty-two!" Charley Graywolf replied. "We can use a hand."

They finished the climb and sprawled on the ground at the knob's crest next to Graywolf. Walt Moon lay to one side and Joe Reeder to the other. Reeder had a bloody rag tied around his left thigh as a bandage, Bo noted.

"I see one of your men got hit," Brubaker said.

"It's nothing," Reeder said as he levered his rifle. "It won't slow me down none."

He pointed the weapon at the log cabin that was located about a hundred and fifty yards on the other side of the knob, next to a small creek, and squeezed off a shot.

"I reckon that's the old man's place," Brubaker said to Graywolf.

"Yeah. His name's George Kinlock. Honest as far as that goes, or at least so I've heard. But he lets Nat and the rest of the gang stay here. That puts him on the wrong side of the law as far as I'm concerned."

"Me, too," Brubaker agreed. "Looks like a pretty sturdy cabin."

"Too sturdy. Nat and the others have holed up in there, and we're going to have a devil of a time getting them out."

Bo studied the layout. On the other side of the

creek, open fields ran into the distance, some of them with brush fences between them. A man might be able to creep closer to the cabin from that direction by using the fences for cover, but that wouldn't get him close enough. He would still have to cross the creek in the open, which would probably result in his painful introduction to a bullet.

On this side of the creek, next to the cabin, was a lean-to shed that was crowded with horses at the moment. Graywolf and his partners might be able to shoot those horses, although the angle wasn't all that good, but they weren't the sort of men to kill helpless animals unless they had to.

Farther off to one side stood a log barn with an attached corral on one side and a muddy hog pen on the other. Several massive hogs rooted happily in the mud, oblivious to the gunfire going on nearby.

"There's too much open ground all around the place," Graywolf said. "If we could get close enough we might be able to set the cabin on fire and smoke them out, but they're good shots. They'd pick off anybody who tried to do that."

"How about shootin' some flamin' arrows down there?" Scratch suggested.

Graywolf made a disgusted noise.

"We're Cherokee, not Comanche. Did you see any bows and arrows among our gear?"

"Didn't mean any offense," Scratch said.

Graywolf shook his head.

"Don't worry about it. Actually, I am a pretty good shot with a bow, and Walt there is even better. But we don't have any. I thought about trying to make some torches and throwing them down there from up here, but it's too far."

"How deep are those creek banks?" Bo asked.

"I don't know. Five, maybe six feet from the look of them."

"What if a man took some torches along with him, unlit, and waded along that creek? He could get closer that way, maybe close enough to light the torches and toss them onto the roof."

Graywolf frowned in thought. After a moment he said, "That might work. But there's a window on that side. If any of that bunch spotted him when he raised up to throw the torches, they could cut him down without much trouble."

"I'm willing to run the risk," Bo said.

"And if I went with him," Scratch added, "I could cover him in case they did see him."

"You'd both get wet," Graywolf warned. "That creek's spring-fed. It runs year-round."

Scratch grinned. "I reckon we could both do with a bath," he said. "What do you say, Bo?"

"It was my idea," Bo replied. "I'm willing to do a little wading."

He knew why Graywolf was concerned. Even though the temperature was above freezing, the air was still very cold. It would feel even colder to the two Texans once they were wet. They shouldn't have to submerge themselves completely in the water, though, Bo told himself. The creek probably wasn't deep enough for that.

"All right," Graywolf said. "We'll give it a try, but only because I don't see any other way to get them out of there. Let's find some branches and put together a few torches."

Bo picked out three suitable branches that were heavy enough he could throw them easily, but short enough that he could carry them under his coat if he needed to. Around one end of the branches he wrapped strips cut from a wool blanket.

"If they're going to burn hot enough to set the roof on fire, we need to soak them in something," he said. "I don't suppose anybody's got any kerosene?"

"Wait here," Brubaker said gruffly. He went back down the slope to the wagon and rummaged in the box under the driver's seat.

When he returned he brought with him not a bucket of kerosene but rather a jug with a cork in its neck. Graywolf grinned at him and asked, "Why, Forty-two, is that a jug of white lightnin'? I thought you marshals were supposed to track down the people who bring firewater into the Indian Nations, not smuggle it in yourself."

"I brung it along for medicinal purposes," Brubaker insisted. "You can ask these two Texans if they've seen me nippin' at it."

"We haven't," Bo said.

"But we ain't been watchin' for it, either," Scratch added.

Brubaker snarled as he shoved the jug into the silver-haired Texan's hands.

"That's enough. Take this with you, and when you

get close enough to the cabin, pour some of it on the torches. They'll light easy and burn strong."

"You're right about that," Bo told him. "Ready, Scratch?"

"Sure. Let's get this done."

The sky had been mostly clear that morning, but clouds had moved in during the day so that now the sky was partially overcast and the sun was hidden. That made the air seem even chillier.

Bo told himself not to worry about that as he and Scratch mounted up and rode about half a mile north. The knob had shielded them, so the men in the cabin wouldn't have seen them depart.

They angled west and came to the creek. As they dismounted, Scratch asked, "Do we start wadin' here?"

Bo shook his head.

"No, we'll leave the horses here and follow the stream on foot as far as we can before we climb down the bank. No point in getting any colder than we have to."

"That sounds good to me. My circulation ain't what it used to be. Remind me again why we didn't suggest that a couple of them young Indian lads do this?"

Bo laughed. "Because we didn't think of it?"

"Yeah, that's what I was afraid you were gonna say. Come on."

Bo carried the torches while Scratch brought the jug of moonshine. The creek bank was choked with brush, which made their progress slow. The shots from the lawmen on the knob continued, as well as the return fire from the cabin, but the pace of the shooting had slowed down now. A stand-off was always like that. After a while, the apparent pointlessness of it made both sides fall into a lull.

With any luck, that would be changing soon, Bo thought.

They came in sight of the area that had been cleared along both sides of the stream for the Kinlock farm. Bo motioned toward the creek. He handed the torches to Scratch and climbed down the bank first. The drop-off was steep but not sheer, so he didn't have much trouble. When he stepped down into the water, he sank to his knees, which put his head just below the top of the bank.

The cold made him take a sharp breath. Scratch asked, "A mite chilly, is it?"

"Just be glad we only have to wade in it and don't have to swim," Bo said.

Scratch handed down the torches and the jug. When he was standing in the creek, too, he shivered and reached out to take the jug from Bo.

"Reckon there's enough in here to spare a swig?" he asked. "Might help warm us up."

Bo shook his head.

"Better not risk it."

"Yeah, that's what I thought you'd say," Scratch replied with a sigh.

They started trudging along the creek. The mud on the bottom sucked at their boots with every step. Their feet were already soaked and icy. Although it probably wasn't happening yet, Bo thought he felt his toes going numb. When this was over, he'd have to be careful about warming them up again, or else he'd be risking frostbite.

The shots from the knob picked up in intensity and frequency. From that height, Brubaker, Graywolf, and the others could see the Texans making their way along the creek, even though the bank shielded them from the view of those inside the cabin. The increased shooting was by design. The lawmen wanted all the attention on them, not on the threat that was creeping up behind the outlaws.

Bo was in the lead. He had just taken a step when suddenly his foot kept sinking through the water. Just as he had fallen into that ravine, he knew instantly that he had stepped into a hole in the creek bottom. He had the torches in his left hand, and as the frigid water closed around him, he thrust that hand into the air as high as he could.

"Bo!" Scratch exclaimed in a half-whisper. He leaped forward to reach for Bo's arm.

The water didn't come all the way up over Bo's head, but when he stopped sinking he was up to his neck in the creek. Its icy grip enveloped him, shocking him so that he wasn't able to move. He knew better than to start floundering. That might just cause him to sink even more.

Scratch's free hand closed around Bo's wrist and hauled up. Bo's boots slid in the mud, but with Scratch's help he was able to get out of the hole. Trying to keep his teeth from chattering, he said, "B-b-b-better circle around this spot."

"Bo, we gotta get you out of here and into some dry clothes!"

"Not yet," Bo said. "We're c-c-c-c-close now."

It was true. The shots from the cabin sounded like they were only a few yards away. The Texans moved on a short distance and then Scratch pulled himself a few inches up the bank.

"I can see the roof!" he whispered to Bo.

They were back in knee-deep water now. Bo was shivering. He told Scratch, "You'll have to light the torches. My matches are soaked."

"Sure. Let's get 'em ready."

Bo held out one of the torches. Scratch used his teeth to pull the cork from the jug, then tipped it just enough to let the clear liquid inside soak into the blanket strips wrapped around the end of the branch. He got them thoroughly wet without spilling much of the whiskey. The stuff would evaporate quickly, so they didn't waste any time as they soaked all three torches.

Then Scratch set the jug on a little shelf of earth that jutted out from the creek bank and dug a tin of matches from his shirt pocket. He snapped one of them to life with his thumbnail and held the little flame to each of the torches in turn.

That was all it took. The whiskey-soaked rags caught fire immediately and blazed up. Scratch took one of the torches from Bo and said, "Let's go!"

They scrambled up the bank, carrying the burning torches. The cabin was about twenty feet away.

The window in the wall facing them was a dark hole. Nobody was looking out.

Fighting off the terrible chills that ran through him, Bo drew back his right arm and let fly with that torch. It spun through the air and landed cleanly on the cabin's roof. Scratch's torch bounced and looked like it might fall off, but then it caught on the rough shakes and came to a stop. Bo's second torch landed close to it. All three continued to burn.

But even though the wooden shakes on the roof quickly started to char and smolder, they didn't actually catch fire. And the flames on the torches were beginning to die down. They looked like they might burn out before they caught the roof on fire.

Scratch cursed and whispered, "Now what?"

Being half-frozen hadn't slowed down Bo's brain any, at least not yet.

"Hand me the jug," he said.

"What are you— Oh, hell," Scratch said as he realized what Bo had in mind. "That ought to do it, all right, but you'd better let me heave it. We'll only get one try, and you're shakin' to beat the band."

"T-t-t-toss it good," Bo urged.

Scratched reached back down and snagged the jug. He gave it a shake.

"Probably half full," he said. "Ought to be enough."

"Let it rip."

Scratch left the cork in the neck of the jug, hooked a finger through the little handle, and drew back his arm. He swung it forward and sent the jug arching through the air toward the top of the cabin.

For a second Bo thought his old friend had thrown the jug too hard. It looked like it was going to go clear over the roof's peak and fall on the other side.

But then it dropped, its weight carrying it down with enough force that when it struck the roof it seemed to explode, spraying moonshine in all directions, including over the still-burning torches.

With a mighty *whoosh!*, flames shot high into the air.

CHAPTER 18

With that added fuel, there was no question now that the cabin roof was going to catch on fire. It did so in a matter of seconds as Bo and Scratch slid back down the creek bank and their feet splashed in the water. A fierce crackling filled the air as the wooden shakes began to burn and black smoke billowed up.

The Texans heard alarmed yelling from inside the cabin. Scratch leaned closer to Bo and said, "I hope there were no womenfolk or kids in there with those outlaws!"

"Me, too," Bo agreed with a nod, "but if there are, none of the f-f-f-fellas up on that knob will shoot them when they come out."

"You're gonna freeze to death if we don't get you in some dry clothes soon."

"I'll be all right," Bo insisted. He drew his Colt from its soggy holster. "We b-b-b-better be ready in case any of them come this way when they run."

Scratch slid his Remingtons from leather.

"Yeah, you're right about that. With that window on this side, they're liable to."

The shooting continued as the lawmen peppered the burning cabin with slugs. Bo and Scratch waited tensely to see if any of the outlaws were going to flee in their direction. That window in the back wall of the cabin would be easy enough to climb out of.

They didn't have to wait very long. A panting, cursing figure appeared, clambering and sliding down the bank about fifteen feet from the spot where the Texans had drawn back and pressed themselves against the slope.

Another man came close behind the first one, saying bitterly, "Damn it, Nat, you claimed they'd never chase us this far!"

The first fugitive, who had to be Nat Kinlock, didn't look back as he said, "Shut up and run, Chester!"

Both of them started to splash across the creek. Bo and Scratch stepped out with leveled guns. The silver-haired Texan shouted, "Hold it right there, boys!"

Neither of them really expected the fleeing outlaws to surrender, and Kinlock and Chester didn't disappoint. The two men twisted around and clawed guns from underneath their long coats.

But they couldn't outdraw guns that were already drawn, and they were no match for the coolheaded accuracy of the drifters from Texas.

Half-frozen Bo might be, but the trembling that had shaken his body disappeared entirely when he had the butt of a Colt in his hand. Flame stabbed from the weapon's muzzle as he fired. Beside him, the twin booms of Scratch's Remingtons filled the air and echoed back from the creek banks.

Kinlock and Chester didn't get off a single shot. Bo's bullet drove into Chester's body and knocked him backward. He landed full-length in the creek with a huge splash that threw water high in the air.

A few feet away, both of Scratch's slugs bored through Nat Kinlock and twisted him around so that he fell face-first in the icy water. The creek was just deep enough that he began to float with his arms splayed out as the water around him took on a reddish tinge from the blood leaking from both outlaws.

"You sons o' bitches!" someone bellowed from the top of the creek bank. Bo and Scratch turned their heads to look in that direction and saw an old man in overalls leveling a double-barreled shotgun at them. Bo had time to realize the old-timer was probably George Kinlock, Nat's grandfather.

He realized as well that he and Scratch had nowhere to take cover and they were about to be shredded by that double load of buckshot.

George Kinlock lurched forward and arched his back just he jerked the Greener's triggers. That pulled the twin barrels up just enough that the blasts went over the heads of Bo and Scratch and tore into the opposite bank instead. The old man dropped the empty shotgun and fell to his knees. He pitched forward and slid head-first down the bank, coming to a stop with his head just above the water as his overalls snagged on a protruding branch. There was a growing bloodstain in the middle of his back.

"One of those fellas on the knob must'a drilled him," Scratch said.

"And saved our lives," Bo said. He pointed his gun at the old man. "I'll keep him covered just in case, while you check the other two."

Scratch nodded and waded along the creek to check carefully and make sure that both Nat Kinlock and the fugitive called Chester were dead. When he was certain, he looked back and gave Bo a grim nod.

"The old-timer is, too," Bo reported. "It's a shame, if he really was mostly an honest man, like Charley said."

"An honest man don't let thieves and cold-blooded killers hide out with him, family or no family," Scratch said. "And if he was just scared of his grandson and didn't have no choice in the matter, he wouldn't have tried to blow us to hell and gone with a scattergun."

Bo couldn't argue with that logic.

"Creel! Morton!" The shout came from Jake Brubaker. "Are you down there?"

"Yeah!" Scratch called back. "Is it safe to come up?"

"Come ahead!" Brubaker replied. "We've cleaned out the rest of this rat's nest!"

The Texans holstered their guns. Scratch took hold of Bo's arm and said, "Let me give you a hand gettin' up that creek bank."

Bo was about to pull away and tell his old friend that he could take care of himself, but then the shakes hit him again and he was glad for the firm grip Scratch had on his arm.

"*G-g-g-gracias*," he said.

"*De nada*," Scratch told him with a grin. "Careful, there . . ."

They climbed up the bank, and by the time they were back on level ground, Brubaker, Charley Graywolf, Walt Moon, and Joe Reeder were gathered around the burning cabin. A couple of bodies were sprawled face-down on the ground near the cabin. Those had to be the other members of Nat Kinlock's gang.

The heat coming from the leaping flames felt wonderful to Bo. As long as he was standing within reach of it, that kept the bone-numbing cold at bay. In fact, his clothes were already starting to dry a little.

"Are you two all right?" Brubaker asked.

"We will be, once we ain't half-frozen," Scratch said. "Our horses are about half a mile upstream. We've got dry clothes in our warbags."

"Walt, can you go fetch those horses?" Graywolf asked.

Moon nodded and said, "Sure, Charley. Be back in a few minutes."

He swung up on one of the horses they had brought with them from the knob and rode away.

Bo used a thumb to point over his shoulder and said, "Nat Kinlock and a man called Chester are in the creek. So is an old man who tried to use a shotgun on us. I'm guessing one of you hombres shot him?"

Charley grinned and nodded toward Brubaker.

"That was Forty-two here. And a heck of a shot it was, too."

"Darn right it was," Scratch agreed. "Saved our bacon, for sure."

"The old man was Kinlock's grandfather?" Bo asked.

Graywolf nodded. "Yeah. If he had come out of there empty handed and not threatened anybody, he'd still be alive. So I'm sorry for what happened to him, but he brought it on himself."

"Most people do, one way or another," Brubaker said.

Bo had warmed up considerably by the time Walt Moon got back with the Texans' horses, but it felt mighty good anyway to get out of the wet clothes and into dry duds. After pulling on fresh socks, both he and Scratch set their boots aside to dry.

Brubaker said, "The way those flames shot up so high, I'm thinkin' that was more than just the roof catchin' fire."

"We sort of had to help it along," Scratch admitted with a smile.

"I thought I caught a glimpse of my jug sailin' through the air. I'm not gettin' it back, am I?"

"Afraid not, Forty-two. But it went for a good cause."

Brubaker sighed. "I suppose so. When we get south of the Red River, we'll pick up another one at some tradin' post. You know, for medicinal purposes. Just in case."

Bo and Scratch nodded solemnly, and Bo repeated, "Just in case."

* * *

Since it took all afternoon to bury the dead outlaws, it made sense to camp there on George Kinlock's farm that night, although they put some distance between themselves and the smoldering, stinking rubble of the cabin. By evening, Bo and Scratch had warmed up and were back to normal as they sat beside the campfire Charley Graywolf had built.

"I just hope you don't catch the grippe," Scratch said. "My ma always said that if you got wet and cold, you'd come down with it, sure as shootin'."

"Your ma said a lot of things that weren't necessarily right," Bo replied.

"Yeah, but she could cook a mighty fine apple pie."

Bo nodded and said, "Yeah, I have to give her credit for that. I could do with a hot slice of your ma's apple pie right now."

Scratch sighed, since his mother had been gone for many, many years.

"So could I, Bo," he said. "So could I."

Walt Moon took over the cooking chores that night. The frybread he made was delicious. Brubaker set aside a portion of the food for the prisoners, and when everyone else had finished eating, he unlocked the door at the back of the wagon.

"Damn well about time you tended to us," Dayton Lowe said.

"They was too busy pow-wowwin' with their redskin friends," Jim Elam added with a sneer on his face and in his voice.

Cara was unusually quiet. She sat with her head down and her shoulders slumped.

"I wouldn't advise tryin' anything," Brubaker warned the prisoners. "We've spent the day killin' outlaws, and nobody's in a very good mood. Give us an excuse to do some more shootin', and you might regret it."

"Just give us somethin' to eat," Lowe snapped. "I'm just about starved in here. I'm a big man! I can't live on two little meals a day."

"You won't starve to death. Not where you're headed."

It was clear what Brubaker meant. Once they reached Tyler, the trial would be a speedy one, and none of the prisoners would live long enough to starve to death.

After they had eaten, Brubaker unlocked their chains and took them out of the wagon one at a time. Cara said, "My arms are gettin' mighty stiff from being pulled back like this all the time. Don't you think you could chain them in front of us for a while, Marshal?"

Brubaker rubbed his jaw as he thought it over. Then he surprised Scratch by saying, "Well, I suppose if I was gonna do somethin' like that, tonight would be the time to do it, since we've got three other lawmen here."

"Injun lawmen," Lowe said. "They ain't allowed to shoot white folks."

"We'll make a special exception in your case, happen you try to get too smart with us," Brubaker assured him. "As far as anybody will ever know, me or one of these temporary deputies will be the fella who ventilated you. Got that, Lowe?"

The big man lowered his shaggy head and growled, but he didn't argue anymore.

When Brubaker took Cara out of the wagon, he told her, "Stand there. Don't try anything. You boys keep her covered, understand?"

Five guns were pointed at Cara while Brubaker unlocked the shackles holding her wrists behind her back. As the chains came loose and she was able to move her arms in front of her again, she closed her eyes and said, "Aaahh!" in obvious relief.

Brubaker slapped the shackles right back on her. She didn't seem to mind. She rolled her shoulders to ease the stiffness in those muscles.

When she looked up, she asked, "What about the other two?"

"Fine," Brubaker said. "But in the mornin', the hands go behind the back again."

"I don't care. Right now I'm just grateful for a little break."

Scratch went along with Brubaker while Cara visited the woods. When they came back into the circle of light from the campfire the Cherokee Lighthorsemen had built, she glanced over at the silver-haired Texan and gave him a shy smile. Looking at her like that, Scratch thought, it was almost impossible to believe that she was a bloodthirsty outlaw.

Luckily, Scratch recalled how she'd tried to slice him up with that razor a few days earlier, so he didn't let his guard down. It would take more than a pretty face to get him to do that.

CHAPTER 19

The night passed peacefully. The overcast remained in place, and as Brubaker studied the gray, leaden skies the next morning, he commented, "Looks like there might be some snow in those clouds."

Charley Graywolf shook his head.

"I don't think so, Forty-two," he said. "It's been mighty dry down in these parts for months now. We haven't had any rain or snow to speak of in a long time. I hear it's even worse down in Texas, where you're headed."

Brubaker snorted. "It's always dry in Texas," he said.

"This is worse than usual. There's a real drought down there, and it's spreading north."

"Well, it can hold off rainin' until we get where we're goin', as far as I'm concerned. This wagon's pretty heavy. I don't want it boggin' down on muddy roads."

Bo agreed with that sentiment. If the wagon were to get stuck, that would make them sitting ducks for Gentry's gang or for the vengeance-seeking Staleys, if either of those bunches should happen to catch up to them then.

As they got ready to move out, Graywolf said, "I'd still like to go with you to the border, Forty-two, especially since you gave us a hand like that, but our orders were to deal with Kinlock and then get back to Tahlequah as soon as we can. The Lighthorse has a lot of ground to cover, and we're stretched pretty thin."

"I know that," Brubaker said. "Don't worry about it, Charley." He held out a hand. "Good luck to you."

"And to you fellas, as well," Graywolf said as everyone shook hands all around.

Earlier, after breakfast, Brubaker had chained the prisoners' hands behind their backs again. Lowe and Elam had complained bitterly about that, but Cara had taken it in stony silence. She seemed to have gotten tired of raising a ruckus about everything. There was a look of dull acceptance on her face . . . not only about the chains, but about her ultimate fate as well.

Before the Cherokee Lighthorsemen headed back east, Brubaker warned them, "Keep your eyes open for Hank Gentry and his gang. I know they've got to be lookin' for these three. Gentry's liable to gun down anybody who gets in his way."

"Don't worry, Forty-two," Graywolf said from the back of his horse. "If we run into them, they won't find out from us that we've seen you."

"Never crossed my mind that they would," Brubaker said.

He got the wagon rolling westward along the

narrow trail again. Bo took the lead, and Scratch rode behind the vehicle to keep an eye on their back trail. Bo was none the worse for being dunked in the frigid creek the day before, other than the fact that his bones maybe ached a little more than they usually did.

At his age, a multitude of aches and pains was normal, though, so he didn't think anything about it.

Charley Graywolf proved to be better at predicting the weather than Brubaker. The gray clouds hung stubbornly in the sky, but they didn't produce any snow or rain. The day passed uneventfully. Late that afternoon the travelers came to a crossroads, although giving it that name was probably an overstatement. A dim, narrow trail running north and south intersected the westerly one they were on.

Brubaker swung the wagon onto the southern trail and announced, "We'll head south to the Red River. There's a good crossing there above Gainesville. Once we're in Texas we'll cut back east to Dallas and then Tyler. Be there in about a week . . . if folks stop shootin' at us and slowin' us down."

Bo wasn't going to count on having that much luck, and neither was Scratch.

The trail angled to the southwest. Brubaker followed it for a couple of miles and then called a halt for the day.

After they had made camp and eaten supper, Brubaker opened the door of the wagon to feed the prisoners. Lowe asked, "Are you gonna move our chains back to the front again?"

"Not hardly," Brubaker answered. "We had those Cherokee Lighthorsemen with us last night to help out if any of you got rambunctious. Now things are back to the way they were before."

"It was sure a lot more comfortable the other way," Cara said.

Brubaker let out a snort of disdain.

"It ain't my job to keep you comfortable," he said, "just to get you to Tyler so Judge Southwick can deal with you as he sees fit."

"Listen, Forty-two," Scratch said. "We've got us a pretty good routine down by now. I don't see that it'd hurt anything if we made things a mite easier on these folks."

"Blast it, don't get taken in by 'em, Morton!" Brubaker exclaimed angrily. "They never made it any easier on the innocent people they killed in their robberies, now did they?"

Scratch shrugged.

"I reckon not. But it seems like it'd be less trouble for us, too. For one thing, we wouldn't have to feed 'em. They could do that themselves. And if we kept on coverin' em all the time the wagon is open, I don't see how they could get away."

Brubaker frowned in thought for a moment, then asked Bo, "What do you say, Creel?"

"Scratch is right," Bo said. "I don't see how chaining their hands in front of them is going to make any difference. It sure won't while they're riding and chained to the floor, too."

What Bo said was true. He couldn't argue with Scratch's claims.

But he did wonder just why Scratch was taking the side of the outlaws. That was very unusual for him. It had to be because of the soft spot Scratch had for womenfolks. If all three prisoners had been hardbitten male owlhoots, he wouldn't have worried about whether they were comfortable or not.

Scratch was just too much of a Southern gentleman. It was bred in him to be chivalrous to a woman . . . even when that woman was a killer.

Bo resolved to keep an eye on his old friend. He wouldn't let Scratch do anything foolish.

After both Texans had weighed in with their opinions, Brubaker gave a reluctant nod and said, "All right. We'll try it for a day or two. But if anything happens, I'm holdin' you two responsible."

"That's fine," Bo said. He didn't really expect any trouble. And if it arose, they would deal with it.

One by one, while the Texans covered them, Brubaker switched the chains on the prisoners. When he was finished with that and Lowe and Elam were padlocked to the rings in the floor again, the deputy said, "All right, Creel, take the woman into the trees. Morton and I will watch these two."

Cara pouted. "Mr. Morton's been takin' me," she said.

"It don't matter who takes you," Brubaker snapped, "just go get your business done."

"Come on, miss," Bo said. He, too, had been raised to be a gentleman, although it wasn't ingrained as deeply in him as it was in Scratch.

Cara seemed to have gotten used to the lack of privacy and didn't let it bother her anymore. She went into the brush and hoisted her skirts without argument. While she was doing that, she asked, "Has Mr. Morton ever been married?"

"Why in the world would you want to know that?" Bo said.

"I'm just curious, that's all. He seems like such a nice man. I figure some woman must've hooked him at one time or another."

"Well, you'd be wrong there," Bo said. "He's never been married. Never even come close, as far as I know, although he's talked about it a few times when he met some widow woman he particularly liked."

Bo didn't say anything about his own tragedy-shortened marriage. Cara hadn't asked about that, and he wasn't just about to volunteer the information. It wasn't that he tried not to think about what he had lost, all those years ago. It was so far in the past that the pain had almost receded to nothing. Almost. But it didn't have any bearing on what went on now.

Instead he asked, "Why do you want to know about Scratch? Seems like I remember you trying to cut him open with a razor not that long ago."

Cara came out of the bushes, straightening her clothes as best she could since the shackles still kept her from being able to move her arms very well.

"I'm sorry about that," she said. "I didn't know him then, and I was just loco to get away. I can't stand to be cooped up anywhere."

"You seem to be standing that wagon pretty well these days," Bo pointed out.

"What choice do I have?"

She had a point there, he thought. Unless Hank Gentry and the rest of the gang showed up to rescue the prisoners, the odds of Cara LaChance ever again experiencing freedom were pretty slim.

She didn't say anything else about Scratch. Bo took her back to the camp and escorted Lowe and Elam into the woods in turn. The prisoners ate supper and turned in for the night, stretching out on the floor of the wagon and wrapping themselves in blankets against the chilly night air.

Bo and Brubaker headed for their bedrolls as well. Scratch stood the first watch. He sat on a log near the fire, his Winchester across his knees, and let his senses reach out into the night, alert for anything that was out of the ordinary. He never looked into the flames for more than a second at a time, knowing that to do so would weaken his night vision. He knew he needed to stay as vigilant as possible.

Time passed slowly, as it usually did when he was standing guard. Scratch was a naturally gregarious sort. He loved talking to people and just having folks around him. He had company tonight, of course, but they were all asleep. He was glad it was cold. The chill probably helped keep him awake.

The sound that drifted to his ears was so soft that he almost didn't hear it at first. Then it came again, and he realized someone was saying, "Psst!"

The little hiss came from the wagon. One of the

prisoners was trying to get his attention. Maybe supper hadn't agreed with whichever one it was, and he or she needed to visit the bushes again. In that case, Scratch thought, he would have to wake up Bo and Brubaker, and the deputy would likely be pretty annoyed.

He stood up and went over to the wagon. Putting his mouth close to the tiny crack around the door, he asked in a whisper, "What do you want?"

"Mr. Morton?" It was Cara's voice on the other side of the door. Scratch could barely hear it because of the snoring that came from Lowe and Elam. "Scratch? Is that you?"

"Yeah, it's me," Scratch replied. He wondered if she had overheard the conversation between him and Bo and Brubaker earlier and had known that he was taking the first shift on guard. "You need somethin'?"

"Just . . . some company, I guess. I'm havin' trouble sleepin'."

He didn't doubt it. The wagon had to be as uncomfortable as all get-out, plus there was the fact that she was on the way to be tried and hanged. Knowledge like that had to weigh heavily on a person.

"I can't let you out of there," he told her.

"I know you can't. But maybe . . . maybe you can talk to me for a little while, until I get to feelin' like I could doze off?"

Scratch glanced at the two bedrolls near the fire. Bo and Brubaker appeared to be sleeping soundly. As long as he whispered, he didn't suppose it would hurt anything for him to talk to Cara for a few minutes. He couldn't let it distract him from being watchful, though.

"All right," he said. "What do you want to talk about?"

"I don't know. I just needed to hear the sound of another human voice. You ever get like that, Scratch? Just so blasted lonely that you think you're gonna shrivel up inside and die?"

"Not hardly," he said. "Bo's always around to talk to."

"You're lucky," Cara said. "Growin' up I never had any real friends."

"You must've had family."

She laughed, but the sound was bitter and humorless.

"Yeah, some family, tryin' to make a livin' out of a hardscrabble farm in the piney woods, down in East Texas. All my ma and pa cared about was how much work they could get out of me, and after I wasn't a kid anymore, all my brothers cared about was what else they could get out of me, if you know what I mean."

Scratch frowned.

"Sorry," he said. "Must've been a pretty hard life. But that's no excuse to go to robbin' and killin'."

"I never killed nobody!" Cara said, and now she sounded vehement. "I know they say I have, but that's all lies. There's nobody who can say they ever saw me kill anybody, because I haven't. It was Hank and the other fellas in the gang who did all the killin'."

"You were there for some of it."

"Well, what else could I do? What happened is, Hank came along a few years ago and I met up with him, and all I could think about was how if I went away with him, I'd get away from that damn farm once and for all. And so when he asked me to, I did. It didn't seem like I had any choice."

"We've always got choices," Scratch said.

"Yeah, but I didn't know that then. I didn't know what Hank was really like, either. I didn't know he was an outlaw until I was part of the gang. And then it was too late. I had to go along with whatever he said. He can be . . . well, he can be really nice when he wants to, but he can be really mean when he wants to be that way, too. I had to keep him happy with me, or else he would've turned me over to the rest of the men. Or worse, just left me somewhere to shift for myself."

Scratch didn't see how that could be any worse than what she was talking about, but obviously she felt differently about it. He said, "If all this is true, I'm sorry for you, miss. But you'll have a chance to tell your side of it at the trial."

"Do you think anybody will ever believe me?"

"Well, considerin' how you came after me with that razor and how you've acted since we left Fort Smith . . ."

"I haven't done anything except yell some, and you'd yell, too, if you thought you were gonna be dancin' at the end of a hang rope for things you didn't do. And as for the razor, like I told your friend Mr. Creel, I was just about out of my head. I can't stand bein' locked up. I was loco to get away." Cara paused, then continued in her soft whisper, "I'm sorry for what I done, Scratch, really and truly sorry. And I'm glad now that I didn't hurt you."

"Huh. You and me both," Scratch said.

A big part of him didn't believe anything Cara was saying to him. She was just playing up to him, he told himself, trying to make him feel sorry for her.

But what if it was true, even partially? Somebody living as hellish an existence at home as she had described might do anything to get away from it, even throwing in with a gang of bandits and cutthroats. And once she was a part of that gang, what else could she have done except go along with whatever its leader wanted? She must have been terrified of Hank Gentry.

So there was a part of him that actually did feel sorry for her . . . *if* she was telling the truth, which she probably wasn't.

"You'd better try to get some sleep now," he told her. This conversation had gone on long enough.

"All right," she whispered. "Thanks for talking to me, Scratch. It eased my troubled mind a little."

"I'm glad to hear that."

She laughed again, and this time it was a more genuine sound.

"You probably thought I was gonna ask you to let me go, didn't you?"

"It wouldn't have done you any good," he told her.

"I know that. That's why I didn't waste my time.

You're not the sort of man who'd turn on his friends for a woman."

"No, I sure ain't."

He started to turn away, when he heard her whisper, "But what about a woman who knows where there's a fortune in greenbacks and gold?"

CHAPTER 20

For a long moment, Scratch didn't say anything. Then he asked, "What are you talkin' about?"

"When me and Hank and the rest of the boys were runnin' wild down in Texas, before we ever came up here to Indian Territory, we had a hideout in some rugged country west of Fort Worth. There's not much out in those parts except rocks and rattlesnakes. So Hank figured it was safe to stash most of our loot there. We kept what money we needed to get by and cached the rest in a cave."

Again, Scratch didn't know whether to believe her or to think that she was making up some story for reasons of her own. It was possible she was telling the truth. Plenty of outlaws hid part of their loot, rather than spending it all right away.

"Are you sayin' that money is still there?" he asked.

"Don't forget the gold," Cara said. "And yeah, it's still there unless somebody found it. Nobody would know to look for it there, so it'd have to be somebody just stumblin' over it. Just blind luck. I'd bet anything it's still there." She paused. "I'd bet my life on that, Scratch."

"Yeah, well, I don't see how that has anything to do with what's goin' on now," he said as a feeling of crawling unease grew inside him.

"I know how to find that cache. I could lead you right to it. There's plenty there to make two people rich."

"Forget it," Scratch said without hesitation. "Bo and me gave our word to Forty-two and to Judge Parker. Anyway, Bo would never go along with it."

"I wasn't talkin' about Bo," Cara snapped. "Or does he do all the thinking for both of you?"

"That ain't the way it is. We're partners. Equal partners."

"Sure," Cara said, but she didn't sound convinced.

Scratch grimaced and rubbed his jaw. He figured now that he never should have come over here to talk to Cara LaChance. He didn't like the direction this conversation was taking.

Bo would like it even less, especially if he knew the thoughts that were going through Scratch's mind at this very minute. He could see how it would all play out, how he could let Cara loose and steal Brubaker's horse, and they could take off together for the tall and uncut . . .

With a fortune in stolen loot waiting for them.

It was enough to tempt any man, especially with Cara herself thrown in as an added prize. He could never fully trust her, of course, but if they were off on their own, he didn't think she would double-cross him.

For one thing, she would need him to keep her safe. She might be hell on wheels, but a woman traveling alone would have a hard time ever making it to that hideout she'd talked about, especially if the country around it was as rugged as she made it sound.

"What about Lowe and Elam?" he asked. "We couldn't take them."

"The hell with them!" Cara whispered savagely. "I don't owe them a damn thing. Brubaker and your friend can take them on to Tyler and the hangman as far as I'm concerned. I promise you, considerin' some of the things I've seen them do, whatever happens to 'em, they've got it comin'."

Scratch thought hard, following the idea to its logical conclusions. As far as he could see, it would work, except for one thing.

"Bo would come after us," he said.

"You think so?"

"I know he would. He'd try to track us down, sure as shootin'." Scratch thought some more. "It'd be better to wait until after we cross the Red River. Then it won't take us as long to reach that hideout. We'll have a better chance of gettin' away with it."

He knew he was talking like he agreed to go along with Cara's suggestion. But he had to do some more thinking about it, and this would give him the time to do so.

"I suppose I could wait a few more days," Cara

replied with obvious reluctance. "Even though bein' locked up like this is makin' me awful crazy, Scratch."

"You can do it," Scratch told her, thinking that the delay would give him a chance to work out every last detail of the plan that had sprung into his mind. He couldn't take a chance on anything going wrong. "It won't be much longer, and then the two of us can be together."

"That sounds good," Cara breathed. "I'm so glad I didn't cut your throat, Scratch."

"You and me both," Scratch said.

The next few days were uneventful, which came as a definite relief after the journey's action-packed beginning. Brubaker kept the wagon rolling from dawn until nearly dark, changing trails several times but always trending in a generally south-to-southwest direction.

They passed a number of farms and skirted around a couple of settlements. Hank Gentry might have spies just about anywhere, Brubaker explained, and he didn't want to make it easier for the outlaws to find them. That made sense to Bo.

They were out of the Cherokee reservation now and were crossing Choctaw land, Brubaker told them. Scratch commented, "You really do know every foot of this country, don't you, Forty-two?"

"Damn straight I do," Brubaker replied. "I've been ridin' for Judge Parker for several years now. A man who don't know where he's goin' winds up dead, more often than not."

"Words to live by," Bo agreed solemnly.

Scratch asked, "How about Texas? You know your way around down there?"

"Why in the hell would I know my way around Texas?" Brubaker replied with a disdainful snort. "I can find my way from one place to another, but it's outta my jurisdiction. No offense to you Lone Star waddies, but I agree with General Sheridan: if I owned hell and Texas, I'd live in hell and rent out Texas."

"I reckon there are plenty of people who feel that way," Bo said.

"But we make allowances for 'em because they don't know no better," Scratch added.

Scratch had been unusually quiet for the past couple of days. This was the first time he had cracked wise in a while. That was because he had a lot on his mind. He hadn't had a chance to talk to Cara again, and he would have to before he made his move. There were still things that he wanted to know.

They reached the Red River, the boundary between Indian Territory and Texas, the next day. The stream, with its banks of reddish clay that gave the water its namesake color, twisted through rugged hills. Brubaker explained that as the trail sloped down toward a low-water crossing, it went between a couple of high cutbanks covered with stunted brush.

Bo was riding in front of the wagon. When he was still a few hundred yards from the river, he held up his hand to signal a stop and turned in the saddle to talk to Brubaker.

"I don't much like the looks of this," he said to the deputy. "This is a good spot for another ambush. How many crossings like this are there along the river?"

"Half a dozen or so," Brubaker replied. "Depends on how far west you go, I guess. You think Gentry's waitin' down there for us?"

"He's bound to have figured out by now that we left the main road back in Arkansas," Bo said. "He might have tried to follow us . . . or he might have decided to get ahead of us instead and wait for us to come to him."

Brubaker shook his head.

"That ain't very likely considerin' that he wouldn't have any way of knowin' which crossin' we'd head for. His gang's not big enough that he could set up an ambush at every place we could cross into Texas."

"Maybe not," Bo said, "but he could send men out to watch every crossing and get back on our trail that way."

Scratch had brought his horse up alongside the wagon while Bo and Brubaker were talking. He asked, "Would Gentry risk crossin' back over into Texas just to rescue these three? Didn't he light out for the Indian Nations to start with because the law made it too hot for him south of the Red River?"

Brubaker chewed at his drooping mustache as he thought about Scratch's question. After a moment he said, "It's true that he and his bunch got out of Texas by the skin of their teeth when the Rangers were after them. But that's been a couple of years ago. Yeah, I think he'd risk it." Brubaker leaned his head toward the back of the wagon. "Gentry sets a lot of store by that girl in there, and Lowe and Elam rode with him for a long time. He has to get 'em all back, or he risks losin' the respect of the rest of the gang."

"Then why don't you wait here," Bo suggested, "while Scratch and I take a look around? We'll scout out the crossing and come right back."

Brubaker nodded. "Sure, go ahead. Just be careful in case there is some sort of trouble waitin' up there."

"We're always careful," Scratch said with a grin. "Sometimes what we do just *looks* reckless."

Bo chuckled and said, "Come on."

While Brubaker sat there with the wagon, the Texans rode on toward the river.

Scratch was thinking as he rode. He figured that what Brubaker had said about Gentry's gang getting out of Texas one step ahead of a posse of Rangers was the answer to one of the things he'd been wondering about. They had left that loot stashed in the cave Cara had told him about because they'd never had a chance to go back and get it. When they rode away from the hideout for the last time, they hadn't known that they wouldn't be able to return.

"See anything?" Bo asked quietly as they approached the cutbanks.

"Not so far," Scratch replied. His keen eyes scanned the brushy bluffs overlooking the river. "You really think Gentry posted watchers at all the river crossin's in these parts?"

"It's possible. They might not even be regular members of his gang, just wild youngsters who want to be outlaws, like Jink and Mort Staley and their cousin Bob. If I was Gentry, I think I'd be waiting with the rest of my men at some central location, so that if one of the watchers saw us cross the river into Texas, he could gallop there and carry the word. Then Gentry and the gang could get on our trail."

Scratch let out a low whistle of admiration.

"That's some devious thinkin' there, Bo," he said. "I think we missed our callin'. We should've been outlaws."

"Maybe so. But I sort of like being able to sleep at night."

Scratch didn't say anything to that.

They rode along the eastern bank overlooking the trail and didn't find anything unusual. Then they doubled back and started checking out the western bank. As they approached the edge that overlooked the river, Bo suddenly reined in and lifted his head to sniff the air.

Scratch did likewise. He smelled the same thing Bo had.

Tobacco smoke.

Somebody was in the vicinity, all right, puffing on a quirly. Whoever it was might be totally innocent, with no connection to Hank Gentry, but they couldn't risk that.

Bo said in a fairly loud voice, "Well, I don't see anybody up here. We might as well go on back to the wagon and tell Deputy Brubaker that it's all right to cross the river."

While he was talking, he swung down from the saddle and handed his reins to Scratch. The silver-haired Texan frowned in concern, but Bo made a reassuring motion with his left hand and drew his gun with his right.

Scratch turned his mount and rode back toward the wagon, leading Bo's horse. To anyone listening, it would sound like they were both returning to the wagon.

Gun in hand, Bo stole forward stealthily. He approached the edge of the bank where it dropped off rather sharply to the river, some twenty feet below. The smell of smoke was stronger now. It drifted up from a brush-choked ledge that ran along the northern riverbank, following the curve of the bank and gradually descending to a flat area next to the water where some scrubby trees grew.

Bo studied those trees closely, and after a few moments he caught a glimpse of movement there. He continued watching until he was able to make out a horse cropping at the sparse grass under the trees. Someone had picketed the animal there, and that somebody had to be hiding in the brush farther up the ledge, watching the crossing.

And foolishly smoking a cigarette, too, Bo thought. That was the only thing that had given away the man's presence. The trees where the horse was hidden were around a small bend, so it was unlikely any of them would have noticed the animal if they had crossed the river without scouting around first.

Bo moved closer to the edge of the bank and peered down into the brush. He thought he might be able to spot smoke rising from the quirly, but the smell was fading now. The watcher had finished his smoke, and he didn't seem to be in a hurry to build another.

He couldn't keep completely still, though, which told Bo that he was probably young. Most experienced frontiersmen had the ability to remain motionless when they had to. A lot of times being able to do so was a matter of life and death.

In this case, the watcher shifted, and Bo spotted the movement. Now that he knew where to look, he was able to pick out the shape of a brown hat among the mostly bare branches. The watcher wore a brown coat, too, which helped him to blend in with the gray branches and the reddish-brown dirt. Sunlight reflected on something beside him. The breech of a rifle, Bo decided.

He could have gunned the man down without much trouble, but that would be cold-blooded murder. Not only that, but Bo couldn't be absolutely certain the watcher was working for Hank Gentry, although that was the only explanation that really made sense. If the man was a member of Gentry's gang, or even if he just wanted to be, he might possess information that would be valuable.

The ledge was about twelve feet below Bo. In absolute silence, he holstered his gun, then rose to his feet and gathered himself. He knew that Scratch and

Brubaker were probably watching him, and as soon as he made his move, Scratch would, too. So he would have help if anything went wrong.

The watcher shifted again, and Bo took a deep breath.

He leaped over the edge of the bank and plunged straight down at the hidden man.

CHAPTER 21

The watcher didn't know he was under attack until it was too late to do anything about it. At the last second some instinct must have warned him, because he twisted around and looked up, revealing a freckled, frightened face.

The next instant, Bo's booted feet smashed into him and drove him to the ground.

The man let out a cry of pain. Bo's weight carried him forward, but he rolled against the bushes and they kept him from falling off the ledge and into the river. As soon as he caught his balance, he came up on one knee and drew his Colt.

He didn't have to worry about the man he had jumped on putting up a fight. The fellow was curled up in a ball clutching his chest with both hands. He gasped, "Holy cow! I think you . . . busted all my ribs!"

The watcher's hat had flown off when Bo knocked him to the ground, revealing him to be young, probably no more than twenty years old. He had a thick shock of rumpled red hair that went with his freckled features. The rifle that lay on the ledge close to the spot where he'd been hunkering on his heels was an old single-shot weapon. As far as Bo could see, the youngster wasn't carrying a handgun.

Bo's hat had come off, too, when he jumped from the edge of the bank. It had landed nearby on top of a bush. Without taking his eyes off the man he was covering, he picked up the black hat and clapped it back on his head.

Then he said, "Don't try anything. I don't want to shoot you, but I will if I have to."

"Didn't you . . . hear me?" the young man asked miserably. "I'm busted all to pieces inside!"

"I doubt that," Bo said. "I didn't hit you that hard. What's your name?"

"Early," the youngster forced out through clenched teeth. "Early Nesbit."

"Why were you lurking in the bushes, Early?" Bo asked. "Waiting for somebody to come along so you could bushwhack them and rob them?"

"No! I . . . I wasn't lurkin'. Can't a fella . . . stop to have a smoke . . . without somebody jumpin' him?"

"You didn't just stop to have a smoke," Bo said. "You were hidden in the brush, and you've been here a while." He gestured toward the ground. "I see what's left of half a dozen quirlies lying there."

An angry, sullen expression came over Early's face.

"I don't have to . . . talk to you. You got no right . . . to ask me a bunch of questions."

Quietly, Bo said, "I reckon this Colt in my hand gives me the right to ask whatever I want."

Early sighed. "All right. I was waitin' for somebody. A friend. He was supposed to meet me here, but he ain't come along yet."

Bo shook his head, apparently sad at hearing the answer Early had given him.

"All right. I guess I'll just have to shoot you. That way you can't go running to Hank Gentry to tell him what you saw. When he gets curious and sends somebody to check on you, and they find your body, he'll figure this must be where we crossed. By then, though, you'll be dead, so it'll be too late for the knowledge to do you any good."

Early's brown eyes widened in fear.

"You'd really shoot me in cold blood? But you're supposed to be lawmen!"

Bo smiled at the young man, who winced as he realized what he'd just done.

"I said too much, didn't I?" Early drew in a deep breath and winced again at the pain that caused him. "Now you really are gonna kill me."

"No, I'm not," Bo said as he stood up. "Or at least I might not, as long as you keep telling me the truth. Are you part of Hank Gentry's gang?"

Early struggled into a sitting position with his back propped against the bank. He shook his head and said, "I ain't never rode with 'em on a job, if that's what you mean. Me and some other fellas just sort of hung around wherever Hank was, hopin' that someday he'd take us with him when he went to rob a bank or hold up a train."

"Where was this?"

Early got that sullen look on his face again.

"I ain't sayin'. I don't turn on my friends that easy. You can just go ahead and shoot me if you want!"

"Hank Gentry and those owlhoots aren't your friends, son," Bo said. "If you're lucky and live long enough, you might figure that out one of these days."

Early glared up at him.

"What're you gonna do with me?"

"Yeah, Bo," Scratch said from the top of the bank, where he'd come up without Early noticing him, although Bo had. "What're we gonna do with him? He's too small a fish. He ain't a keeper."

Early leaned forward and twisted his head to look up at the silver-haired Texan.

"You better go ahead and kill me!" he raged. "If you don't, I'll hunt you down and shoot you both!"

"Settle down," Bo told him. "This isn't some dime novel. Ranting and making threats isn't going to do you any good." He picked up Early's rifle. "Can you get to your feet?"

"I . . . I don't know."

"Why don't you try?" Bo suggested.

"My ribs—"

"Aren't broken, or you wouldn't be able to breathe and talk the way you are."

"Well, by God, they *feel* broken!"

Bo motioned with the Colt and said, "Up."

Muttering curses under his breath, Early struggled

to his feet. When he made it, he said, “There! You satisfied?”

“It’ll do for a start,” Bo told him. “You’re here alone, aren’t you?”

“That’s right.” Early’s jaw jutted out defiantly. “Hank trusted me to handle this job by myself. He knows I’m a good man.”

Bo had counted on the young man’s pride to get him an honest answer to the question, and he was convinced Early was telling the truth.

He looked up and said, “Scratch, go tell Forty-two that he can bring the wagon on across. We’ll collect Early’s horse and meet you at the ford.”

“You’re not gonna shoot him?” Scratch asked.

“Not yet, anyway.”

Scratch shook his head. “Forty-two ain’t gonna like havin’ another prisoner to take care of.”

“Well, if Early gets to be too much trouble, I’m sure there are buzzards and coyotes on the other side of the river, too.”

Early swallowed hard at the grim implications of that seemingly casual comment. Bo managed not to grin. He figured that right now, keeping the young man good and scared was the best way to get him to cooperate.

Bo wiggled the revolver’s barrel again.

“Get moving,” he ordered. “Down the ledge and around the bend to where you left your horse.”

“You’re gonna be mighty sorry about this,” Early threatened as he moved gingerly along the ledge in front of Bo. "Hank don't take kindly to hombres who mistreat his friends."

"I told you, you're not Hank Gentry's friend. A man like that doesn't have any real friends, only people that he uses to get what he wants. Where are you from, anyway? Seems like I hear some Texas in your voice."

"A little town called Tioga," Early replied grudgingly. "It ain't too far from here."

"I've heard of it," Bo said. "What made you decide to cross the Red River and become an outlaw?"

"That's none o' your damn business!" After a moment, though, the youngster went on, "You ever pick cotton, mister?"

"I sure have," Bo said.

"Well, my daddy works a cotton patch on shares, and he expects all of us kids to work, too. I just couldn't see spendin' the rest of my life bent over pickin' those damn bolls, so as soon as I got big enough, I lit out."

"Just because you don't want to be a cotton farmer doesn't mean you have to become an outlaw."

"Maybe not, but it seemed like the quickest way to get rich."

"That's all you want to do, get rich?"

"Don't you?" Early asked.

"Can't say as it ever interested me all that much," Bo answered honestly. "Having a bunch of money seemed like more trouble than it was worth. You'd have to be worrying all the time that something might happen to it."

"Not having money doesn't worry you?"

"Not all that much. I'm not so old that I can't do an honest day's work for an honest day's pay."

"What are you gonna do when you *are* too old to do that? How you gonna take care of yourself then?"

That question brought a frown to Bo's face as they reached the bottom of the ledge. It was something he had thought about from time to time. He didn't have any close relatives who would take him in, and as far as he knew, neither did Scratch. There had been some lonely nights on the trail when they got to talking and wondering about such things, and neither of the Texans had an answer for the problem.

On the other hand, Bo told himself, the sort of lives they led, the way trouble followed them around, it was more likely they'd get shot or knifed before they got so old they couldn't fend for themselves. There was a lot to be said for dying with your boots on.

Early's horse was a placid-looking chestnut gelding. Bo untied the animal and swung up into the saddle.

"Hey!" Early protested. "Are you stealin' my horse?"

"No, just riding back down to the crossing on it."

"How am I supposed to get there?"

"You can wade along the edge," Bo told him.

"Why do I have to wade while you get to ride?"

"Well, for one thing, I'm older than you, and you should respect your elders. For another, I've already been wading one time this week, and I don't have any hankering to do it again. Now move."

The crossing was only a hundred yards or so from where Early had left his horse. He slogged through the reddish mud and shallow water at the edge of the river, and Bo rode behind him, covering him with the Colt. By the time they reached the crossing, Scratch and Brubaker were waiting for them just on the Texas side of the river. They all went up the trail between the cutbanks to the flats at the top.

Bo dismounted and told Early, "Climb on top of the wagon."

Brubaker frowned. "What've you got in mind to do with the boy, Creel?" he asked.

"I don't want to put him in with those three prisoners," Bo said. "But I don't want to have to shoot him off his horse if he decides to light a shuck, either. So I figured we could tie his hands and feet and he could ride on top."

"I'll fall off," Early complained.

"Try not to," Scratch drawled. "Sounds like a pretty good idea to me, Bo."

"Why are we even takin' him along anyway?" Brubaker wanted to know.

"Well, Forty-two, you're the boss," Bo said, "so if you don't want to bring him, I reckon we can just tie him up and leave him here. Somebody *might* come along to turn him loose before he starves to death. I just thought that if we took him with us, he might be able to tell us some more about Gentry and the rest of that bunch."

"I told you, you're wastin' your time," Early said. "I ain't a double-crosser."

"Also," Bo went on, "we'd have him to use as a hostage if we needed to."

Early let out a bark of laughter.

"Now you really are loco," he said. "If Hank Gentry wants to kill you, he won't let me stand in the way. Why, he'd—"

The youngster stopped short as he realized what he was saying.

"That's right," Bo said. "He'd just shoot you to get to us, because he doesn't care whether you live or die, Early. Are you starting to understand now what I've been trying to tell you?"

Early just glared and muttered something, probably a curse.

Brubaker said, "All right, you convinced me, Creel. Get up there, kid. Morton, you got some rope I can use?"

"I sure do," Scratch said.

A few minutes later, Early Nesbit was sitting on top of the wagon with his hands tied together behind his back and his legs stretched out in front of him with the ankles roped together. As long as he made an effort to stay balanced, he wouldn't be likely to fall off. Bo tied the youngster's horse to the back of the wagon, alongside Brubaker's saddle mount.

"Ready to go," he told the deputy with a nod.

"Let's get movin', then," Brubaker said. "Right now, the more distance we put between us and Indian Territory, the better as far as I'm concerned."

CHAPTER 22

Taking Early Nesbit along with them was a complication in the plan Scratch had come up with, but it couldn't be helped. It wasn't really safe to leave him behind, because there was no telling when some of Gentry's men might come along and find him, and at the same time discover that Brubaker had taken the prisoners across the river at that spot.

And no matter what else, killing the boy in cold blood wasn't an option, despite what they'd made Early believe.

Nightfall found them making camp several miles south of the Red River. Early had complained a lot, but at least he wasn't as obscene about it as Cara and the other two had been during the early stages of the journey. He had gotten on Brubaker's nerves enough, though, that the deputy had threatened to gag him if he didn't shut up.

After that, Early had just muttered and mumbled.

Scratch took Cara when she had to go visit the bushes that evening. When they were far enough away from the camp, she said, "All right, we're in Texas now, like you wanted. When are we gonna make our break for it, Scratch?"

"I was thinkin' maybe tonight," he said, keeping his voice pitched low so he wouldn't be overheard.

"Oh, thank the Lord! I wasn't sure I could take one more day of bein' cooped up inside that damn wagon!" She paused, then went on, "Listen, you'll have to knock out Dayton and Jim, otherwise they'll raise a ruckus when they see that I'm escapin' and they ain't."

"I can do that," Scratch said. "I've been wonderin' . . . don't they know where that hideout is, too?"

"Sure, they were ridin' with Hank back in those days, just like I was."

"Won't they figure that's where you're headed and tell Brubaker where to find you?"

"Not hardly," Cara answered without hesitation. "They'll still be hopin' that Hank will get them loose somehow, and they'll know that if they spill the location of that cache to the law, he'd kill 'em faster than some judge ever could. They'll wait until he rescues them, then tell Hank what happened and where they think I went. But by then it'll be too late, even if Hank does free them. And if he doesn't, well, they might break down on the gallows and tell about it, but it'll be too late to stop us by then, too."

"You've thought it all out," Scratch mused.

"Of course I have," she said. "I learned a lot while I was riding with Hank. He's pretty smart."

"All you needed was to figure out which one of us

was the most likely to help you, so you'd know who to bat your eyes at and play up to."

"Now, it wasn't like that, honey," Cara said with a pout in her voice. "I never would've said anything to start with to Brubaker or your friend Bo. I've known plenty of stiff-necked, upright bastards like them. They're too blasted stubborn to know what's good for 'em. But a man like you . . . you're smart enough to see the possibilities. That's why I liked you right from the start. Well, once we got past that part about tryin' to cut you with a razor blade, anyway."

Scratch laughed. "You are a caution, Cara La-Chance."

"You don't know just how right you are," she said.

"What about that kid? You know him from when you were still with the gang?"

"Early?" Cara emerged from the brush and shrugged her shoulders as much as the heavy chains would let her. "I remember seein' him around a few times. Don't know that I ever talked to him. There were always kids suckin' around Hank, wantin' to be desperadoes. He said that was just part of bein' famous."

"I may have to knock him out, too."

"Go right ahead," she told him. "Kill him if you need to. He don't mean nothin' to me." Cara nodded toward the camp. "We'd better get back. We've been out here a while, and we don't want them gettin' suspicious when we're this close to makin' our move."

"You're right," Scratch said, noting to himself that

she was already taking charge. He was starting to wonder just who had really been running that gang. He thought that the story she had told him about being scared of Hank Gentry and going along with everything he said might have been embellished just a mite.

Back at the wagon, Early was complaining because his hands were still tied behind him.

"As long as my feet are tied, I can't go anywhere," he argued. "So why can't my hands be tied in front of me?"

"Where you can grab a gun, if any of us was foolish enough to get within reach of you?" Brubaker asked. He let out a disgusted snort. "Not likely, kid."

"Look, Marshal, I'm startin' to think that maybe I ain't so keen on bein' an outlaw after all. If you were to turn me loose, I give you my word I'd go on back to Tioga and you'd never see or hear from me again. And I wouldn't help Hank Gentry find you, neither."

"Forget it," Brubaker said. "You should've thought of that before you started runnin' with that no-account trash. What I'm gonna do, since we need supplies anyway because the trip is takin' longer than I expected, is go to Gainesville. We can provision up there, and I'll leave you locked in the city jail with instructions for the marshal to hold you there until I wire him to let you loose."

Early stared at him for a second, then burst out, "You can't do that! Why, I . . . I didn't even break any laws! I was just sittin' there smokin' a cigarette when that old galoot jumped on me and like to busted all my ribs!"

The youngster jerked his head toward Bo, who smiled.

"You've admitted knowin' Gentry," Brubaker said, and his voice was as cold as the night air. "That makes you a witness, and I can hold a witness in custody for as long as I damned well please."

"But it ain't fair!"

"Goes to show what a babe in the woods you really are, Nesbit, hollerin' about fair. There ain't no fair in this world. There's only the law, them that follow it . . . and them that don't."

Early leaned back against the rock where he'd been sitting. He fell into a sullen silence as he glared at Brubaker and the Texans.

A short time later, Bo said, "I'll stand first watch tonight. Scratch, you want the second turn?"

"Sure," Scratch replied. "That'll leave you to finish up, Forty-two."

Brubaker nodded curtly and said, "Sure. Fine by me."

Scratch yawned. "Reckon I'll turn in, then," he said. "Want to be wide awake when it's my turn to stand guard."

He wrapped up in his blankets and fell asleep almost right away, without even thinking about what would happen later. On the frontier, a man grabbed whatever chances he could to rest.

After several hours, Bo woke him to take over. The fire had burned down quite a bit. Bo had fed it just enough wood to keep it going and provide a slight bit of warmth. Mostly, though, it was another cold winter night.

The wagon was dark and quiet. Brubaker lay motionless in his blankets, snoring softly. Not far away, Early Nesbit was wrapped up in blankets as well, sleeping restlessly because it was difficult to get comfortable when you were tied hand and foot.

"Anything unusual goin' on?" Scratch asked Bo in a whisper.

"Not a thing. Night's as quiet as can be."

Scratch nodded and said, "Just the way I like it."

Taking his rifle, he went over and sat down on the wagon tongue. He watched Bo crawl into the other bedroll, turn to face away from the fire, and pillow his head on his saddle. Within moments, Bo was breathing deeply, steadily.

Scratch waited some more.

When half an hour had passed, he stood up. Moving with the stealth and silence that decades of experience had taught him, he approached the recumbent Brubaker. The deputy didn't stir as Scratch lifted his rifle and then brought the butt crashing down.

Swiftly, wasting not even a second, Scratch whirled away from Brubaker and took a couple of quick steps that brought him within reach of Bo. The rifle rose and fell again, brutally.

Then Scratch turned back and bent over to reach into Brubaker's coat pocket. He brought out the heavy key that unlocked the padlocks.

He had just started toward the wagon when Early

Nesbit started up off the ground as much as his bonds would let him, apparently startled out of sleep. He started to say, "Wha—"

Scratch's boot crashed against the young man's jaw, stretching him out on the ground, senseless.

Scratch went to the wagon, thrust the key into the padlock, and turned it. When he opened the door, Cara was already awake and waiting for him. She whispered, "Knock out these two, quick!"

"No need," Scratch told her. "Bo and Brubaker are dead. I stove in their skulls. Got to thinkin' about it and decided why take chances?"

"You . . . killed them?"

"Yep." Scratch unfastened the padlock holding Cara's chains to the ring in the floor.

She began to laugh. Lowe and Elam both stirred, and Lowe rumbled, "What's goin' on here?"

"I'm gettin' away, that's what's goin' on, you damned fool!" she told him.

Scratch unlocked the shackles on her ankles, then the ones on her wrists.

"Hey!" Elam said. "Let us loose, too!"

"Sorry, boys," Cara said. "Scratch and I are the only ones ridin' away from here tonight."

"You bitch!" Lowe roared. "You double-crossin' bitch!"

"I'll see you in hell for this," Elam snarled.

"Not if I see you first," Cara taunted. She bent over for a moment to rub her ankles and get better circulation in her feet, then stood up and said to Scratch, "Let's get out of here."

"You'll have to lead the way," he told her. "I don't know this part of Texas."

"Fine. Come on."

She climbed down from the wagon without any trouble. Behind her, Lowe and Elam bellowed futile curses. Cara told Scratch to close the door and lock it again.

"I'm tired of listenin' to those two," she said. "I hope they both starve to death before somebody finds them."

Scratch replaced the padlock on the door and snapped it shut. He gave it a tug to make sure it was secure.

"We're gonna be rich, Scratch, just you and me," Cara went on. "I'm takin' your friend's horse, all right?"

"Fine with me," Scratch said. "He don't need it anymore."

Moving quickly, he saddled his own horse and Bo's mount. They climbed onto the animals. Cara looked at the Winchester sticking up from Bo's saddle boot, and for a second Scratch thought she was going to pull out the rifle and put a few slugs into the motionless forms of Bo and Brubaker for good measure.

But then she turned the horse and said, "Let's ride!"

Her reckless laughter rang through the cold night as she kicked the horse into a run despite the darkness. Scratch followed close behind her.

When the sound of rapid hoofbeats had dwindled

away completely, Bo pushed his blankets aside and stood up.

"They're gone, Forty-two," he said.

Brubaker sat up and said, "This is the biggest damn fool stunt I ever did see. I don't know how in blazes I let you two Texans talk me into it."

Bo grinned. "It was Scratch's idea. But you've got to admit, using Cara to lead us right to all that loot the gang stashed is probably the only way the law would ever find it."

"I know, I know," Brubaker grumbled as he got to his feet. "But he came damn near to actually hittin' me with that rifle butt! If he'd missed a little and hit me instead of my saddle, my skull'd be cracked now."

Bo checked on Early. The young man was unconscious and had a bruise starting up on his jaw, but he would be all right.

Profane yelling still came from inside the wagon. Brubaker walked over to it and slapped a hand on the side a couple of times.

"Shut up in there!" he roared. "Or else I won't feed you breakfast in the mornin'!"

A stunned silence came over the wagon. After a few seconds, Jim Elam said tentatively, "Marshal? Is that you?"

"Who the hell else do you think it'd be, Colonel George Armstrong Custer? Now settle down, the both of you."

Dayton Lowe began to laugh. It was a low, rumbling sound.

"That treacherous little hellcat ain't as smart as she thinks she is!" he said.

"Maybe not, but you ain't, either," Brubaker said. "Shut up and go back to sleep."

He left the prisoners and walked back over to where Bo was standing and gazing off in the direction Scratch and Cara had taken when they rode away from the camp.

"Judge Parker's gonna have my hide for goin' off on my own like this," Brubaker said quietly. "And if those prisoners manage to escape . . ."

"They won't," Bo said. "The county jail in Gainesville is plenty sturdy, and Gentry won't have any reason to look for them there. They'll be fine for a week or so, until we get back. And then we'll have not only Cara, but all the loot that Gentry hid before he headed for Indian Territory, too. The judge will understand."

"Maybe," Brubaker said. "Or maybe that gal will outsmart us, and we'll all wind up dead."

Bo nodded slowly as he peered into the darkness and hoped Scratch knew what he was doing.

CHAPTER 23

As far as Scratch could tell from the stars, he and Cara angled southwest when they rode away from the camp where they had left Bo and Brubaker pretending to be dead. Everything had gone off pretty much the way the three of them had planned during the past few days in quiet conversations out of earshot of the wagon.

Brubaker hadn't been easy to convince when Scratch first laid out the idea. He had insisted in no uncertain terms that Scratch was plumb loco, completely out of his head, to even be considering letting Cara LaChance escape, no matter what the reason.

"She's tellin' the truth about that cache of loot, though, Forty-two," Scratch had argued. "I can hear the greed in her voice when she talks about it."

"You know she doesn't really plan to split the money with you, don't you?" Bo had asked.

"Oh, shoot, yeah. She's figurin' she'll put a bullet in my back just as soon as it's convenient for her. Might not be as soon as we get to the hideout, because she might need my help totin' the loot out of there, but as soon as we're close enough to a town so that she could make it without me, it'd be adios, José."

"I didn't figure you for bein' part Mexican, Morton," Brubaker had commented.

"It's just an old sayin'. Anyway, I'm goin' into this with my eyes wide open, fellas. I know she don't aim to split the loot with me, and I know my manly charms don't really make her heart go pitty-pat, neither. I figure she'll do whatever she has to in order to get what she wants, though."

Brubaker had frowned and said, "It'd be like beddin' down with a she-panther. You couldn't ever tell when she was fixin' to rip you to shreds. But that ain't none of my business." He had studied Scratch intently. "You ain't plannin' to double-cross us, are you? Seems to me you might be playin' a mighty deep game here, mister."

Bo had shaken his head and said, "There's no game, Forty-two. Scratch and I have been partners for more than forty years. He'd never double-cross me. Besides which, he's a law-abiding man—"

"Most of the time," Scratch had put in.

"Most of the time," Bo had gone on, "and he wouldn't let an outlaw and a killer get away. At least not permanently."

In the end the Texans had persuaded Brubaker to go along with the idea. They had figured out how they would do it, and Bo and Scratch had decided that it would be best to wait until the party crossed the Red River into Texas before putting the plan into operation.

"We know that area where she says the hideout is pretty well," Bo had explained. "She must mean over in Parker or Palo Pinto County, deep in the Cross Timbers. That's rugged country, all right. Rocks and rattlesnakes and ravines, everywhere you look. And plenty of places in those hills for outlaws to hide themselves and their loot."

"It'll take two or three days of ridin' to get there," Scratch had said. "But Cara and me will have to take the back trails and try not to be seen, while the two of you can use the main roads and make better time. Even with stoppin' off at Gainesville to lock up those prisoners, you ought to get to the area about the same time we do."

"How will we ever find your trail once we're there?" Brubaker wanted to know.

Scratch had grinned and said, "I'll send up smoke signals. If Cara thinks you're dead, she won't be expectin' anybody to be followin' us. So she won't be suspicious if I build a nice big campfire."

"Just try not to be too obvious about it," Bo had advised.

"Don't worry, I'll be careful."

And so far, he had been, Scratch thought as he rode alongside Cara through the darkness, their way lit only by a three-quarter moon and a multitude of stars glittering brightly in the cold heavens.

Knowing that she had a rifle within easy reach made his skin crawl a little. Maybe she'd been telling the truth when she claimed that she had never killed anybody, but he wasn't going to bet his life on it.

Although, Scratch mused, that was sort of what he was doing . . .

Cara had ridden hard and set a fast pace when they left the camp behind, even though she didn't have any reason to expect pursuit. Probably that was just instinct, Scratch thought, with her wanting to get as far away from the scene of her captivity as she could.

Now she had slowed Bo's horse to a more reasonable gait, especially considering the fact that they couldn't always see where they were going.

If things had worked out that way, Scratch would have suggested that Cara take Early Nesbit's horse. But when she wanted Bo's mount, Scratch didn't think it was reasonable to refuse her. Early's horse was a decent one. Bo could use it, since Early wouldn't have any need of the animal while he was locked up in the county jail at Gainesville.

"How come you don't know this part of the country?" Cara asked as they rode. "You're from Texas, aren't you?"

"Yeah, but from down around Hallettsville and Victoria. That's pert near four hundred miles from here. Not only that, but Bo and me left Texas a long time ago, and we ain't been back much since."

That wasn't far from the truth, Scratch thought. It *had* been a long time since they rode away from the Lone Star State, following the deaths of Bo's wife and children.

But they had been back often enough that they had

crisscrossed the state several times and knew all of it pretty well, from the piney woods of East Texas to the mountain desert of West Texas. Scratch knew the area they were going now, knew its thickly wooded hills and dark valleys. The Brazos River angled down across the region, and fifteen years earlier, it had marked the western boundary of civilized Texas. Beyond the river lay Comancheria, shrouded in mystery and menace, home to some of the most ruthless, dangerous warriors in the history of mankind, the Comanches.

But in that intervening decade and a half, a lot had changed. The bounds of the range controlled by the Comanches had been pushed back farther and farther, and the army had broken their power bit by bit, climaxed by the decisive Battle of Palo Duro Canyon. Since then the threat of the Comanches, while not eliminated entirely, had been reduced to sporadic raids and skirmishes. In the area where they were headed now, Scratch knew they would be in more danger from white savages than red ones.

"I'm sure I can find the place," Cara went on. "I helped Hank pick it out. Just be glad it's winter. During the summer, the rattlers are mighty thick out there."

"I ain't fond of snakes. I won't bother them if they don't bother me."

"They'll all be curled up in their holes at this time of year."

"Like in that cave where the loot's stashed?"

Cara laughed. "Don't worry. I'll go in first if you're scared."

"Never said I was scared," Scratch replied. "Just that I don't like snakes."

They rode on through the night. At one point, when they were on high ground, Scratch caught sight of some lights several miles to the east. That would be Gainesville, he thought. Bo and Brubaker would be there first thing in the morning, locking Lowe, Elam, and Early Nesbit in the jail. The county sheriff might not be too fond of the idea, but with Brubaker being a federal marshal, he woudn't have much choice but to go along with it.

Finally Cara brought Bo's horse to a stop in a thick stand of trees and said, "We'll make camp here. We need to get some sleep, and then we can push on in the mornin'."

"You sleep," Scratch said. "I'll stand guard. I got some sleep earlier, before Bo woke me up."

"We'll both sleep. Hell, Scratch, nobody's comin' after us. Nobody knows where we are. We're as safe as we can be."

Part of Scratch wanted to stay awake all the time Cara was awake, just so he'd be ready if she tried to double-cross him, but he knew that wasn't going to be possible. Sooner or later, he'd have to trust her, at least a little, so it might as well be now, he decided.

And if she cut his throat while he was asleep . . . well, he knew that Bo would catch up to her sooner or later and settle the score for him.

As he was picketing and unsaddling the horses, he realized that they had only one bedroll—his—which he'd picked up and lashed on behind his saddle before they left camp.

That would have been fine if they had taken turns sleeping, as Scratch had sort of figured they would do. But from what Cara had said, she planned on them sharing the blankets.

Under other circumstances, that might not have been so bad, although Cara was young enough that would have made Scratch a little uncomfortable. But her youth combined with the fact that she was an outlaw and quite possibly a murderer gave him the fantods for sure.

Still, he didn't see what else he could do except play along with whatever she wanted.

She had already crawled into the bedroll when he finished with the horses. She held back the blankets for him and said, "Here."

Scratch took off his hat and boots, then unbuckled his gun belt and coiled it around the holstered Remingtons. He set the revolvers on the ground next to the blankets, within easy reach.

He slid into the bedroll with Cara. He had put his saddle down for a pillow, and as he rested his head on it, she snuggled against him and laid her head on his shoulder. Her curly blond hair tickled his cheek as she moved closer to him.

He cleared his throat and said, "You know this, uh, this saddle of mine is older than you are, don't you?"

"Oh, hush," she said sleepily. "I'm tired, and it's damned cold. I've just about froze every night since we left Fort Smith because I wasn't just about to curl up with those two varmints I was locked in the wagon with. I figure with you it's different."

"Different, eh?" Scratch wasn't sure if he liked the sound of that or not.

"Well, you're older. Maybe not *too* old. But we'll see about that later. Right now, I just need some sleep."

"Me, too," Scratch said. "Good night."

"Night . . ." she murmured as she pressed closer against him, seeking warmth.

If this didn't beat all, Scratch thought. Curled up in his blankets with a beautiful young gal who was probably plumb loco and a killer to boot, and the two of them on their way to retrieve a small fortune in stolen money and gold from an outlaws' cave that might be full of rattlesnakes.

Well, he thought as he drifted off to sleep, she might cut his throat before morning, but at least he wasn't likely to die of boredom.

CHAPTER 24

Scratch was cold when he woke up in the morning, which meant two things, one good and one maybe not so good.

The good thing was that he woke up at all, which meant he was still alive. Cara hadn't killed him while he slept, after all.

The fact that he was cold meant that she was no longer huddled in the blankets next to him. He sat up quickly, thinking that she might have slipped away and taken both horses with her, leaving him stranded here. He hated to think that she could do such a thing without waking him, but maybe it was possible . . .

"Good morning," she said. He heard the crackle of a fire and suddenly smelled coffee brewing. When he turned his head she was there, hunkered on the other side of a small campfire. She had gotten the coffeepot from his gear and started the Arbuckles' boiling.

"Where'd you get the water?" Scratch asked.

"There's a little creek just the other side of these

trees," Cara said. "And I told you good morning. You ain't very polite, old man."

Scratch grunted, and then a grin spread across his leathery face.

"Good mornin'," he said. "You sleep all right?"

"Better than I have in a while," Cara replied. "You?"

"Just fine," Scratch admitted. If he could just forget the errand they were on and the sort of woman she really was, this little adventure wouldn't be so bad.

But he couldn't forget. Not hardly.

"You want me to fry up some bacon?" Cara went on. "I'm not very good at it. I can make coffee, but that's about all. So if you're thinkin' that just because I'm a woman I'm here to wait on you hand and foot—"

"The thought never crossed my mind," Scratch said.

"Good. We'll head toward Decatur today. I want to stay away from big towns like Fort Worth. Too many blasted people there. Somebody might recognize me."

Scratch almost came out with *Eighter from Decatur, the county seat of Wise*, but he remembered in time that he wasn't supposed to know this area, so he probably wouldn't have heard that little saying about the town.

Instead he told Cara, "You lead the way, darlin', and I'll go along with you."

He climbed out of the bedroll, his muscles creaking a little and his breath fogging in front of his face in the cold air, and got busy frying bacon and cooking some biscuits. They had slept until after dawn, and the sun was well up by the time they finished breakfast and were ready to ride.

They spent the day continuing to head southwest, avoiding farmhouses and little crossroads settlements and trying not to skyline themselves atop the rolling hills. Late in the afternoon they skirted east around the town of Decatur that Cara had mentioned that morning. They made camp alongside a slowly moving stream that Scratch guessed was one of the several forks of the Trinity River.

The day had warmed up considerably, enough so that Scratch had taken off his buckskin jacket while he was riding in the sun. Cara removed her coat, too, and paused from time to time to run her fingers through her thick, curly hair. Whenever she did that, Scratch thought, Lord, she was beautiful, but there were plenty of things in this world that looked pretty but could kill you in a hurry if you let your guard down, he reminded himself.

Once the sun was down it quickly started getting cold. After supper, Scratch and Cara once again curled up together in the bedroll. She went to sleep immediately. Scratch lingered on the edge of wakefulness long enough to wonder how Bo and Brubaker were doing and how things had gone with the sheriff in Gainesville. Scratch had every confidence in the world that when the time came, Bo would be there. In all the years they had traveled together, Bo had never let him down.

The next day they followed the river southward. Scratch grinned and said, "If we had a boat, we could float down to where we're goin'."

Cara snorted disdainfully. "Except when it's floodin', the Trinity's not deep enough in these parts to float anything more than a little rowboat. Anyway, I'd rather be on horseback. I don't like boats." She sniffed. "I can't swim."

"You can't?"

"Never learned. There was no place around where I grew up that was big enough to swim in. We had a little pond on our farm, but it was barely deep enough for the crawdads to paddle around." She got a reminiscing look on her face. "One time up in the Nations, Hank wanted to go skinny-dippin' in a creek. I told him I'd take my clothes off, but I wasn't gonna swim."

"You were quite a hellion, weren't you?"

She grinned over at him.

"I still am. You got a problem with that, Scratch?"

He shook his head and said, "Nope, not me."

They had gone only another mile or so when the horse Cara was riding suddenly broke its gait and started limping. She reined in and glared in annoyance.

"What's wrong with this jughead?" she asked.

Scratch swung down from his saddle.

"Let me take a look," he said.

He lifted the horse's hoof that seemed to be causing the trouble and studied it. Taking a clasp knife from his pocket, he opened it and pried at the horseshoe with the blade.

"Shoe's loose and it's picked up a rock," he announced after a moment. "We need to find a blacksmith."

"Can't you take care of it?" Cara asked.

"Maybe, if I had the right tools, which I don't. Anyway, we'll be better off lettin' somebody who knows what he's doin' handle it. You don't want to be left a-foot out here, and if we have to ride double we couldn't get away very fast if we needed to."

"I wanted to steer clear of towns until we got to the hideout."

"I know," Scratch said, "but this can't be helped. We'll see if we can find some little settlement where there's no law and nobody will know you."

"All right, all right," she said with a disgusted tone in her voice. She waved a hand toward the west and went on, "There's a wide place in the road over that way called O'Bar. Might be a blacksmith there. We needed to start headin' in that direction anyway if we're gonna avoid Fort Worth."

"Sounds good," Scratch said. "Why don't you climb up here with me, so your horse won't have to carry you? We can ride double for that far."

Cara agreed with that idea. She dismounted and handed him the reins to Bo's horse. Scratch took his left foot out of the stirrup and let her use it to swing up behind him. When she was settled down behind the saddle and had her arms around his waist, he heeled his mount into motion again and started off, leading Bo's horse.

Cara told him which way to go. This was still

wooded, hilly country, although not as rugged as it would be farther west, where the Gentry gang's old hideout was located. It took them about an hour to reach O'Bar, which turned out to be a one-street settlement with a couple of blocks of businesses and a few dozen houses scattered around its outskirts. Scratch spotted a church steeple that stuck up on the other side of some cottonwood and Post oak trees lining the banks of a creek just west of town.

"You see a blacksmith shop?" Cara asked anxiously.

Scratch nodded to a building on the left side of the street. It had double doors that stood open, and smoke came from a chimney in the middle of the roof.

Scratch reined to a halt in front of the doors. Cara slid down from the horse first, then he dismounted, too, as a stocky man with rusty hair and a close-cropped beard emerged from the building.

"Got a horse with a loose shoe that picked up a rock," Scratch said. "I got the rock out, but the shoe still needs work. Reckon you can take care of it for us?"

"Not a problem," the blacksmith replied with a nod. "I got one job to finish up first, but I can get to it in a little while. That be all right?"

Scratch turned to look at Cara, but she wasn't there. He stiffened in surprise for a second before he spotted her walking across the street. He nodded to the blacksmith and said, "Yeah, that'll be fine, thanks," and started after her.

She was headed for a squat building made of red

sandstone. The place had a tiled roof that was a darker shade of red. A sign on the overhang above the flat, flagstone porch proclaimed the place to be the RED TOP CAFÉ AND SALOON. Several horses were tied at the hitch racks in front of the porch.

Scratch's long legs allowed him to catch up to Cara before she reached the café.

"I thought you didn't want to call attention to yourself," he said quietly.

"We're already here anyway," she said. "I figured it wouldn't do any harm to get a meal that amounted to more than just bacon and biscuits."

"Well, that's not a bad idea," Scratch admitted.

He opened the door, and they stepped into warmth that was thick with the delicious aromas of food cooking. The Red Top was more saloon than café, he saw. There was a lunch counter to the left that formed an L with the long side of it running toward the back of the low-ceilinged room and serving as a bar. The right-hand wall had several booths with leather-covered seats, and round tables were scattered over the open area between the wall and the bar. A poker game with four cowboys playing was going on at one of those tables.

A couple of punchers were at the bar nursing mugs of beer, while two men sat at the lunch counter with plates of food in front of them. Out of habit, Scratch quickly scanned the faces of all the men in the place. He didn't see anybody he recognized, which came as no surprise. He had never been to O'Bar before, leastways that he could remember.

The patrons glanced at the newcomers, curious as anybody would be about strangers in their midst, and several of the cowboys took a second, longer, more appreciative look at Cara. Scratch didn't think that any of them seemed to recognize her. Like all young men, they were just interested in the sight of a pretty girl.

They probably thought he was her grandfather, Scratch told himself. He didn't care one way or the other. He didn't intend for them to stay in O'Bar any longer than they had to in order to get that horseshoe fixed.

Cara sat down on a stool at the lunch counter. Scratch took the stool beside her. A short, burly man with salt-and-pepper hair rested thick-fingered hands on the counter and said, "Howdy, folks. What can I do y'all for?"

Cara gave him a dazzling smile.

"I'd love a nice juicy steak with all the trimmin's," she said.

The counterman grinned back at her.

"I reckon we can do that for y'all," he said. "How about you, old-timer?"

Considering the gray in the man's hair, Scratch didn't think he was all *that* much older than the hombre, but he let it pass and said, "A steak sounds good to me, too."

"Comin' up," the counterman said with a nod. He shouldered his way through a swinging door into the kitchen, which let out even more appetizing odors into the air.

Scratch leaned closer to Cara and said quietly, "If the idea was for you not to attract much attention, you ain't goin' about it the right way."

He nodded toward the cowboys watching them.

Cara gave a toss of her head that made her mass of blond hair swirl enticingly around her shoulders.

"Oh, them?" she said. "To tell you the truth, I don't even notice it that much anymore. Men have been lookin' at me like that since I was fourteen."

Scratch didn't believe for a second that she didn't notice the attention. She saw it, all right, and she liked it. But that wasn't important at the moment. They would eat their meals, pick up Bo's horse when that shoe had been repaired or replaced, and then shake off the dust of O'Bar's single street as quickly as possible.

At least, that was the plan. But one of the poker players at the table threw in his hand in disgust, announced, "I'm out," and scraped his chair back. Cocking his Stetson at a jaunty angle, he sauntered toward the lunch counter.

And all Scratch had to do was look at him to know that trouble was walking toward them.

CHAPTER 25

"Hello, sweet thing," the young cowboy said to Cara as he came up and rested a hand on the counter next to her. He gave her a grin that was cocked at a jaunty angle just like his hat. "You don't live around here, do you? I don't remember seein' you around these parts before."

"You know everybody who lives around here, do you?" Cara asked him coolly.

"I can promise you, if you lived in O'Bar, I'd know it. Fact of the matter is, I'd have been courtin' you before now. My name's Joe Reynolds."

"Well, you're right, Mr. Reynolds, I don't live around here," Cara told him. "We're just passin' through."

"Travelin' with your grandpa, are you?" Reynolds asked, sparing Scratch barely a glance.

"Oh, he's not my grandpa." Cara linked her arm with Scratch's and leaned her head intimately on his shoulder. "This here is my husband."

"Husband!" Reynolds exclaimed in obvious amazement. "This old codger? You can't be serious."

"He's all the man I need, and then some," Cara said with great solemnity.

"What in blazes do you think you're doin'?" Scratch asked her in a whisper.

Cara ignored him. She kept giving Reynolds that daring, go-to-hell smile of hers. She even ran her tongue over her lips in a deliberately provocative gesture.

"Well, all I got to say is that this is the biggest pure-dee waste of a beautiful woman that I ever did see." Reynolds sneered at Scratch. "Why don't you let this gal spend a little time with a real man, Gramps?"

A low growl sounded in Scratch's throat. He was about to lose his patience with this young pup, even though Cara was egging him on.

"Listen, son—" he began.

"Don't worry, honey, I can handle this," Cara said. She looked at Reynolds and went on, "I reckon you're the real man you think I should spend a little time with?"

"That's right," he said.

"Yeah, I can tell by lookin' at you that it'd be a little time, all right. A real little time."

"What do you— Hey! What do you mean by that, gal?"

Cara laughed. "You know what I mean," she said.

Reynolds crowded closer to her, saying, "I don't appreciate some stranger talkin' to me that way!"

Cara didn't flinch. Instead she leaned toward him and said, "Do you appreciate this?"

Before Reynolds knew what was going on, Cara had snaked the young cowboy's gun out of its holster. She jammed the muzzle up under Reynolds's chin and eared back the hammer with an ominous, audible click.

The talk around the poker table stopped abruptly, and the men in the Red Top who weren't already watching the confrontation turned to see what was going on.

Cara had taken Scratch by surprise, too. He'd had no idea she was about to grab the cowboy's gun. If he had known, he would have tried to stop her.

But Cara herself probably hadn't known what she was about to do until she was already doing it. She was acting on pure wild impulse, Scratch sensed.

Reynolds's eyes widened until they looked like they were about to pop out of their sockets. He came up on his toes in an effort to lessen the pressure as the gun muzzle dug into his neck, but Cara just forced it up even harder.

"Wha . . . what are you doin'?" he managed to gasp. "Are you loco?"

"Loco?" Cara repeated. "You come over here and look at me like I'm a whore instead of a lady and you insult this fine gentleman, and you ask me if I'm loco? You're the one who's loco, buckaroo! And it seems to me like you need a lesson in manners, too."

Scratch said, "We don't need to do this. Why don't

you just let that hammer down easy-like, and we'll get out of here."

"Not until we've had our steaks!" she insisted. "Which are gonna be on you, aren't they, cowboy?"

The burly counterman had emerged from the kitchen, only to come to a shocked halt as he saw Cara holding the gun on Joe Reynolds. Reynolds swallowed as best he could and cut his eyes toward the counterman.

"Y-you heard what the lady said, Larry," he stammered out. "Their steaks are . . . are on me!"

"Look, ma'am, we don't want any trouble here . . ." the counterman began.

"There's no trouble," Cara said. With her thumb on the hammer, she eased it down as Scratch had suggested. Again, she moved so fast it was hard to follow what she was doing as she lowered the gun and slid it back into Reynolds's holster. "Joe here is just leavin', but he'll pay you later for our meals."

"Yeah, I . . . I sure will," Reynolds said. Now that the gun wasn't pressing into his throat anymore, he moved back a step. He watched Cara like a small, terrified animal would watch a snake advancing toward it.

But his pride wouldn't let him just turn tail and run. He looked at Scratch, and the belligerent expression appeared again on his face. He said, "Listen, mister, you need to get this woman of yours under control!"

Scratch stood up and moved a step away from the counter so he could face the cowboy squarely.

"I like her just fine the way she is," he said. That

wasn't true, not by a long shot, but this young peckerwood annoyed the hell out of him.

Reynolds's gaze dropped to the pair of ivory-handled Remingtons on Scratch's hips. It was pretty obvious that the silver-haired Texan knew how to use the guns.

After a moment, Reynolds muttered, "All right, it's none of my business if you want to let her act like a hellcat. I gotta get back to work."

He turned and stalked out of the Red Top. Cara's merry laugh followed him. That was the only sound in the place. The other customers still seemed a little stunned by how close Reynolds had come to getting his head blown off by the beautiful blonde.

The counterman finally cleared his throat and said, "Them steaks y'all wanted ought to be just about ready. I'll go fetch 'em."

"Much obliged," Scratch said with a nod.

The other two men sitting at the counter laid down coins and left. Once they were alone on the stools, Scratch asked quietly, "What was the idea of that little fandango?"

"I just can't stand cocky cowboys like that," Cara said. "They rub me the wrong way."

"Maybe so, but now folks around here are gonna remember us. That ain't what we wanted."

Cara shrugged. "It doesn't matter. Tomorrow we'll be where we're goin', and after that we won't have to worry about anything. We'll be rich."

"Bein' rich don't always mean that trouble can't find you," Scratch observed.

"I plan on goin' so far away that nobody will *ever* find me," Cara said.

The counterman returned with their food. The steaks were fried just right, and the potatoes and other fixin's were good, too. The way things had turned out, Scratch would have rather they had just waited at the blacksmith shop, but he had to admit that this was the best meal he'd had since leaving Fort Smith.

When they were finished, Cara said to the counterman, "You won't have any trouble collectin' from Reynolds, will you?"

"No need for that," the man said. "It's all on the house."

"You don't have to do that," Scratch said.

"It's my pleasure."

"Well, if you're sure . . ."

Scratch figured the only thing the man was really sure of was that he wanted the two of them out of his place before any real hell broke loose.

Scratch helped Cara down from the stool, and they walked arm in arm out of the Red Top. Together they angled across the street toward the blacksmith shop.

As they stepped through the open double doors into the shaded interior of the shop, Scratch looked around for the proprietor. He didn't see the man, but he spotted their horses standing tied to a post. He picked up the hoof that had caused the trouble and checked it. The horse had a new shoe nailed onto that hoof.

"Hey," Scratch called as he lowered the horse's leg

and straightened. "Anybody home? What do we owe you? We're ready to settle up."

"You'll settle up, all right, you old bastard, you and the bitch both," Joe Reynolds said as he stepped out of the shadows behind the forge with a rifle in his hands.

CHAPTER 26

Scratch reacted instinctively to the threat, shoving Cara aside with his left hand while his right dipped to the Remington on that side and drew the long-barreled revolver.

Reynolds brought the rifle to his shoulder and fired, but Scratch was already moving the other way. The bullet whipped harmlessly through the air between him and Cara, who let out a startled cry as she lost her balance and fell on the dirt floor of the blacksmith shop.

Scratch triggered the Remington just as Reynolds ducked for cover behind the forge. The Texan bit back a curse as he saw splinters leap from one of the thick beams holding up the roof. His shot had missed.

He scrambled farther to his right as the rifle cracked wickedly again. He hated using the horses for cover, but that was all he had. He hurried behind the animals as they started tossing their heads and stamping their hooves. The gunfire had spooked them. Normally they were coolheaded and accustomed to the sound of shots since Bo and Scratch had been riding them for several years, but the blacksmith shop's low ceiling made the echoes boom deafeningly.

Scratch snapped a shot at the forge and heard the bullet whine off the brick. More splinters flew as a slug chewed into the wall above his head. He couldn't see Cara anymore, and he hoped that she had taken advantage of the chance to scramble out of the shop to safety.

No such luck. He heard her scream a curse, and a second later Reynolds yelled in anger and alarm. It sounded like they were struggling. Scratch burst out from behind the horses and headed for the forge.

He spotted Cara wrestling with Reynolds over the rifle. She had both hands on the barrel and was trying to wrench it out of his hands as she forced the muzzle toward the roof, but he hung on stubbornly.

With the two of them so close together, Scratch couldn't risk a shot. There was too great a chance he would hit Cara, and he still needed her to lead him to that hidden loot. Besides, she was a woman, and his upbringing still wouldn't allow him to forget about that.

So he charged in, figuring that he could thump Reynolds over the head with the Remington. However, before he could get there Reynolds let go of the rifle with one hand and used that fist to drive a punch into the middle of Cara's face. Her head snapped back from the impact of the blow, and her grip on the rifle slipped. Reynolds tore the weapon out of her hands.

He swung around to meet Scratch's charge and brought the rifle butt up. It crashed into Scratch's jaw and brought him up short. Reynolds lowered a shoulder and bulled into him, driving him backward. Scratch lost his balance and fell.

Reynolds aimed a kick at him. Scratch rolled aside just in time to avoid it. He had dropped his revolver when Reynolds knocked him down, so he reached up with both hands, grabbed the man's leg, and heaved. With a startled yell, the vengeful cowboy went over backward.

Scratch rolled away from him, snatching up the Remington along the way. As he came up on one knee, from the corner of his eye he saw several of O'Bar's citizens gathered in the open doorway of the blacksmith shop. They had come to see what all the shooting was about.

Reynolds had dropped the rifle when he came crashing down on the hard-packed dirt. As Scratch leveled the Remington, Reynolds scrambled after the fallen rifle.

"Hold it!" Scratch yelled.

Reynolds gave up on retrieving the rifle, but that didn't mean the trouble was over. He twisted around and clawed at the Colt on his hip instead.

"Damn it, stop!" Scratch ordered as Reynolds's gun cleared leather. "I don't want to—"

What he wanted didn't matter anymore. Reynolds's

gun was coming up, and Scratch didn't have any choice.

He fired.

Flame licked from the Remington's muzzle. Reynolds was on his knees. The bullet punched into his chest and drove him halfway around. He dropped his gun and crumpled.

"The stranger shot Joe!" one of the onlookers yelled in outrage. "Get him!"

That was what Scratch had been afraid of. Reynolds had friends here. The silver-haired Texan and Cara didn't.

As he turned toward the doorway, Scratch saw most of the townspeople scattering. Three remained, and Scratch recognized them as the men who had been playing poker with Reynolds in the Red Top. They looked like cowboys, too, and probably rode for the same spread as him.

Two of them had their guns out, and the third man was trying to draw his. Still on one knee, Scratch palmed out his left-hand Remington. With his hands full, he triggered a pair of swift shots from both guns.

The bullets smashed into the men who already had their guns drawn and sent them reeling backward. The third man had finally cleared leather, but as Scratch turned toward him, a rifle shot cracked and the man was knocked backward, his Colt flying from his hand as his arms flung out. He landed hard on his back in the street, dust flying up around him.

Scratch glanced over and saw that Cara had grabbed the rifle Reynolds had dropped. The blonde's lips were drawn back from her teeth in a grimace of hate. Smoke curled from the repeater's muzzle.

Reynolds was down, lying on his side, apparently not breathing. The other two men Scratch had shot had dropped their guns and fallen in the street. One of them clutched his side and moaned as he writhed around in the dirt. The other lay still, but his chest was rising and falling, and as the echoes of the shots faded away, Scratch could hear the rasp of the wounded man's breathing.

The man Cara had blasted lay on his back, arms and legs spraddled out. Scratch had a hunch he was dead.

So, two men dead, more than likely, and two more wounded.

That wasn't a very good way for him and Cara to avoid drawing attention to themselves.

They got to their feet at the same time. Cara worked the lever on the rifle to throw another shell into the chamber. She looked like she was ready to put some more slugs into the fallen cowboys, just on general principles.

Scratch said sharply, "Wait a minute. Don't shoot anymore, Cara."

"Some of them are still alive!" she protested, as if that state of affairs couldn't be allowed to continue.

"I know it, but we don't want to kill any more of 'em than we have to."

Her mouth twisted in a snarl.

"Anybody gets in my way, they deserve killin'!"

Well, if he'd had any lingering doubts about her, if

he'd wanted to talk himself into believing that she was really sweet and innocent and she'd only done the things she did because she was terrified of Hank Gentry, that kind of attitude pretty well took care of it, Scratch thought.

Cara LaChance was a loco, cold-blooded killer . . . just like she had seemed to be all along. It was the other part that was an act.

Keeping one eye on Cara because there was no telling what she might do, Scratch took a closer look at Reynolds and confirmed that the cowboy was dead.

"Stay here," he ordered firmly. "I'm gonna check on those other fellas."

"Be careful that somebody else in this hick town doesn't try to shoot you from ambush."

Scratch was well aware of that danger. Before he emerged from the blacksmith shop, he looked up and down the street as best he could. He didn't see anybody moving around. The citizens of O'Bar seemed to have retreated into the buildings in case any more bullets started to fly.

Scratch stepped out into the street. With both Remingtons still in his hands, he approached the man Cara had shot. The man's glassy eyes staring sightlessly at the sky left no doubt that he was dead.

The man who'd been moaning had fallen silent. He was still breathing, though, and as far as Scratch could tell without really examining the wound, he thought that a bullet had just plowed a furrow in the man's side. He had lost some blood and likely passed out because of it, but he ought to survive, Scratch decided.

He wasn't so sure about the fourth man, who'd been shot through the body. He seemed to be breathing without too much strain, though, so maybe with luck he would pull through, too.

Scratch was glad to see that. He wasn't just about to feel guilty for shooting any hombre who was trying to shoot him, but even so, he'd just as soon not be part of a massacre if he could avoid it.

The potential for a massacre might not be over, though. Scratch heard a door open and glanced up to see two men emerge from the Red Top. He recognized one of them as the counterman from the café and saloon, and the other man was the stocky, redheaded blacksmith.

Both of them wore grim expressions and brandished shotguns as if they intended to splatter Scratch all over the street.

CHAPTER 27

Scratch stiffened and brought up his Remingtons.

"You fellas hold it right there!" he shouted. "I don't want to kill you!"

The two men stopped short and lowered their scatterguns. The man from the Red Top said hurriedly, "Wait a minute, wait a minute, mister! We don't mean you any harm. We were comin' to help you."

Scratch frowned in confusion.

"What do you mean?" he asked. "Help me how?"

"In case some of those varmints are still alive and might try to shoot you again," the counterman said.

"Wait a minute. You ain't on their side?"

The blacksmith snorted in contempt.

"That son of a bitch Reynolds came into the shop and clouted me on the head when I wasn't lookin'," he said. "Knocked me out and dragged me into the back so he could hide there and get the drop on you, mister. When I came to and realized what was goin' on, I went out the back door and ran around to the café to get some help. Larry loaned me a Greener."

"Then you ain't friends with this lowdown bunch?" Scratch asked.

"Not by a long shot!" the counterman exclaimed. "They've been comin' into town, gettin' drunk, and causin' trouble for months now. They've shot up the place and hoorawed folks more than once."

"Then why didn't you get the law on them, or do somethin' about it yourselves?"

Both men shrugged.

"We're not gunfighters," the blacksmith said. "They're probably not really good enough to call them by that name, either, but they're slicker on the draw and better with their guns than anybody else around here."

"And as for the law," the counterman put in, "there's a deputy sheriff who comes out this way from Fort Worth every now and then, but Reynolds and his friends were always on their best behavior when he was around. He wasn't of a mind to do anything about it."

Scratch began to see that he and Cara had done these folks a favor by gunning down Reynolds and the other three wild cowboys. This wasn't the first time he had seen an entire town treed by a bunch of self-proclaimed badmen, and it probably wouldn't be the last.

"All right," he said as he holstered his left-hand Remington and started reloading the other gun. "Two of these fellas are shot up but still alive. You got a doctor around here who can take a look at 'em?"

The counterman nodded and said, "Somebody's

already gone to fetch Doc Steward. He'll be here directly."

"The other two need buryin'."

"We can take care of that," the blacksmith said. "I build coffins, too."

"I saw that you changed the shoe on that horse before Reynolds buffaloed you."

The blacksmith nodded. "That's right. I'd just finished up the job when the son of a bitch came in."

"What do we owe you?"

The man shook his head.

"Not a blamed thing, mister," he declared. "We're square. It's worth the cost of a horseshoe and a little labor to get that bunch cleaned up. Now O'Bar can go back to bein' a nice, friendly place to live."

Scratch grunted. You never could tell how things were going to work out. No matter how much you thought you knew, life still held plenty of surprises.

He supposed he wouldn't want it any other way.

He finished reloading his guns and turned to Cara, who stood in the doorway of the blacksmith shop holding Reynolds's rifle, still looking like she really wanted to shoot somebody.

"We'd better be movin' on," he told her. "And we'll leave that rifle here."

"Yeah, I don't reckon we need it now," she said as she leaned it against a wall of the shop. "But it sure came in handy for a minute."

"It did," Scratch agreed. He led the horses out of the barnlike building, and they both swung up into their saddles.

More of O'Bar's citizens had emerged. Some of them were carrying the corpses over to the side of the blacksmith shop while another man set a black doctor's bag down next to one of the wounded men and knelt beside him to check on the wound. That would be the local sawbones, Scratch thought.

He lifted a hand in farewell to the blacksmith and the counterman from the Red Top as he and Cara rode out of the settlement. The townsmen returned the wave.

Cara followed a trail that dipped down to cross a wooden bridge over the creek, then climbed to go past the church Scratch had spotted earlier.

"Where are we headed now?" he asked.

"We'll camp between here and Weatherford," she said. "Then tomorrow we'll cut north of there and make for the hills where the hideout is. We ought to be there by late afternoon." She grinned over at him. "And then we'll be rich."

"Can't be soon enough to suit me," Scratch said. He was glad to be closing in on the end of this deception.

Now all he had to do was hope that Bo and Brubaker would be able to hold up their end of the deal.

On their way to Gainesville, Brubaker had predicted that the county sheriff was going to give them trouble about locking up the prisoners, and he was right. The man had complained bitterly about having to feed and house federal prisoners out of his jail budget.

"Write a letter to Judge Parker at Fort Smith and take it up with him," Brubaker had told the sheriff in his usual blunt manner. "Maybe he'll reimburse you for the cost."

The lawman had gone along with that, finally, and transferred Lowe, Elam, and Early Nesbit under heavy guard into cells. As Bo and Brubaker rode away, Bo on Early's horse, the Texan asked, "What do you think the chances are that Judge Parker will cover those expenses for the sheriff?"

Brubaker snorted. "Slim and none," he said. "The judge is thrifty to a fault. He'll tell the sheriff to take it up with the Justice Department, and we know how often things actually get done in Washington. No, he'll never get any of that county money back, but that ain't my worry. All I'm concerned about is recapturing Cara LaChance and recovering all that stolen loot." Brubaker shook his head. "I still say I never should've let you and Morton talk me into this. No good's gonna come of it."

"We'll see," Bo said.

They had left the wagon at a stable in Gainesville, since they would need it when they returned to pick up Lowe and Elam. Brubaker planned to leave Early Nesbit locked up there long enough to let him get to Tyler with his prisoners, and then the local law could let Nesbit go as far as he was concerned.

From Gainesville they rode south to Denton and

spent the night there, then angled southwest toward Decatur and Weatherford.

The Cross Timbers was nice enough country in the summer, Bo thought, with its wooded hills, wide valleys, and abundance of creeks. Right now, though, in the middle of winter and with this part of Texas suffering through a terrible drought as well, all the vegetation was dead. The landscape was parched and ugly. If it was like that farther west, where the terrain was more rugged to start with, things were going to be pretty harsh.

Brubaker addressed that issue by asking, "What's this country like where we're goin'?"

"Rough," Bo said. "Lots of gullies and bluffs, thick brush, rocky ground, and plenty of snakes and scorpions, although we shouldn't have to worry about varmints like that at this time of year."

Brubaker snorted and said, "What's it good for? From the sound of it, not much."

"Some of the valleys are fertile enough for farming, or at least they were before this drought," Bo explained. "For the most part, though, it's ranching country. Longhorns are hardy enough that they do well just about anywhere. There are quite a few spreads scattered through the hills. Over time there'll be more. It wasn't that many years ago that the Comanches represented quite a threat. Anybody who tried to settle west of the Brazos River was running a mighty big risk. Plenty of ranches were raided and burned out."

"Folks kept moving in out there anyway, though, didn't they?"

Bo nodded. "That's what people do. Pioneers, anyway. They push out ahead and make their own way."

They spent the second night in Weatherford, in a small hotel on the courthouse square, and when Bo woke up the next morning, the first thing he heard was the wind howling outside the window. Thinking that a blue norther must have blown through, he got up and pushed back the curtain, expecting to see a gray, leaden sky that held the threat of snow.

Instead he blinked at the bright sunshine that flooded in through the window. The sky was a cloudless, brilliant blue. The U.S. and Texas flags flying from a flagpole on the courthouse lawn stood straight out in the hard wind, snapping and popping as the gusts caught them.

Bo got dressed and went downstairs to the hotel dining room to find Brubaker already there, sipping coffee. The deputy nodded to him and said, "That wind's blowin' like a son of a bitch out there."

Bo nodded. "It'll do that," he said, "especially from this time of year on through the spring. We'll have to hold on to our hats today."

"We'll catch up to Morton and the LaChance woman today, that's what we'd better do," Brubaker said.

"That's the plan. Scratch will find a way to signal us."

"He damned well better. If he decides to take off

with that gal and the loot, I'll hunt him down, and you'd be wise not to try to stop me, Creel."

"I'm not worried about that," Bo replied with a shake of his head. "Scratch isn't going to double-cross us."

They ate breakfast at the hotel, then paid their bill and walked down the street to the livery stable where they had left their horses. The wind was still blowing fiercely out of the west.

The elderly hostler greeted them with a jerky nod, and Bo frowned as he sensed that something seemed to be making the man nervous.

Or some*one*, Bo corrected himself as three men slouched into the doorway behind him and Brubaker. Bo glanced over his shoulder at them and knew right away they seemed familiar.

A second later he understood why as the man in the lead, a white-haired hombre with a seamed, weathered face, said in a hard, gravelly voice, "I hear you two are lawmen from Arkansas. Is that right?"

Bo and Brubaker turned slowly. Brubaker glared at the three men and asked, "What business is that of yours, mister?"

"My name's Leander Staley. You killed my boys Jink and Mort and my nephew Bob, and now that I've tracked you down, it's time for you to pay."

CHAPTER 28

As soon as Leander Staley opened his mouth, Bo recognized his voice from their previous encounter in Indian Territory. So he knew right away this was trouble, and Brubaker must have, too, because the deputy didn't wait, didn't try to talk Staley out of anything.

No, Brubaker just hauled his gun out and commenced to shooting.

Bo had no choice but to follow suit, since Staley and his two companions clawed their irons from leather and returned the fire. As Bo's Colt began to roar and buck in his hand, he angled to his left, away from Brubaker, who was lunging to the right. Splitting up like that kept their three opponents from concentrating their fire.

Behind Bo, the hostler let out a screech. Bo hoped the old man was just scared and not wounded, but he couldn't check on the hostler now. Besides, he hadn't called this tune, Leander Staley had, and the vengeful Staley was the one ultimately responsible for whatever happened.

Staley and his partners were spreading out, too. One of them stumbled and clapped a hand to his side as a bullet ripped through him. That gave Brubaker the chance to put a well-placed slug through his head. The man went down like a puppet with its strings cut.

Bo dropped to one knee behind a post holding up the stable's hayloft. It was meager cover but better than nothing. He ducked as a bullet smacked into the post above his head and sent a chunk of wood flying into the air. The Colt in his hand blasted again. The other younger man doubled over as Bo's bullet punched into his belly.

That left Leander Staley still on his feet, and the vengeance-seeking old man was hit. Under his open coat, blood stood out on his flannel shirt like bright flowers in a couple of places.

But he wasn't going down easily. The hatred he felt for Bo and Brubaker kept him upright. He was even able to stalk forward, still triggering his gun. Bo and the deputy fired at the same time, flame spouting from the muzzles of their guns, and that pair of slugs hammering into Staley's chest was finally enough to knock him down. He went over backward.

Even when he was on the ground, though, Staley struggled to raise his gun and fire again. Brubaker, who was crouched near a parked wagon, straightened and strode over to him. Staley rasped a curse.

"You . . . killed my boys!" he managed to say as blood trickled from the corner of his mouth.

"They had it comin'," Brubaker said. He kicked the gun out of Staley's hand. "And so do you."

Brubaker lined his gun on Staley's face and clearly was about to pull the trigger again when the old man gasped and arched his back. When he relaxed a second later, the breath came out of him in a death rattle.

"You'd be wasting a bullet, Forty-two," Bo said from behind Brubaker.

"Yeah, I know." Brubaker let out a disgusted curse. "And now we're gonna have to waste time talkin' to the local law. They'd better not hold us until we can't catch up to Morton and that gal!"

Bo didn't think that was likely. Brubaker's deputy U.S. marshal badge would smooth over any ruffled feelings the local star packers might have about this shoot-out in their bailiwick.

But any delay might prove costly, Bo thought, and he couldn't forget that Scratch was risking his life just by riding along with Cara LaChance.

Scratch and Cara camped on a high ridge that gave them a view of the countryside for several miles around. Scratch built a good-size campfire that sent smoke climbing upward. He didn't know if Bo was already in these parts, but if that was the case, he might spot the smoke and realize that was Scratch sending him a signal.

Things had changed by the next morning. The wind had been from the south the day before, continuing the warming trend, but by morning it had turned around to the west. On the ridge it was particularly strong, snatching Scratch's Stetson from his head when he went to saddle the horses. He had to run after the hat and catch it, which made Cara laugh at him.

Scratch pulled the Stetson down tighter on his head and frowned at her.

"You won't think it's so funny when that dang wind blows you off your horse," he told her.

"That's not gonna happen," she said. She grew more serious as she went on. "We'd better have a cold camp this morning. With the wind blowing like that and as dry as everything is, it wouldn't take much to start a wildfire."

Scratch knew she was right about that. The grass, the brush, and many of the trees were dead, which meant the whole countryside was tinder-dry. Charley Graywolf had warned them that the drought in Texas was bad, and obviously, the Cherokee Lighthorseman had been right.

"I'll miss my coffee," Scratch said, "but maybe we can find a place later where we can risk a little fire. Like inside that cave of yours where the loot's hidden."

Cara nodded and said, "Yeah, that ought to be all right. Let's get on the trail. We've still got some jerky. We'll gnaw on that and call it breakfast."

The wind was cold in their faces as they rode west. Not icy, as it might have been, and the bright sunshine helped warm things up a little, but Scratch felt the chill in his bones, anyway.

Cara didn't seem to mind. She was excited at the prospect of arriving at the hideout and claiming that stash of loot before the day was over, and she wasn't going to let some wind bother her, even a howler like the one blowing today.

By the middle of the day, the terrain had grown rougher and they had to slow down their pace as they fought their way past gullies choked with dry brush, up rocky slopes where their horses' hooves slid on loose pebbles, and around rugged bluffs that were impossible to climb. At times they made their way along dark, narrow valleys that seemed to be trying to close in on them. Atop the ridges on either side, the bare branches of dead trees waved in the wind and reminded Scratch of skeletal fingers clawing at the empty sky. He didn't know why such a grim thought crossed his mind, but once it did, he couldn't shake that ghastly image from his brain.

"Is any of this startin' to look familiar to you?" he asked Cara around midday.

"It all looks familiar to me," she replied, "but things weren't nearly as dry the last time I was here. Another couple of hours and we'll be at the hideout. We've actually made pretty good time."

Scratch supposed that she knew what she was talking about. He tugged his hat down, lowered his head, and rode on into the wind.

Sometime later—he wasn't sure exactly how

long—he lifted his head and sniffed. Cara, riding beside him, had her head up, too.

"You smell it, don't you?" Scratch asked.

"Yeah," she replied, her voice growing taut with worry. "Smoke."

They were down in a hollow and couldn't see very far. Scratch heeled his horse into a faster pace, and Cara did likewise. The smell of smoke grew stronger in the air as they trotted toward a rise about a quarter of a mile away.

By the time they reached the top of that rise, Scratch wasn't surprised to see clouds of gray smoke billowing into the air in the distance. Both riders reined in sharply, and Cara exclaimed, "Damn it!"

"I reckon that was the way we were goin'?" Scratch asked as he nodded toward the smoke.

"That's the right direction," Cara said. "What I can't tell is how far away the fire is. I think it's on the other side of the hideout."

"Maybe so, but the wind's blowin' it this way mighty fast. You reckon we can get to the cave and get out before the fire reaches it?"

"I don't know," Cara said, "but I sure as hell intend to try."

She leaned forward in the saddle, jabbed her boot heels into the flanks of Bo's horse, and sent the animal lunging forward in a gallop.

"Cara!" Scratch shouted after her. "Dadgum it, come back here!"

She ignored him and kept riding. For a second, Scratch pondered pulling out his Winchester and trying to shoot the horse out from under her. He decided against it because he wasn't going to do that to Bo's horse, for one thing, and for another it wasn't easy to hit a target moving that fast. He might kill Cara with the shot instead.

And maybe she was right, he thought. It was difficult to judge distances where smoke was concerned. That blaze could be fifteen miles away, maybe even more. They might be able to reach the hideout, retrieve the loot, and then flee ahead of the flames. It was worth a try, at least until he had a better idea how close the fire really was.

With that decision made, Scratch sent his own mount galloping after Cara's.

She was a good rider, and she maintained the short lead over him as she raced along draws, over ridges, and around jutting piles of rock. The pillar of smoke in the distance had climbed high enough into the sky that it was visible even when they were riding over lower terrain. The gray column stood out in sharp, menacing contrast to the bright blue sky. Scratch thought it was a little wider, too, which meant the leading edge of the fire was spreading out and growing broader.

The air was so dry it tasted like dust in his mouth. That, combined with the high winds and the dead vegetation, was a recipe for pure, unadulterated hell.

Up on the Great Plains, Scratch had witnessed a number of prairie fires, and they could be awesome in their destructiveness. Nothing was a match, though, for a Texas wildfire with its sheer deadly speed. The only natural disaster Scratch could think of that was close to a wildfire's equal was a tornado, and even those usually weren't as bad because their paths of devastation weren't as broad.

As they came out on the lip of a rise overlooking a valley, Cara hauled back on the reins and drew her horse to a stop. She leveled an arm and pointed at the long, rugged ridge on the other side of the valley, a couple of miles away.

"The cave is in that ridge," she told Scratch. "And the fire is still on the other side of it."

She was right. The spreading smoke was beyond the ridge, but it was impossible to tell just how far away the fire really was.

"We can get the loot," Cara said. "Then we'll head east, away from the fire."

"Until it overtakes us," Scratch warned. "That wind is blowin' faster than these horses can run."

"We can make it," she insisted. "Come on!"

She kicked the horse into a gallop again, taking the downward slope at a breakneck pace. Scratch rode after her. He couldn't help but keep casting glances at the steadily advancing smoke.

Those two miles or so across the valley seemed a lot longer with the threat of the wildfire looming over them. Eventually, though, they reached the ridge and Cara started following a winding trail that twisted and turned its way upward. The face of the ridge was such a jumble of boulders that Scratch could understand how the entrance of a cave could be hidden up here. They probably wouldn't be able to see it until they were right on top of it.

He had caught up to Cara and was right behind her when she suddenly reined in. She jerked Bo's Winchester from the saddle boot.

"What is it?" Scratch asked as he brought his mount to a stop alongside hers.

"I saw somebody above us," she said tensely. "Riders comin' down this way."

"Folks tryin' to get away from the fire, more than likely," Scratch guessed.

"Maybe, but we're close to that cache now, and I don't trust anybody." She jerked her horse toward a cluster of rock slabs that had slid down the face of the ridge in ages past. Over her shoulder, she told Scratch, "We can hole up over here and bushwhack whoever it is!"

Scratch wasn't of a mind to bushwhack anybody, but there was no point in arguing with Cara right now. Once she saw that those riders she had spotted weren't any threat to them, they could go on with their own business.

Scratch coughed as he followed Cara into the rocks. The smoke was getting thicker in the air. You didn't just smell it; now it irritated the nose and eyes and throat. The horses didn't like it, either. They were getting harder to control.

Scratch and Cara dismounted where they could watch the trail leading down from the ridge without being too noticeable themselves. Scratch hadn't seen the riders, but he trusted Cara's eyesight. His own eyes were starting to water a little from the smoke.

He listened intently for hoofbeats, and for the crackle of flames as well that would warn them the wildfire was almost on top of them. He didn't hear that telltale crackling, but after a moment he caught the steady thud of hoofbeats. Someone was coming down the trail, all right.

Cara lifted the Winchester. Her hands were tight on the weapon.

"Whoever that is, they better not've got into that cache," she said. "I'll kill 'em before I let anybody steal my loot."

That struck Scratch as funny, but he didn't have any laughter in him at the moment, not even a dry chuckle. Instead he waited in silence, holding the reins of both horses while Cara edged forward beside one of the massive slabs of rock to get a better look at the trail.

One by one, half a dozen riders came into view. As they drew closer, Scratch studied them intently. They were all rugged-looking, well-armed hombres. The man in the lead wore a flat-crowned black hat and a black vest over a white shirt. He had a hawklike face and a dark mustache.

Close behind him rode a burly man in a buckskin jacket. He was bare headed and had a wild shock of long gray hair. The next man was lean, with red hair and a face like a fox. The other three were typical hard cases, roughly dressed and with several days' worth of stubble on their faces. Each of those three was leading a packhorse.

Scratch had never seen any of the men before.

That wasn't the case with Cara, though. A shock went through him as he realized that she was staring at the men in stunned recognition, especially the man riding in the lead.

Then she cried out, "Hank! Over here! Hank!"

The words were barely out of her mouth when she swung the rifle in her hands toward Scratch and pulled the trigger.

CHAPTER 29

Brubaker reined in and pointed to the towering column of smoke rising in the distance.

"Morton said he'd send us a smoke signal," the deputy commented. "You reckon that's it?"

"That looks like too much smoke to be a signal," Bo replied with a worried frown. "That's from a big fire."

"But it's in the direction we're headed, ain't it?"

"It is," Bo said. "So I guess we don't have any choice but to keep going." He paused, then added, "I just hope that Scratch isn't right in the middle of it."

As expected, the Parker County sheriff hadn't been happy to have three dead men lying in the street outside the livery stable. Neither was the Weatherford city marshal.

At least the elderly hostler had yelped because he was scared and diving for cover, not because he'd been hit by one of the flying bullets. If an innocent citizen had been cut down, that would have made the local star packers even less inclined to cut Bo and Brubaker any slack.

As it was, Brubaker's standing as a federal lawman, plus the fact that the dead men were all members of a somewhat shady clan from Arkansas, convinced the local authorities to allow Bo and Brubaker to go on their way.

"I'm gonna send a telegram to that Judge Parker in Fort Smith, though," the sheriff had said, "just to make sure you really are who you say you are. If you're not, I'll hunt you down, mister, and see that you answer for these killin's."

"Go ahead," Brubaker had said. "The judge'll confirm my story."

After they rode out of Weatherford, though, Brubaker hadn't been quite so sanguine about it.

"Judge Parker's liable to pop a vein when he finds out I'm a couple of hundred miles away from where I'm supposed to be, and goin' in the wrong direction, to boot."

"He was already going to find out when he heard from the sheriff up in Gainesville," Bo had pointed out.

"Yeah, but that fella said he was gonna send a letter, not a telegram. That'll take longer, and I was hopin' we'd have this whole mess cleaned up by then."

"When you recover all that stolen loot, His Honor won't be able to complain too much."

"If, not when," Brubaker groused. "And you don't know the judge as well as I do."

Bo couldn't argue about that, but a short time later they spotted the column of smoke and forgot about Judge Parker. They might have much bigger worries before the day was over.

"The way the wind's blowin', that fire's gonna move fast," Brubaker said. "And as dry as everything is . . ." His voice trailed off, and he shook his head. "Anybody who got caught out in front of a blaze like that would be in a heap of trouble."

"I know," Bo said. "I've seen some pretty bad wildfires. I'm not sure I've ever been around one when the conditions are as perfect for destruction as they are today, though."

A grim expression on his face, Brubaker nodded and said, "We'll keep an eye on that smoke. If it starts to get too close, we'll have to turn around and head back, at least until the fire burns itself out."

"And what about Scratch?" Bo asked, his own features taking on a solemn, worried cast.

"I reckon he'll be on his own," Brubaker said. "The same way he has been ever since he rode off with that devil woman."

As soon as the name Hank came out of Cara's mouth, Scratch knew what had happened. He didn't have any idea how or why, but he was certain that Hank Gentry and the rest of the gang had somehow beaten them to the hideout.

Scratch knew this meant that Cara had no need of him anymore. No need whatsoever.

And to her warped mind that would mean she might as well go ahead and shoot him.

So he ducked, shot out a hand, and grabbed the rifle's barrel as she pointed it at him. He wrenched it up and to the side just in time. The blast was stunningly loud and he felt the sting of burning powder grains against his cheek, but the bullet tore harmlessly past his ear.

Cara cried out in frustration as Scratch ripped the Winchester out of her grasp before she could work the rifle's lever and try again to shoot him. He didn't throw the gun aside because he heard horses pounding toward them and knew that Gentry and the other men were responding to her cry.

He was outnumbered six to one, so he didn't hold out any hope of surviving this fight, but he planned to take as many of the varmints with him as he could. So he might need the Winchester.

He didn't get the chance, because Cara, shrieking incoherently, threw herself at him. Her fingers, hooked like talons, clawed for his eyes. When she slammed into him unexpectedly, he had to take a step back to catch his balance. She kept driving against him as he tried to fend off her harpy-like attack, and the rifle slipped from his fingers and clattered to the ground.

He felt a couple of her fingernails gouge fiery lines down his cheeks before he was finally able to grab her wrists and hold her off.

But by then it was too late, because the six riders

surrounded them, and every man had a gun in his hand pointing at the silver-haired Texan.

"Cara!" Hank Gentry exclaimed in astonishment. "Is it really you?" He threw back his head and boomed out a laugh. "By God, it is! It really is!"

The big man with the shaggy gray hair growled, "You'd better let go of her, mister. At this range, we can blow you to doll rags without hittin' Cara."

Scratch knew the threat was true. He looked intently into Cara's face, only inches from his, and played the only card in his hand.

"I'm gonna let you go, but don't come after me again," he said. "You got no reason to want me dead. I've done nothin' but help you."

He let go of her wrists and took a step back, lifting his hands so they would be well away from his Remingtons. These outlaws might well kill him anyway, but he didn't want to give them an excuse to start shooting.

"You!" Cara cried. "You haven't done anything but help me? If you hadn't stopped me in Fort Smith, I would've gotten away! I wish I'd cut your throat then!"

She looked like she was about to start after him again, but Gentry reached down from the saddle and rested a hand on her shoulder.

"Cara, take it easy," he said. "It's a miracle we all wound up here together, but you need to settle down. Who is this old fella?"

"He's a lawman!" Cara practically spat. "He's workin' for that damn Judge Parker!"

Gentry regarded Scratch coolly.

"Is that true, mister?" he asked. "You're a deputy U.S. marshal?"

"I was, but only temporary-like," Scratch replied. The way he saw it, as long as they were talking, they weren't shooting. "A saddle pard and I signed on to help one of Parker's full-time deputies deliver some prisoners to Texas. But I gave up on that job when somethin' better came along."

His glance at Cara made it clear what that something better was.

Gentry's face hardened slightly.

"You been up to your old tricks, Cara?" he asked. "Playin' up to a fella to get him to do whatever you want, like you did with me?"

Cara just folded her arms across her rapidly rising and falling breasts and glared at Scratch.

"And you probably didn't care that he's old enough to be your grandpa," Gentry went on. "You figure that anybody wearing pants is fair game for your little schemes, don't you?"

Scratch said, "You've got it all wrong, mister. I just wanted to help out the little lady. She told me she never set out to be an owlhoot, that she was forced into it."

Gentry let out another laugh.

"She told you that, did she?" Now Scratch could tell that the outlaw leader wasn't really upset. He told his men, "Keep him covered," and holstered his own gun. He swung down from the saddle and pulled Cara into his embrace.

She struggled for a second, then used both hands to grab the back of his head and hold him while she plastered her mouth to his in a frenzied kiss that lasted for a long moment before Gentry pulled back and asked her, "What are you doing here? Where are Dayton and Jim?"

"I wasn't able to get them loose and bring them with me," Cara said. "I barely escaped myself."

Gentry nodded toward Scratch.

"By getting this old-timer to help you?"

"That's right."

"You had to know that I was coming after you," Gentry said. "You knew I would never let you hang."

"I knew that."

"So why did you come after the loot that was hidden here?" Gentry asked.

"I figured I'd retrieve it so we'd have it when you caught up to me," Cara answered without hesitation. "Indian Territory's too hot for us now, Hank, just like Texas was. I was thinkin' we ought to head west. To Arizona, maybe, or California."

"Speaking of hot," the fox-faced man said, "that fire's getting closer while we're sitting here jawing."

"Bouchard's right," Gentry agreed with a nod. "We'll hash out everything later, Cara. Right now I'm just damned glad to see you again." He looked at Scratch. "The question is, what do we do with you, mister?"

"Morton," Scratch said.

"What?"

"That's my name, Scratch Morton." Figuring that

they were likely to shoot him anyway, Scratch spoke bluntly. "Listen here, you owe me for gettin' Miss LaChance loose from the law and bringin' her here. She'd have been locked up by now in Tyler if it wasn't for me. If you want to be fair about it, you'll take me with you."

"Make you part of the gang, you mean?" Gentry asked harshly.

"I've turned my back on my old pard and the law," Scratch said. "I got nothin' to go back to. I've skirted pretty close to the shady side plenty of times in my life. Might as well go all the way."

Gentry grinned. "You've got gall, I'll give you that."

Scratch shrugged and said, "At my age, why the hell not?"

Gentry looked at Cara and asked, "What do you think? Take him along . . . or kill him?"

A couple of tense seconds ticked past before she said, "Oh, hell, we might as well take him, at least for now. He's pretty good in a fight."

Gentry nodded and looked at Scratch.

"Do I need to ask you to turn your guns over, Morton?"

"You don't think I'm loco enough to slap leather against all six of you boys, do you?" Scratch asked.

"I guess not. But I'll be keeping my eye on you, and if you try anything even a little funny, I'll blow a hole in you."

"Fair enough." Scratch cast a glance at the billowing clouds of smoke filling the sky to the west. "Right now

I just want to get out of here before that fire catches up to us."

"I don't blame you for that. We'll ride south until we're clear of it and then swing to the west."

Gentry pulled Cara against him for another quick kiss, then they both mounted their horses. The other men holstered their guns, but they watched Scratch closely as he swung up into his saddle.

Somehow he was still alive, and he was more than a little surprised by that. If he could stay that way, he thought, maybe Bo and Brubaker would catch up to them and be able to pull his fat out of the fire.

Of course, with the smell of hell itself thick in the air, that might not be the best way of thinking about it, he told himself. But no matter how you put it, he knew that his life was now in the hands of his old friend and the deputy marshal from Arkansas.

And whatever fate guided the wildfire that was now racing across the Texas countryside toward them.

CHAPTER 30

Brubaker uttered an emphatic, heartfelt curse as he lowered the field glasses from his eyes.

"That's Gentry, all right," he told Bo, who had been watching the men through field glasses of his own. "The big fella with the shaggy gray hair is his second-in-command, Chet Ryan. The redheaded hombre is named Bouchard. He's been with Gentry for quite a while, too. The other three are just run-of-the-mill hard cases. I've probably got reward dodgers on 'em somewhere, but I can't recall their names."

"I thought Gentry had more than a dozen men riding with him," Bo said.

"He did. I reckon the others must've split off on their own up in Indian Territory."

"I thought he was going to try to rescue those prisoners, too, and yet he's here in Texas. From the looks of the loads on those packhorses they've got with them, they've already been to the hideout and recovered the loot."

"Don't ask me how some damn outlaw thinks,"

Brubaker snapped. "But if I had to guess, I'd say he was plannin' on leavin' Cara and the other two to the hangman and takin' off for parts unknown with the money. Once Cara figures that out, I'd sleep with one eye open, if I was Gentry."

"We can't give them enough time for that to happen," Bo said. "They're taking Scratch with them. We have to go after them and help him."

Brubaker nodded and said, "That's the plan. And if we can kill or capture the whole bunch while we're doin' it, that's even better."

The deputy didn't fool Bo. He knew that if it came down to the nub, Brubaker would sacrifice Scratch's life in order to kill Hank Gentry and the other outlaws.

And Bo would let them escape if it meant saving Scratch's life, so he supposed things sort of evened out.

Had it not been for the glint of sunlight on metal as they topped the rise where they sat their horses now, they might not have noticed the men on the other side of the valley. But Bo's keen eyes had spotted that reflection, and he and Brubaker had reined in while they were still in the shadow of some live oaks. The trees were clinging to life with a few green leaves still on their branches, but the drought had caused most of the leaves to turn brown and drop off.

If the wildfire reached this spot, the dry, dying trees would go up like torches.

Bo and Brubaker didn't have time to worry about that. They had to figure out a way to get the drop on those outlaws and hope that the fire gave them time to do so.

That might be a forlorn hope. The huge clouds of smoke filled fully half the western sky now, and they towered so high they were starting to block the sun. It was like a biblical apocalypse, Bo thought as they put away the field glasses and started riding southwest, angling across the valley toward the ridge on the opposite side so that their course would intersect that of the outlaws.

They stuck to whatever cover they could, not wanting Gentry's men to spot them as they closed in. The smoke grew thicker, causing both Bo and Brubaker to cough from time to time. Bo kept a wary eye on the gray clouds, and after a while he said, "It looks like Gentry intends to skirt the southern edge of the fire, but I'm not sure they can get around it."

"Yeah, I was thinkin' the same thing," Brubaker said. "If they'd headed east, they would've come right to us. We could have set up an ambush."

"They're abandoning Lowe and Elam, like you said," Bo speculated. "Taking that loot and heading west for greener pastures."

Brubaker snorted. "No honor among thieves, that's for damned sure," he said. He let out a curse and pointed. "Look yonder."

Bo looked to the south. Like a giant gray finger pointing to the heavens, another column of smoke had sprung up.

"This wind can carry sparks a long way," he said. "Looks like another fire has broken out."

"And it won't take long at all for that bigger one to join up with it," Brubaker predicted. "They'll never get around the fires goin' that direction now. They're gonna have to turn back." He reached for the butt of his Winchester and drew the rifle from the saddle boot. "And when they do, we're gonna be ready for them."

Hank Gentry and Cara LaChance were riding in front of the group, and they both slowed their horses as gray smoke began to climb into the sky ahead of them.

Scratch saw it, too, and knew what it meant. The wildfire had been spreading rapidly, and the main body of smoke now loomed over the valley where they rode. But this was a new fire, caused no doubt by sparks flying from the first conflagration and carried by the wind, and once the blazes linked up they would bar the way completely.

The gray-haired man called Ryan said, "We better turn around, Hank. Looks like we can't get through to the south and west anymore."

Gentry and Cara had brought their mounts to a halt, causing the others to follow suit. The outlaw leader frowned at the smoke in the sky. Cara lifted a hand to point at the gray columns.

"Look," she said. "Those are still two separate fires. We can go between them."

Gentry's lieutenants cast apprehensive glances at

each other. Ryan cleared his throat and said, "It's too risky. We'd have fires closing in from both sides."

"But if we make it, no one will ever catch us," Gentry said. He nodded as he came to a decision and heeled his horse into motion. "Come on."

He rode toward the open area between the massive clouds of smoke to the right and the smaller column to the left. Cara didn't hesitate. She urged her horse forward right alongside his.

Scratch saw Ryan and Bouchard look at each other again and knew that Gentry's men were considering a mutiny. That might be his best bet for getting away.

But then Ryan shrugged and Bouchard nodded. They sent their horses after Gentry and Cara.

"Get movin', Gramps," one of the other outlaws ordered Scratch in a hard voice. All three of them were behind the silver-haired Texan, so he knew he had no choice but to go along with what they said.

The riders headed more toward the southwest now, angling for that narrow gap and moving fast. It was a race against the flames and the wind, a race that Scratch figured they were destined to lose.

He wasn't going to let the fires claim his life. That was no way for a man to cross the divide. If it came down to it, he thought as the smoke stung his eyes and rasped in his nose and throat, he would whip out the Remingtons and open fire, gunning down as many of the outlaws as he could before they killed him. At least that way his death would accomplish something, and it would be quick.

They all had their eyes on the sky as the fire to the

west advanced. The column of smoke in front of them was spreading to the east with the wind whipping it onward.

"This is crazy!" one of the owlhoots behind Scratch suddenly yelled. "We can't make it, Hank! We've got to turn and head for Weatherford!"

Gentry slowed his horse enough to twist in the saddle and look back at the others.

"We're not turning back!" he said. "We have to keep moving. That's our only chance!"

He was wrong, Scratch knew. They had already lost their chance. The wildfire was moving too fast. The two areas of smoke were almost touching ahead of them now.

The outlaw who had objected said again, "Hank, we can't—"

Gentry hauled back hard on the reins, wheeling his horse in a tight turn that left him facing the others, who also brought their mounts to a stop. Reaching down to his holster, Gentry pulled his gun and leveled it at the man who was complaining.

"You want to cut and run the other way, go ahead, Temple. But you'll go without your share of the loot, understand?"

"Damn it, Hank—"

Gentry eared back the hammer of his gun. Even over the growing crackle of flames that was now audible, everybody heard the sinister metallic ratcheting sound of the revolver being cocked.

"It's up to you," Gentry said in a low, menacing

tone, "but make up your mind fast, because we're running out of time."

Temple swallowed hard, then said, "All right! All right, blast it. Let's go. I don't want that fire to get me."

Gentry lowered the hammer of his gun and slipped the weapon back in its holster.

"I'm glad you came to your senses. Let's ride!"

The delay, brief though it had been, had just made the situation worse, Scratch saw. The gap in the smoke had almost closed. As the riders reached the southern end of the valley and started up a long, fairly steep slope, the billowing clouds to the west surged even nearer. Scratch leaned forward in the saddle as a cough racked him.

The heavily loaded packhorses couldn't climb the rise very quickly. The group of riders strung out, with Gentry and Cara in front, followed by Ryan and Bouchard, then Scratch, then the three outlaws leading the packhorses bringing up the rear. As Scratch looked around, he realized this might be his last chance to make a break for it.

Up ahead, Gentry and Cara reached the top of the slope. Scratch saw them bring their horses to frantic, skidding stops. Then they whirled the mounts around and raced back toward the others.

A wall of flame exploded over the rise and shot after them like a thing alive.

"Move, move!" Gentry yelled as he waved an arm toward the east. His stubborn determination to make it through to the other side of the fire and use the flames to cut off any pursuit had vanished in the face of the inferno. They had to flee as if hell itself were after them.

Which it pretty much was.

The riders scattered, spreading out as they tried to outrace the blaze. Scratch glanced over his shoulder and saw that the flames were leaping six to eight feet in the air. The sound from them wasn't a menacing crackle now. It had turned into a roar of devastation.

Trees caught fire and turned into charred, skeletal remains in a matter of instants. Brush disappeared, swallowed up completely by the flames. The dead grass on the ground might as well have been kerosene, it burned so swiftly and violently.

In all his years of living, Scratch had never been this close to such a fire. He liked to think he was a pretty courageous hombre. He had been in plenty of tight spots and never panicked, not even facing Santa Anna's vast army decades ago at San Jacinto, when he was only a kid.

But just looking at the monster blaze coming after him roused a primitive terror inside him like none he had ever experienced before. Every instinct in his body screamed for him to run. He controlled that fear, but it required an iron will and a considerable effort.

"Head for the hideout!" Gentry screamed. "We'll be safe there!"

That wasn't a bad idea, Scratch thought. In a situation like this, being in a cave under the ground might be safer than being above. There was still the danger that the smoke might kill them as it rolled over the ridge where the hideout was located, but they had a better chance of surviving that than they did of outrunning the fire.

The problem was that it might be too late. The flames had advanced to the north, too, and the cave might be cut off from them. The blaze seemed to be closing in on them from both sides, as if it were intent on cupping them in fiery fingers.

The cave was a couple of miles away, and as they drew close enough to see the area of the ridge where it was located, Scratch saw that flames had already engulfed it. The others realized that as well and pulled their horses to a stop.

"We can't make it back there," Bouchard said. "Now what do we do?"

"We'll make a run to the east," Gentry said grimly. "That's all that's left."

There was a good reason for his bleak tone. The two arms of the fire had started angling toward each other, threatening to close off the only remaining escape route. All that the dashing around they had done had accomplished was to put them in a position where the flames might soon encircle them.

Cara let out an inarticulate cry of frustration and fear.

"How can it do that?" she said. "It's like the wind's blowin' from all directions at once!"

There was some truth to that, Scratch thought. The wind was strong enough to start with, and the heat of the blaze just whipped it up more. Folks were mostly helpless in the face of a disaster like this. The fire went where it wanted to go and did what it wanted to do, and people had to just stay out of its way as best they could and pray that they survived.

He wondered where Bo and Brubaker were. They were supposed to rendezvous with him in this area, but surely the smoke had warned them of the danger and they'd had sense enough to stay away.

It was bad enough that he was probably going to die here, Scratch thought. He didn't want his old friend to meet the same fate.

CHAPTER 31

Bo grew more worried as he and Brubaker crossed the valley toward the fire. The column of smoke to the south was getting bigger all the time, and the original fire continued to rush eastward. Any sane man would turn his horse around and ride hell-bent-for-leather away from here.

Bo wasn't sure that Brubaker was completely sane anymore, though. The deputy had a look of intense determination on his face, as if he wouldn't let hell itself stand between him and the outlaws he intended to bring to justice.

And Scratch was still out there somewhere, too, threatened by the fiery onslaught. After all they had been through together, Bo wasn't just about to abandon his old friend without making every effort to find him.

He had tried to keep his eye on the distant riders, but the terrain and the ever-thickening smoke made that impossible. Bo didn't know where Scratch and the others were anymore. He and Brubaker were just riding blindly up and down the valley now, searching for any sign of them.

Brubaker hunched his shoulders and coughed several times before saying, "We ain't gonna be able to stand this much longer, Creel. I hate to say it, but the fire's probably caught up with 'em by now."

"I don't believe that," Bo said.

"You don't want to believe that. But it's true."

"Maybe Scratch *is* dead," Bo said, although it hurt him to admit that. "But I'm not going to believe it until I see it with my own eyes."

"And I ain't turnin' back as long as there's still a chance I can corral Gentry and the LaChance gal and the others. So I reckon that means we keep goin'."

Bo nodded. "We keep going," he said.

They rode on warily, not wanting to run right into their quarry without any warning, although that was becoming more and more possible as the visibility worsened. Some instinct made Bo lift his head and look up at the top of the ridge. Flames danced among the trees there, giant flames that leaped and cavorted madly as the wind whipped them.

Hades had to look and feel something like this, he thought, and that howling wind might as well have been the devil's laughter.

Like an army charging into battle, once the flames topped the ridge they rushed down the slope. Their speed was incredible. As the heat beat against their faces, Bo and Brubaker were forced to swing their horses around and gallop away from the tongues of fire reaching out for them.

"What the hell?!" Brubaker yelled. "It's on all sides of us now! How did it—"

His voice was lost in the huge roar of the firestorm.

Bo spotted something in front of them that might represent a faint hope of survival. A line of trees marked what might be the course of a creek. He reined his horse closer to Brubaker's and slapped the lawman's shoulder to get his attention. He pointed to the trees.

Brubaker nodded and kicked his horse into a faster run. Both men galloped toward the trees, which would provide more fuel for the fire when the flames reached them but might also signify a place of sanctuary, perilous though it might be.

As Bo came up to the trees, he saw how the earth dropped away on the other side of them, forming a deep gully. At the bottom of it flowed a creek no more than five feet wide. From the looks of the banks, in normal times the creek was bigger and deeper than it was now, but the drought had shrunk it. It had to be fed by springs in the surrounding hills, or it would have gone dry entirely by now.

Bo was swinging down from his saddle by the time his horse came to a stop. He yanked his Winchester from the saddle boot and swatted the animal on the rump with the barrel. The horse let out a startled cry and leaped forward.

"The horses can't get down there!" he yelled to Brubaker, who had also dismounted and was pulling his rifle from its sheath. "We have to let them go!"

Brubaker nodded. They might be consigning the animals to a fiery death, but there was nothing else they could do. Without the weight of their riders, the horses might be able to outrun the flames. That is, if they didn't panic and turn around so that they raced right into the inferno.

Either way, the horses were on their own now, and so were Bo and Brubaker.

They half-climbed, half-slid down the steep banks of the gully until their boots splashed into the water. The banks were mostly dirt and rock, which was good. Only a few gnarled bushes that had grown there stubbornly would burn.

Cinders began to rain down around the two men.

"Get in the water!" Bo shouted. It only came up to his knees, but it would provide some protection. He set his Winchester on the ground next to the creek and stretched out on his back, letting the water flow over and around him. Just downstream, Brubaker did likewise.

Bo took his hat off and soaked it in the creek, then draped it over his face, which he lifted out of the water so he could breathe. He was starting to gasp. He had heard about men dying from breathing smoke, and also because the fire burned up all the air. The wet hat trapped a little air right over his face, but he didn't know how long it would last.

The creek water was cold, and that helped because the heat of the flames was intense. Even with his ears underwater, Bo heard the inferno's roar. His eyes were squeezed closed, but red sparks shot across his vision anyway. He felt the world start to spin crazily around him and knew he was on the verge of passing out.

"So . . . long . . . pard," he managed to whisper, and he prayed that wherever Scratch was, he heard that farewell.

"Wait!" Cara screamed as they were about to make their desperate, doomed run. "Look! Up there!"

Scratch looked where she was pointing, and hope leaped in his chest. This was a different section of the ridge from the one where the gang's hideout had been located, but the dark blotch on the side of the slope could only be the mouth of another cave.

"Come on!" Gentry yelled. "Bring those packhorses!"

Just like an outlaw, Scratch thought with a grim chuckle. Even caught in the middle of a hellish nightmare like this, Gentry wanted to save the loot.

The nearness of the fire made the horses more skittish than ever. The riders had to fight to control them and send them in the direction of the onrushing flames. They managed to do it, though, and climbed slowly but steadily toward the cave.

It wasn't really much of a cave, Scratch saw as they came closer. It was more of an overhang with a sheltered area underneath it. But the whole area was rock, and that meant there was nothing there to burn.

Right now, that was mighty welcome.

The heat and smoke combined to make every

breath searingly painful. Floating ashes filled the air and stung bare skin when they landed on it, as well as charring holes in clothing. If by some miracle he lived through this, Scratch thought as they crowded into the cavernlike space, he would never look at a campfire the same way again.

The area under the overhang was barely big enough for seven men, one woman, and ten horses. The panicky animals presented the biggest problem.

"Whatever you do, hang on to those packhorses!" Gentry ordered his men. "Let your saddle mounts go if you have to, but don't lose that loot!"

Scratch found himself pressing his back against the rock wall at the rear of the protected space. The burly, gray-haired outlaw named Ryan was to his left. To his right were Gentry and Cara. The leader of the gang looped one arm around the blonde while he used his other hand to hang on to the reins attached to their horses.

Smoke drifted through cracks in the rock around them and made it hard to breathe. Coughing, Cara said, "Hank, I . . . I have to know something. What made you . . . come out here . . . to the hideout . . . instead of tryin' to rescue me?"

"I was going to rescue you," Gentry insisted. "You know I never would've let you hang, sweetheart. I planned to save Dayton and Jim, too, while I was at it, but you're the one I really care about."

"But Brubaker was takin' me to Tyler! That's more than . . . a hundred miles east of here. And you weren't followin' us . . ."

"I sent men to the crossings along the Red River, once I realized that lawman was cutting across Indian Territory," Gentry explained. "I had to find out where you were."

"I know . . . about that. We ran into some kid named Nesbit."

"Early Nesbit," Gentry agreed. "He was working for me, Cara. I planned to go back and check with all those spies and find out which way you'd gone."

"That's what the kid said. But it doesn't make sense, Hank. Even if you'd doubled back after you got the loot, you wouldn't have had time . . . to find us and get us away from that lawdog . . . before we were locked up in Tyler!"

So she had figured it out, Scratch thought. Well, he wasn't surprised. Cara was loco, but she was smart, too, and especially cunning when it came to saving her own hide.

And she had to realize now that Hank Gentry hadn't had any intention of trying to rescue her and Lowe and Elam from the law. Oh, maybe at first that had been his plan, Scratch mused. Gentry might have even been sincere when he sent Early Nesbit and those other would-be owlhoots to keep an eye on the Red River crossings.

But sometime since then, he had decided that it just wasn't worth the time and trouble. He had come to the conclusion that it would be better to let the three prisoners stand trial and hang while he and the rest of the gang lit a shuck for their old hideout, recovered the loot stashed there, and then shook the dust of this part of the country off their boots. Scratch had no doubt that if the fire hadn't interfered with their plans, Gentry and the other outlaws would be riding west right now, headed for California.

A nervous tone had crept into Gentry's voice as he said, "Don't worry about any of that, Cara. We're together now, and that's all that matters. We were lucky enough to find this place, and as soon as the fire goes on past us, we'll get out of here. Folks around these parts will be too busy trying to recover from this disaster to worry about us. We'll be out of Texas before you know it."

"Maybe," Cara said, but Scratch thought she didn't sound convinced.

All the outlaws were coughing now. Ryan suggested, "Better get your bandannas out and soak them with water from the canteens. Then tie 'em around your face and breathe through 'em."

That was a good idea, Scratch thought. He soaked his bandanna and tied it on, and that helped with the smoke. The others really looked like outlaws now with their faces masked, and he supposed he did, too.

This cavelike area was about fifty feet up the face of the ridge. Down below, the flames had reached the valley. The grass and the trees and the brush were burning furiously, sending even more smoke into the air. Scratch's lungs burned and ached. His hope now was that the wind would keep blowing as hard as it had been all day, because then the fire would move on quickly and burn itself out behind the leading edge of the flames, once all the dry vegetation was consumed.

Right now, though, it was still pretty bad out there. If Cara hadn't spotted this sanctuary, they would all be dead by now.

Gentry suddenly exclaimed, "Cara, what are you—"

"Shut up, you lyin' son of a bitch!" she screamed.

Scratch's head jerked around. He looked over to see Cara holding a revolver in both hands and pointing it at Gentry. Gentry's holster was empty, which told Scratch that Cara had snatched the weapon from it.

He had been pretty sure that Gentry hadn't sweet-talked Cara out of her suspicion of him, and what was happening now confirmed that.

"Cara, stop it!" Gentry said. "Put that gun down, damn it."

"No," she said. "You double-crossed me, Hank. I never would have believed it of you, but you did. I kept tellin' Creel and Morton and Brubaker that you'd be comin' after me, and I knew with all my heart that you would. I knew you'd never let me hang." Even with the heat from the fire making it almost unbearable under here, her voice was as cold as ice as she went on, "But you would have. You didn't care if they hanged me, as long as you got your money."

She had moved away from him a little and had her back pressed tight against the rock so that nobody could get at her. Gentry held out a hand toward her and said, "Cara, you're not thinking straight. You know I love you. I'd never let any harm come to you."

"If that was true, you wouldn't have made a beeline for that loot," she snapped. "You'd have come after me, instead. You're a son of a bitch, Hank. I don't like it, but it's true."

Gentry's lip abruptly curled in a sneer.

"You think I couldn't find a dozen more women like you, you little harlot? With my share of this loot, I could get a hundred women like you!"

"You're wrong, Hank," she said, her voice little more than a whisper now. "You don't know how wrong you are, but you're about to learn."

Gentry looked around at the other outlaws and said, "Somebody take that gun away from her."

Nobody made a move toward Cara.

"I don't hold anything against these other boys," she said. "They were just doin' what you told 'em to. But you, Hank, you were supposed to come for me, and you didn't. You let me down, and now you're gonna pay for it."

Gentry laughed wildly.

"You can't fight all of us!" he said.

"I don't have to." Cara tossed her head defiantly, like Scratch had seen her do a dozen times before. "I'm the boss of this gang now. Ain't that right, boys?"

Bouchard said, "All we want is our share, Cara."

"You'll get it," she promised.

"You bastard!" Gentry screamed at Bouchard. He looked over at Ryan. "Chet, don't let them get away with this!"

"I'm startin' to wonder if we might not be better off workin' for Cara," Ryan said. "She planned most of our jobs anyway, didn't she, Hank?"

"You . . . you . . ." Gentry looked and sounded flabbergasted, as well as outraged.

Scratch just watched. Whatever happened now, it was out of his hands.

Cara jabbed the gun toward Gentry.

"Get out of here," she ordered. "I can't stand the sight of you anymore!"

"But there's nowhere to go!" Gentry protested. "The whole world's on fire out there!"

"That's your problem. Back away from me, Hank. I swear, if you don't I'll shoot you dead where you stand."

Gentry looked around desperately and tried one last appeal.

"Fellas, I'll give up my share. You can split it among you, just stop this crazy bitch."

Bouchard smiled thinly and said, "I think you're giving up your share anyway, Hank."

Gentry backed toward the edge of the area under the overhang. He stared at the blonde and said, "Cara, you can't do this. Not after all we've meant to each other. Please."

Cara took a deep breath and said, "Oh, hell."

A smile tugged at the corners of Gentry's mouth.

He believed that he had won her over at last, Scratch thought.

He found out a second later just how wrong he was as Cara lowered the barrel of the gun a little, squeezed the trigger, and blew his right knee apart.

CHAPTER 32

The blast was deafening in the close confines under the overhang. Gentry screamed in agony as his wounded leg folded up underneath him. Blood welled like a crimson river from the shattered knee. Somehow he pushed himself to his feet and said, "Cara, please—"

The gun in her hands roared again as she blew his other leg out from under him.

Bone and blood sprayed in the air as the bullet demolished his left knee. Screeching from the inhuman pain, Gentry went over backward. The slope was steep enough that he started to roll, out of control as he bounced and plunged.

He landed in the middle of a stretch of blazing brush.

Scratch wouldn't have thought it was possible, but Gentry's screams grew even louder as the flames engulfed him. Like a tortured soul trying to escape from the pits of hell, Gentry used his burning arms to pull himself forward since he couldn't stand up on his destroyed legs. His clothing was ablaze, and his hair was on fire. He kept screaming.

Ryan muttered a curse. Holding his rifle, he stepped forward and asked, "Cara, you mind?"

Cara had moved up to the edge so she had a better view of her former lover's torment. She lowered the gun as she stared raptly at Gentry.

"He had it comin'," Scratch heard her say quietly. "He let me down, and he had it comin'. But I reckon he's been punished enough."

She looked over at Ryan and gave him a curt nod.

The burly man lifted the rifle to his shoulder, took a second to make sure of his aim, and then fired. Gentry's head snapped back as the slug drilled cleanly through his brain, putting him out of his misery.

Cara turned to face the other men, obviously putting Gentry behind her for good.

"Anybody have any objection to me runnin' things from now on?" she asked. They could all hear the defiant challenge in her voice.

"We never did have any objection," Bouchard said. "As far as we were concerned, you and Hank were always both in charge of this bunch."

"All right," she said. "We'll wait until the fire dies down, and then we'll head west."

Mutters of agreement came from the men.

"Scratch," Cara went on, looking at the silver-haired Texan, "you're welcome to ride with us if you want to." She glanced around at the others, again challenging them to disagree with her. "Ain't that right?"

Nobody spoke up.

The last thing Scratch wanted to do was join up with an outlaw gang, especially one ramrodded by a beautiful but pure-dee loco blonde.

He had a hunch that if he said that, though, she'd just shoot him, too.

So instead he grinned and said, "I'm much obliged for the invite, Cara."

She smiled at him, and when she did, she appeared as sweet and innocent as ever.

Until you looked past her down the slope and saw the smoking husk of Hank Gentry.

For now, Scratch thought, he had to play along with her. But Bo might be out there somewhere, and Scratch intended to find out what had happened to him.

Until then he would do whatever he needed to in order to stay alive.

Bo kept slipping in and out of consciousness, aware only of the heat, the cold water and mud in which he lay, and the shortness of breath that made his lungs ache. Finally it was water going up his nose that brought him back to sputtering, flailing awareness.

He saw a streak of blue overhead, and it seemed to take him an hour to figure out what he was looking at.

The smoke was thinning. That was a strip of blue sky up there above him.

That meant . . . he struggled to hold the thought . . . that meant the fire had moved on.

And he was alive.

Coughing and hacking, he rolled onto his side. His hat had started to float away on the creek. Without thinking too much about what he was doing, he reached out to snag it. Then he lifted his head and looked around.

Jake Brubaker was still lying in the little stream, too. At first Bo thought the deputy was dead, but then he saw Brubaker's chest rising and falling and knew that he had just passed out, the same way Bo had.

He pulled himself through the mud until he was lying next to Brubaker. Putting a hand behind the lawman's head, he dipped up some water in his hat and splashed it in Brubaker's face.

Brubaker thrashed and shook his head violently. He shoved himself up on his elbows and looked around like he was searching for someone to fight.

"Take it easy, Forty-two," Bo told him. "You're all right. We both made it through the fire."

"Wha . . . what . . . Creel? Is that you?"

"Yeah," Bo said. "We're both alive. The smoke's thinning out overhead. The fire's moved on."

With Bo's help, Brubaker managed to sit up. The clothes of both men were soaked and covered with mud.

Brubaker declared, "We look like a couple of hogs in a wallow."

A grin stretched across Bo's muddy face.

"At least we're not a couple of dead hogs," he said.

"Yeah." Brubaker hunched over and coughed. "Feels like my insides are blistered."

"Yeah, mine, too," Bo said. His voice sounded odd to his ears because it was so hoarse. "We both breathed too much smoke. It'll be a while before we get over it."

"That won't keep me from tryin' to find those varmints we're after." Brubaker shook his head. "We should've just taken those prisoners to Tyler and been done with it."

In hindsight, that was probably right, Bo thought. But Cara's approach to Scratch had given them the chance to recover that missing loot, so he had thought it was a gamble worth taking.

Not all bets paid off, though.

And this one might have cost Scratch's life.

That thought made Bo's face settle into grim lines. As he climbed to his feet, he said, "We need to see if we can find Scratch and the others."

"The fire's bound to have gotten them," Brubaker said with a shake of his head. "Nothin' could've lived through that inferno."

"We did," Bo pointed out.

"That was just a stroke of blind luck. If we hadn't found this creek, we'd be dead now."

"Maybe they had some luck, too," Bo said. "We have to find out."

"I don't know how we're gonna do that without horses." Brubaker sighed. "But I guess the first thing to do is climb out of this gully, ain't it?"

Bo helped Brubaker to his feet. Both men clapped their dripping hats on their heads and picked up their rifles. They kept sliding back down as they tried to make their way up the bank, but eventually they reached the top and crawled out of the gully that had saved their lives.

They found themselves looking at a landscape out of a nightmare.

Except for the patches of blue in the sky, all the color appeared to have been blasted out of the world. There was nothing but gray and black as far as the eye could see. Ashes covered the ground. Gaunt black skeletons of trees jutted up here and there. The brush was just a tangle of charred limbs, and in some places it had burned all the way to the ground, leaving sharp little stobs sticking up.

"Good Lord," Brubaker muttered. "I ain't never seen anything like this before."

"I have," Bo said. "Scratch and I rode through the Yellowstone country a while back after they'd had a big fire like this one that was probably started by lightning. It looked about like this. Miles and miles of nothing but destruction." Bo summoned up a smile. "But it grew back. The next time we were there, you couldn't even see any signs of the fire unless you looked for them, and even then it was hard to find them. New growth had come along and repaired all the damage. Nature's like that."

"Maybe so. But this sure looks terrible right now."

"I can't argue with that," Bo said. "We'll have to watch where we're walking. There are still places that will be pretty hot. Might burn right through our boots."

Brubaker nodded and said, "I reckon we should head for the ridge. That was the last place we saw Morton and that bunch."

Bo agreed with that decision. They started trudging toward the ridge, which was about half a mile away. With every step, fine gray ashes puffed up around their feet and swirled in the air.

They hadn't gone very far when Bo stopped short. He put a hand on the deputy's arm and said, "Listen. Do you hear that?"

Brubaker lifted his head and listened with a look of intense concentration on his face. After a few seconds, his eyes widened in surprise.

"That sounds like horses!" he said.

Bo nodded and said, "Those are hoofbeats, all right. And I don't think anybody else is likely to be moving around out here except the folks we're looking for."

"How in the world did they survive?" Brubaker asked. "And with their horses, too."

"I don't know, but maybe we can find out. We'd better hunt some cover until we're sure what we're dealing with."

Brubaker jerked his head in a nod.

"Damn right." More ashes swirled around his legs as he hurried toward some rocks. "Come on."

The rocks weren't big enough to provide much cover, but they were better than nothing and certainly better than the burned trees and brush, which wouldn't conceal much of anything. Bo and Brubaker knelt behind the largest of the boulders and waited as the steady thudding of hoofbeats came closer.

Bo's breath caught in his tortured throat as the first rider came into view around a little knob. He recognized Cara LaChance instantly. She rode with a rifle held across the saddle in front of her, and she had gotten hold of a holstered revolver and gun belt, which she had strapped around her waist.

The next rider was the slender, redheaded, foxlike man Brubaker had called Bouchard. Bo's heart sank. He had hoped to see Scratch following Cara.

Then his spirits leaped as the third rider appeared. The fancy duds and the cream-colored Stetson were grimy from smoke and ashes, but there was no mistaking Scratch. As far as Bo could tell, his old friend was all right. He didn't see any bloodstains on Scratch's clothes, and the silver-haired Texan was riding easily enough.

Big, shaggy Chet Ryan came next, followed by the three hard cases leading the packhorses. Brubaker leaned closer to Bo and whispered, "Where in blazes is Gentry?"

"Blazes is probably right," Bo replied, equally quietly. "The fire must have gotten him."

All the other members of the gang seemed to be fine, other than some coughing and sniffling from breathing too much smoke. At the front of the group, Cara rode with her head held high, and her attitude made it clear that she was now in charge of this bunch. Bo supposed that she had inherited leadership of the gang from Hank Gentry.

That didn't really matter. What was important was that the surviving members of the gang were here, and so was the loot they had come after. This was the chance to round them up and recover the stolen money. They wouldn't be expecting anyone else to be around in this burned-out devastation.

Bo looked over at Brubaker. The deputy nodded, tightened his hands on his rifle, and suddenly stood up, leveling the Winchester at the outlaws.

"Hold it right there!" Brubaker bellowed. "You're under arrest!"

CHAPTER 33

Scratch had seldom been more surprised—or more relieved—than he was when Bo and Brubaker stood up from behind those rocks and threw down on the gang.

After leaving the little cavelike area under the overhang and seeing the terrible destruction that the wildfire had wreaked on the countryside, Scratch had figured that nothing could have lived through it. If Bo and Brubaker had been caught out here, surely they had perished.

But that wasn't the case, he now knew. He had never seen two more muddy, bedraggled figures, but they were definitely alive.

For now.

But that might not be the case for very long, because Cara whipped up her rifle and the other outlaws clawed at their guns as the blonde screamed, "Those damn lawmen! Kill them!"

She kicked her horse and caused the animal to

leap aside just as Brubaker fired. The bullet went harmlessly past her.

Cara didn't return Brubaker's fire. She let the others do that, as a storm of lead from Bouchard, Ryan, and the other three hard cases made Bo and the deputy leap for cover behind the rocks again.

Cara swung her Winchester toward Scratch instead.

"You double-crosser!" she cried. "You led them to us somehow!"

That wasn't exactly true. That had been the plan, all right, but fate had intervened. Because of the apocalyptic blaze, Scratch had never had the chance to send any sort of signal to his friends. But that same fate, and stubbornly sticking to the general plan they had worked out, had brought Bo and Brubaker across their trail anyway.

Scratch palmed out his Remingtons and guided his horse with his knees as he sent the animal plunging to the side. Cara's rifle cracked, but the shot missed. Scratch heard the slug scream past his ear. He brought up both pistols and triggered them. It was too late to worry about the fact that he was shooting at a woman.

Bouchard's horse gave a skittish leap just as Scratch fired, taking him into the path of one of the bullets from the silver-haired Texan's guns. The slug smashed into Bouchard's right shoulder from behind and rocked him forward in the saddle as he cried out in pain.

Scratch's other shot missed Cara, who whirled her

mount and kicked it into a run. A gray cloud of ashes boiled up behind her as she galloped across the hellish landscape.

Scratch hated to leave Bo when he had just seen his old pard for the first time in days, but he didn't want Cara to get away. He sent his horse leaping past Bouchard's wildly cavorting mount and leaned forward in the saddle as he pounded after her. He pouched his left-hand iron and used that hand to grip the reins.

He was a little surprised that Cara was fleeing. He would have said that she was crazy enough, she would want to stay and fight it out. But maybe for once self-preservation had gotten the best of the insane rage that filled her.

Regardless of the reason, Scratch knew he had come too far to let her get away now. He urged his horse on as the two riders tore across the burned landscape at breakneck speed.

Bo's Winchester kicked hard against his shoulder as he knelt behind the rock and fired. He worked the rifle's lever so fast it was a blur. His bullets sprayed across the space between him and the outlaws. One of the men with the packhorses pitched out of the saddle as a slug tore through him.

Next to Bo, Brubaker kept up a deadly fire as well. Bouchard was wounded, and that made it hard for him to control his plunging horse. The deputy drew a bead on him and pressed the trigger. Bouchard's head jerked as the lawman's bullet drilled him.

Outlaw lead whined all around them. Brubaker suddenly grunted and went over backward. Bo glanced over at him.

"I'm all right, damn it!" Brubaker yelled. "Keep shootin'!"

Bo knew that Brubaker was hit, but they were still outnumbered three to two. There wasn't time to check on how badly the deputy was hurt. Bo swung his rifle and lined the sights on Ryan's broad chest. Ryan's six-gun spurted flame at the same instant that Bo's rifle cracked.

The black Stetson flew off Bo's head with a neat hole through its crown from Ryan's bullet. Bo's shot had found its mark. Ryan rocked back in the saddle as the bullet drove into his chest.

But he didn't fall. Instead, roaring out his defiance, he sent his horse lunging forward, straight at the rocks where Bo and Brubaker had taken cover. He kept firing, slamming shots at the two of them.

Brubaker had made it back to his knees. His left arm was clumsy because that was where the bullet had ripped through his flesh, but Bo could tell the bone wasn't broken because Brubaker managed to lift his rifle again. He and Brubaker both fired, and Ryan jerked again, more bloodstains springing out on the outlaw's buckskin shirt like crimson flowers opening.

Ryan still didn't go down. His bullets whined off the rock that shielded Bo and Brubaker, coming close enough to make them dive to the sides, one in each direction. Lying on his side on the ground, Bo triggered off the last two rounds in the Winchester. One of them smashed through Ryan's throat and traveled upward at an extreme angle through his brain.

That was finally enough to kill the big man. He dropped his gun and flew out of the saddle as his horse came to an abrupt, skidding halt. The massive body crashed facedown across the rock where Bo and Brubaker had taken cover.

Lying on his belly, Brubaker sighted in on one of the remaining outlaws and broke the man's right arm with a well-placed slug. That left just one of them, and as Bo tossed his empty rifle aside and came up with Colt in hand, that man turned to light a shuck out of there. Bo sent two shots racketing over his head. The outlaw hauled back on the reins and then thrust his hands into the air.

"Don't shoot!" he cried. "I give up, damn it! Don't shoot!"

Brubaker was already drawing a bead on the man. Bo said, "He's surrendering, Forty-two. You shoot him now and it'll be murder."

"Not if nobody knows about it," Brubaker said. He growled in disgust. "But I reckon you're right. I ain't in the habit of gunnin' down prisoners, no matter what some of those no-account lawyers back in Fort Smith would have you believe."

Bo kept the remaining owlhoot covered as he approached and said, "Get your guns on the ground, mister, and be mighty careful about it. I may need an excuse to shoot you, but I don't need much of one."

"I'm not gonna give you any," the outlaw said. He dropped his pistol on the ground, then used his left hand to pull his rifle from the saddle boot and toss it aside, too.

Brubaker checked on the other men and made sure they were dead while Bo got the remaining outlaw off his horse and tied his hands behind his back. He marched the man back to the rocks and had him sit down on one of them.

"All the others are done for," Brubaker announced, "and those packhorses have run off. We're gonna have to catch some of the saddle mounts and round them up."

"What about Scratch and Cara?" Bo asked.

The deputy shook his head.

"They're gone. She took off for the tall and uncut, and Morton went after her. I lost sight of 'em while we were swappin' lead with the others."

Bo's forehead creased in a worried frown.

Brubaker went on, "I don't know if he was tryin' to capture her, or if he's really thrown in with her."

"Scratch would never do that," Bo said without a shred of doubt. "He'll bring her back . . . or die trying."

A second later, as a flurry of shots rang out in the distance, he wished he hadn't said that.

* * *

The fire had burned off all the vegetation, but it hadn't had any effect on the basic terrain. The ridges, the gullies, the rocks all remained, and they prevented Scratch and Cara from racing their horses at top speed.

Scratch stayed stubbornly behind her, matching her pace as best he could. At any moment, either of the horses might take a spill in this rugged landscape, but somehow the animals managed to avoid that.

Cara topped a rise and disappeared. Scratch reached the crest a moment later and expected to see her descending the far slope.

Instead, as his eyes scanned the burned-out wasteland, he didn't spot her. The land fell away in front of him for about a mile in a series of natural terraces, and at the bottom lay a wide stream dotted with sandbars.

That was the Brazos River, Scratch realized. On the other side of it, more hills rose, but these held at least a hint of green. The drought had muted the color, but it was there, signifying that the fire hadn't burned that side of the river. The blaze must have started somewhere around here, Scratch thought.

He didn't really care about that. What mattered was that Cara seemed to have disappeared into thin air. That just wasn't possible, Scratch told himself as he reined in and twisted his head from side to side, searching for her.

He didn't see the little gully tucked away in a fold of the hills until she fired at him from it. Powder smoke spurted as the shot rang out. At the same instant, Scratch heard the wind-rip of the bullet past his ear.

The Remington in his hand roared as he kicked his horse down the slope toward the gully. He squeezed off three shots that had Cara ducking for cover.

Scratch was on top of the gully before he realized it. Suddenly aware that his horse couldn't stop in time, he booted the animal's flanks again and sent it lunging into the air in a daring leap that carried horse and rider all the way over the gully.

The horse landed awkwardly, though, and lost its footing. Scratch yanked his feet out of the stirrups and left the saddle in a dive. A cloud of ashes rose around him and choked him as he landed on his shoulder and rolled. Pain shot through him. His old bones didn't take kindly to such punishment.

But he was all right, and he came up on a knee with both guns drawn as Cara burst out of the gully mounted on her horse. The revolver in her hand blasted at him. He threw himself to the side and returned the fire as her bullets smacked into the ground beside him, kicking up dirt and more ashes.

She was past him in the blink of an eye. Scratch's right-hand Remington was empty, but the left-hand gun still held a couple of rounds. He lifted it and squeezed them off just as she twisted in the saddle and flung one final shot back at him.

Scratch had time to see her body jerk as if she were hit, then something slammed into his head with tremendous force, knocking him down so that he was stretched out on his back. He tried to get up, but his muscles refused to obey him. The fire must have started up again, he thought crazily, because red, leaping flames seemed to fill his brain. He was vaguely aware that the drumming of hoofbeats continued, then a terrible roaring sound welled up and drowned them out. That roar was his own blood inside his skull, he realized.

And Cara was getting away. There was nothing he could do to stop her now. Consciousness had started to slip away from him, and when it went, it would probably take his life with it, he knew.

"S-sorry, Bo . . ." he whispered through lips crusted with bitter ashes.

Then the darkness took him.

CHAPTER 34

There had been a drought in East Texas, too, but nowhere near as bad as the one that gripped the country west of Fort Worth. So even though it was still winter, the countryside around Tyler was considerably greener than it had been over there in the Palo Pinto Hills where Bo, Scratch, and Brubaker had fought their battle with the Gentry gang.

The three men looked considerably better, too, as they left the courthouse. They were dressed in clean clothes again, Bo had a new hat to replace the one with the hole shot through it, and although Brubaker's left arm was in a black silk sling and Scratch had a bandage around his head so that he had to wear his hat cuffed back a little, those were the only outward signs of their injuries. Bo hadn't been wounded at all during the ruckus.

All three men were still a little hoarse when they talked, though, and from time to time fits of coughing seized them.

One such fit struck Brubaker now. The deputy

stopped and pulled a handkerchief from his pocket, coughing into it until the spasms subsided. He glared at the dark stains on the handkerchief and rasped, "I think I'm gonna be coughin' up ashes the rest of my borned days."

"You'll get over it sooner or later, Forty-two," Bo told him.

"Yeah, but it'll be a long time before the smell of smoke stops givin' you the fantods," Scratch added. "Maybe never. I feel the same way."

"Well, at least the job's done now," Brubaker said as he put away his handkerchief. "And none too soon to suit me. I'll be glad to get back to Fort Smith. I plan on headin' that direction as soon as I've seen the sentence carried out, so I can tell Judge Parker I saw the last of the Gentry gang swing with my own eyes."

"Only it ain't the last of 'em, is it?" Scratch asked quietly.

"You said you thought you hit Cara with your last shot," Bo pointed out. "She may not have made it."

The three of them had just come from Judge Josiah Southwick's courtroom, where the esteemed federal jurist that Bo and Scratch still knew from their youth as "Bigfoot" had sentenced Dayton Lowe, Jim Elam, and Cutter Brown to be hanged by the neck until dead. Brown was the outlaw who had surrendered in the violent aftermath of the wildfire, but he had only postponed his fate by doing so.

Bo had galloped over the hills and found Scratch lying unconscious on the slope overlooking the Brazos River. Blood and ashes had painted a ghastly pallor over Scratch's face, but he'd been breathing, and once Bo had cleaned up the wound he had seen that his old friend was only grazed on the side of the head, enough to knock him out but not enough to kill him. When Scratch had come to, Bo had informed him that that cast-iron skull of his had saved his life again.

"Cara got away," Scratch had said then, bothered by that more than he was the head wound.

"I know," Bo said. "But wherever she is, she's somebody else's problem now."

It had taken the rest of the day to round up some horses and recover those pack animals loaded down with stolen loot. Bo found his horse, which had survived the fire although its hide was singed in places. They never found any sign of Brubaker's mount.

Nobody wanted to spend the night out there in that smoky wasteland, so they had ridden through the darkness back to Weatherford with their prisoner. The wildfire had burned itself out before it reached the town, but it had left a wide swath of devastation through the Cross Timbers. The area would be a long time recovering from this . . . but as Bo had said, it *would* recover.

From Weatherford, Brubaker sent a wire to Fort Smith explaining the situation to Judge Parker. Brubaker kept the details of the judge's reply to himself, but Bo got the feeling that Parker had pretty well burned up the telegraph wires.

Brubaker didn't seem worried, though. With the exception of Cara LaChance, the entire Gentry gang was either scattered, wiped out, or due to hang, so they no longer posed a threat to Indian Territory.

Losing Cara was a bitter pill to swallow, but telegrams would go out to the chief marshals across the frontier, warning them to have their men keep an eye out for her. If she was still alive, she would turn up sooner or later.

The local sawbones had insisted on keeping Scratch in the hospital for a couple of days "to make sure that bullet didn't addle your brain any more than it already was to start with," as Bo put it. When the doctor pronounced Scratch well enough to travel, the three of them set out for Gainesville, taking their prisoner with them.

Once there, they had picked up Brubaker's wagon, loaded Lowe and Elam into it along with Brown, and headed for Tyler to finish the long journey at last. Brubaker told the local lawman to go ahead and release Early Nesbit, since they didn't have to worry about Hank Gentry coming after them anymore.

Scratch had told them how Cara killed Gentry, confirming for all of them, as if they needed confirmation, that the blonde was plumb loco.

When they reached Tyler, Bo and Scratch had had a rather uproarious reunion with Bigfoot Southwick, who momentarily lost the dignity that normally accrued to a federal judge and slapped his old friends on the back, boisterously bellowing, "Bo Creel and Scratch Morton! Hell, I figured some other judge would've hung you sidewindin' scoundrels a long time ago!"

"There wouldn't be no justice in that," Scratch had told him with a grin. "If anybody should've shook hands with the hangman, it's you, Bigfoot."

"You can call me that once," the burly, white-bearded Southwick had said, holding up a finger, "but if you do it again, I'll have to hold you in contempt of court!"

Now as the three men paused on the steps of the courthouse following the conclusion of the speedy trial, Brubaker asked, "Are you gonna stay to watch the hangin', too?"

Scratch made a face and shook his head.

"I've never cared overmuch for hangin's," he said.

"We'll trust you to see that justice is done, Forty-two," Bo added.

A rare smile appeared on the deputy's face.

"You know, we never did play a game," he said.

"You need four people for that," Scratch pointed out.

"I know. One of the jailers said he'd be glad to sit in and make a fourth. We'd have to play at the jail, though, while he's on duty tonight."

Bo smiled and said, "I guess we could stay around that long."

They started down the steps. As they did so, a buggy pulled up in the street. A little old lady in a black dress and shawl was handling the reins. Beside her sat another elderly woman dressed the same way.

Bo's eyes suddenly narrowed as he caught a glimpse of bright yellow hair under the second woman's shawl. His instincts shot a warning through him, and he was already reaching for his Colt as he shouted to his companions, "Look out!"

Cara LaChance leaped from the buggy, throwing back the shawl so that her blond curls spilled free around her shoulders. Her hands dipped and came up with a pair of revolvers from the folds of her dress. Her beautiful face was twisted in a snarl of bloodlust that turned it ugly as she began to fire. Flame jetted from the muzzles of both guns.

Brubaker rammed a shoulder against Scratch and knocked him aside. The deputy grunted and stumbled as lead thudded into his body. Scratch caught his balance and whipped out both Remingtons. Bo's Colt was already in his hand. Gun-thunder rolled across the courthouse steps as the three revolvers roared in unison.

The bullets smashed Cara to the ground. Behind her, the old woman who had driven up in the buggy shrieked, "Don't kill me! She made me bring her here! Please don't kill me!"

She didn't wait to see whether anybody was going to shoot at her. She slashed the whip at the buggy horse and sent it down the street with the buggy careening behind it.

Brubaker had crumpled to the steps. Scratch dropped to a knee beside him and exclaimed, "Damn it, Forty-two, how bad are you hit?"

"I . . . I don't know," Brubaker said through gritted teeth. "It hurts like hell."

Scratch pulled the lawman's coat back and reached inside it to check the wound. He let out a laugh.

Brubaker glared up at him and said, "I'm glad my dyin' . . . strikes you as funny."

"I don't think you're dyin'," Scratch said. "Looks like Cara only hit you once, and the bullet busted the hell out of that set of dominoes in your coat pocket before it went on in. The slug didn't penetrate very far. I can feel it with my finger."

"If that don't . . . beat all," Brubaker gasped. "Still hurts, though."

Meanwhile Bo had gone on down to the bottom of the steps, keeping Cara covered as he did so. Her blue eyes still held some life in them when he reached her, but it was fading fast.

"You just had to have your revenge, didn't you?" Bo said.

"You can . . . go to hell!" Cara gasped. She laughed. "You and Morton both! And when you get there . . . I'll be waitin' for you!"

Her face twisted, her back arched, and when she relaxed a second later, she was gone.

A crowd was gathering, and a lot of people were yelling questions. It wasn't every day there was a shoot-out right in front of the courthouse.

Bo had a question of his own: what turned a smart, beautiful young woman like Cara LaChance into a mad-dog killer?

He knew he would never have an answer. He wasn't sure one even existed.

He turned, holstered his gun, and started back up the steps, glad to see that Brubaker was sitting up with Scratch's arm around his shoulders. The deputy didn't look like he was hurt too bad.

Maybe they would get that game in, after all, before he and Scratch started south toward home.

Turn the page for an exciting preview!

William W. Johnstone's legendary mountain men have fought their battles and conquered a fierce frontier. Now, three generations of the Jensen clan are trying to live in peace on their sprawling Colorado ranch. But for men with fighting in their blood, trouble is never very far . . .

INTO THE EYE OF A STORM

They are strangers in a strange land—a band of German immigrants trespassing across the Jensen family spread. Led by a baron fleeing a dark past in Germany and accompanied by a woman beautiful enough to dazzle young Matt, the pilgrims are being pursued by a pack of brutal outlaws hungry for blood, money—or maybe something else . . . The Jensens are willing to help the pioneers get to Wyoming. But they don't know the whole story of their newfound friends, or who the outlaws really are. By the time the wagon train reaches Wyoming the truth is ready to explode—in a clash of hard fighting and hard deaths in a violent land . . .

The Family Jensen:
The Violent Land

By William W. Johnstone
with J.A. Johnstone

On sale now, wherever
Kensington Books are sold!

CHAPTER 1

The seven men rode into Big Rock, Colorado, a few minutes before noon. Nobody in the bustling little cowtown paid much attention to them. Everyone went on about their own business, even when the men reined their horses to a halt and dismounted in front of the bank.

Clete Murdock was their leader, a craggy-faced man with graying red hair who over the past ten years had robbed banks in five states and a couple of territories. He had killed enough men that he'd lost track of the number, especially if you threw Indians and Mexicans into the count.

His younger brothers Tom and Grant rode with him. Tom was a slightly younger version of Clete, but Grant was the baby of the family, a freckle-faced youngster in his twenties who wanted more than anything else in the world to be a desperado like his brothers.

Until a year or so earlier he had lived on the family farm in Kansas with their parents, but illness had struck down both of the elder Murdocks in the span of a few days, so Grant had set out to find his black-sheep brothers and throw in with them.

Ed Garvey was about as broad as he was tall, with a bristling black spade beard. He wasn't much good with a handgun. That was why he carried a sawed-off shotgun under his coat. As long as his partners in crime gave him plenty of room, he was a valuable ally. They were careful not to get in his line of fire when he pulled out that street sweeper.

The tall, skinny towhead with the eye that sometimes drifted off crazily was Chick Bowman. The loco eye gave him the look of somebody who might not be right in the head, but in reality Chick was fairly smart for an outlaw who'd had very little schooling in his life.

The one who wasn't all there was Denny McCoy, who followed Chick around like a devoted pup. Denny was big and barrel chested, and he had accidentally killed two whores by fondling their necks with such enthusiasm that they couldn't breathe anymore. Chick had gotten Denny out of both of those scrapes without getting either of them lynched.

The member of the gang who had been with Clete the longest was a Crow who called himself Otter. He had worked as a scout for the army, but after coming too damned close to being with Custer when old Yellow Hair went traipsing up the Little Big Horn to his death, Otter had decided that the military life wasn't for him. He knew Clete, who had been a sergeant before deserting, and had looked him up.

Clete's prejudice against redskins didn't extend to Otter, the only man he knew who took more pure pleasure in killing than he did.

As the group tied up their horses at the hitch rack in front of the bank, Otter moved closer to Clete and said quietly, "Lawman."

Clete followed the direction the Crow's eyes were indicating and saw a burly, middle-aged man moving along the boardwalk several buildings away.

"Yeah, I see him," Clete said. "His name's Monte Carson. Used to have sort of a name as a fast gun, but he's been totin' a badge here for several years and people have pretty much forgotten about him. I wouldn't underestimate him, but I don't reckon he poses much of a problem for us, either."

"Anything goes wrong, I'll kill him first," Otter said.

Clete nodded in agreement. Otter would stay with the horses and watch the street. If shots erupted in the bank, the Crow would lift his rifle and drill Sheriff Monte Carson immediately so he couldn't interfere with the gang's getaway.

Otherwise, Otter would wait until the other outlaws left the bank, and if anyone tried to follow them and raise a ruckus, *then* he would kill Carson.

Either way, there was a very good chance the sheriff would die in the next few minutes.

Clete glanced at everyone else and got nods of readiness from all of them except Denny, who just did what Chick told him to, anyway. The six of them stepped up onto the boardwalk and moved toward the bank's double doors.

Otter's head turned slowly as his gaze roamed from one end of the street to the other. This town had been peaceful for too long, he thought wryly. If that hadn't been the case, someone surely would have noticed the seven human wolves who had ridden in together, not even trying to mask their intentions as they closed in on the bank.

Otter frowned slightly as he thought about the name of the town. Big Rock . . . There was something familiar about that. He knew he had heard of the place for some reason. But he couldn't put his finger on exactly what it was.

It didn't matter, anyway. After today Big Rock would be famous because the Murdock gang had cleaned out the bank and killed a few of the citizens.

A broad-shouldered, sandy-haired man in range clothes rode past on a big gray stallion. Otter noticed the horse—a fine one, indeed—but paid little attention to the rider, even when the man reined in and spoke to the sheriff. Otter couldn't hear the conversation between Carson and the broad-shouldered man.

He didn't think any more about it, convinced of its utter unimportance.

"Matt and Preacher are coming here?" Sheriff Monte Carson asked with a grin.

"That's right," Smoke Jensen said as he rested his hands on his saddlehorn and leaned forward to ease his muscles after the ride into Big Rock from his ranch, Sugarloaf. "In fact, they should be riding in today, according to the letter I got from Matt."

"I'll be glad to see 'em again," Monte said. "Good Lord, Preacher must be a hundred years old by now!"

Smoke chuckled.

"He's not quite that long in the tooth yet, and he never has looked or acted as old as he is. I reckon he'll slow down one of these days, but the last time I saw him he seemed as spry as ever."

Sometimes it seemed to Smoke that he had known the old mountain man called Preacher his entire life. It was hard to remember that he had been sixteen years old when he and his pa first ran into Preacher, not long after the Civil War. Preacher had been lean, leathery, and white haired even then, and he hadn't seemed to age a day in the years since.

It was Preacher who had first called him Smoke, after seeing young Kirby Jensen handle a gun. So fast that the sight of his draw was as elusive as smoke, Preacher claimed. The young man's hand was empty, and then there was a gun in it spitting fire and lead, and there seemed to be no step in between. Preacher had predicted then that Smoke would become one of the fastest men with a gun the frontier had ever known, and he was right.

But Smoke was one of the few men who had overcome his reputation as a gunfighter and built a respectable life for himself. Marrying the beautiful schoolteacher Sally Reynolds, whom he had met while he was living the life of a wanted outlaw under the name Buck West, probably had a lot to do with that. So had establishing the fine spread known as Sugarloaf and settling down to become a cattleman.

Despite that, trouble still had a way of finding Smoke. He had to use his gun more often than he liked. But he hadn't been raised to run away from a challenge, and anybody who thought that Smoke Jensen wasn't dangerous anymore would be in for an abrupt awakening if they threatened him or those he loved.

An abrupt and usually fatal awakening.

Preacher wasn't the only visitor headed for Big Rock. He and Matt Jensen had agreed to meet in Denver and come on to the settlement together. In the same way that Preacher was Smoke's adopted father, Matt was his adopted brother, although there was nothing official about it in either case. Smoke had taken Matt under his wing when the youngster was still a boy, the only survivor from a family murdered by outlaws, and with Preacher's help had raised him into a fine young man who took the Jensen name when he set out on his own.

Although still relatively young in years, Matt had gained a wealth of experience, both while he was still with Smoke and afterward. He had already drifted over much of the frontier and had worked as a deputy, a shotgun guard, and a scout. He had tangled with outlaws, renegade Indians, and badmen of every stripe.

Twice in the fairly recent past, Smoke, Matt, and Preacher had been forced by circumstances to team up to defeat the schemes of a group of crooked politicians and businessmen that had formed out of the ashes of the old Indian Ring. This new Indian Ring was just as vicious as the original, maybe even more so, and even though they seemed to be licking their wounds after those defeats, Smoke had a hunch they would try something else again, sooner or later.

He hoped they wouldn't interfere with this visit from Preacher and Matt. It would be nice to get together with his family without a bunch of gunplay and danger.

Those thoughts were going through Smoke's mind as he realized that Monte Carson had asked him a question. He gave a little shake of his head and said, "What was that, Monte?"

"I just asked what time Matt and Preacher are supposed to get here," the sheriff said.

"I don't know for sure. They're riding in, and I figure they'll be moseying along. Preacher doesn't get in a hurry unless there's a good reason to. I thought I'd go over to the café, get something to eat, then find something to occupy my time while I'm waiting for them."

Monte grinned.

"Come on by the office," he said. "We'll have us a game of dominoes."

Smoke was just about to accept that invitation when gunshots suddenly erupted somewhere down the street.

CHAPTER 2

There were several customers in the bank when Clete and his men walked in, but they didn't appear to be the sort to give problems. The men looked like storekeepers, and a woman stood at one of the teller's windows, too, probably some clerk's wife depositing butter and egg money.

The two tellers were the usual: pale, weak hombres not suited for doing a real man's work, or anything else. At a desk off to one side sat the bank president, fat and pompous in a suit that wasn't quite big enough for him.

Clete hated all of them, just by looking at them. They were sheep, and he was a wolf. They deserved to have their money taken away from them, to his way of thinking.

And their lives, too, if they got in his way.

The banker glanced up from his desk as the men entered the bank, then looked again with his eyes widening in shock and fear as he obviously realized what they were and what was about to happen. He started to get to his feet, but Clete already had his gun out and pointed it at the man.

"Stay right where you are, mister," Clete ordered. "We're just here for the money, not to kill anybody."

What he left unsaid was that he and the others wouldn't hesitate to kill anybody who interfered with them getting that money.

The other five men spread out and closed in around the customers. Ed Garvey swung his sawed-off toward the tellers, both of whom raised their hands in meek, fearful surrender.

Clete raised his voice and said, "Everybody just take it easy. No trouble here, no trouble. We just want the money. Tellers, clean out your drawers. Put everything in the sack."

With practiced efficiency, Tom Murdock had taken a canvas bag from under his coat. He shouldered aside the townie at one of the windows and thrust the bag across the counter toward the stunned teller.

"In the sack," Tom snarled at the teller, who swallowed hard and started plucking bills from his cash drawer and stuffing them into the bag.

Denny approached the female customer, who was fairly young and pretty. She was pale and trembling at the moment. She tried to shrink away from Denny as he stepped up to her, but she had her back against the counter and there was no place for her to go.

"Pretty," Denny said. His gun was in his right hand, but his left was free. He raised it and started to take hold of her neck. There was nothing he liked better than caressing a pretty woman's neck.

Chick said, "Not now, Denny, we ain't got time for that."

"Pretty!" Denny insisted, as if that explained everything.

"I know that, but—"

The woman screamed as Denny's hand was about to close around her throat.

Chick exclaimed, "Dadgum it, Denny!"

And on the other side of the counter, the teller shouted, "Leave her alone, damn you!"

His hand dropped below the counter, and when it came up, there was a Colt Lightning in it. The teller jerked the trigger three times fast, and the double-action revolver sent all three .41-caliber rounds crashing into Denny's face. The bullets turned the big man's features into a hideous red smear as his head rocked back.

"Denny!" Chick cried. Enraged, he started firing. His bullets sprayed the woman and the teller, knocking them both off their feet as blood welled from their wounds.

"Son of a bitch!" Clete bellowed. "Tom, grab all the money you can!" He turned back to the bank president, who had started impulsively to his feet, and shot the man in the belly.

Grant looked around wildly, unsure what to do. He had taken part in several robberies with his brothers, but none of them had gone this bad, this quickly. None of the gang had even been wounded in those jobs, let alone killed. Denny wasn't dead yet—he had fallen to the floor, where he was thrashing around—but he couldn't last long, shot in the head like that.

The other teller had thrown himself on the floor and lay there behind the counter with his arms held protectively over his head, as if that would stop a bullet. Tom Murdock didn't take the time to shoot him. Instead, as Tom leaned over the counter, he reached into the cash drawer and grabbed as many greenbacks as he could, stuffing them into the canvas sack. They would get *something* out of this foul-up, by God!

But who could have predicted that that meek little teller would try to turn into Wild Bill Hickok? The fella must have been sweet on the woman, and all he had thought about was protecting her from Denny.

The air inside the bank was thick with gunsmoke now. The sharp tang of it stung Clete's nose as he swung toward the doors.

"Let's go, let's go!" he called. He was confident that Otter would be covering their retreat.

"But Denny—" Chick began.

"He's done for!" Clete yelled. "Come on!"

The five men charged out through the double doors, guns up and ready for trouble.

They weren't ready for what they got.

Reacting instantly, Smoke twisted in the saddle to search for the source of the shots. They were coming from the direction of the bank, and as Smoke spotted the seven horses tied at the hitch rack in front of that establishment, his mind leaped to the conclusion that the bank was being robbed.

The sight of a stranger, a tall, lean Indian in a black hat, standing next to those horses was more evidence supporting that theory.

The fact that the Indian jerked a rifle to his shoulder and pointed it at Monte Carson confirmed the hunch.

That lookout was aiming at the wrong man. He should have paid more attention to the hombre on the big gray stallion. Smoke's Colt appeared in his hand as if by magic, and two shots blasted from it so close together they sounded like one.

Even though Smoke was firing from the hip and the distance was fairly long for a handgun, his almost supernatural abilities sent both slugs hammering into the Indian's chest. The rifle in the Indian's hands went off as his finger jerked involuntarily on the trigger, but the barrel was already pointing harmlessly at the sky as he toppled backward against one of the horses.

The animal shied and bumped into the other horses, and they got skittish, too. All seven mounts started jerking at their reins, trying to get loose and bolt.

Monte drew his gun and broke into a run toward the bank, but instead of dismounting, Smoke heeled his horse into motion. The stallion pounded down the street. Smoke arrived in front of the bank just as several men burst out through the doors.

The strangers were all carrying guns. The one in the lead saw Smoke and opened fire on him. Smoke ducked and snapped a shot at the man. The slug caught the bank robber in the shoulder and drove him halfway around. He stayed on his feet, though, and continued shooting.

One of the other men, a short, bearded, thick-bodied varmint, bulled forward and swung up a sawed-off Greener. Smoke saw the scattergun and went diving out of the saddle just as the awful weapon boomed like a huge clap of thunder. One of the horses screamed in pain as buckshot peppered its hide.

Smoke had landed in the street, rolled over, and come up on one knee. He had to throw himself to the side in order to avoid being trampled.

At the same time, bullets were still flying around him. Clouds of dust swirled, kicked up by the hooves of the fear-maddened horses. It was utter chaos in the street and on the boardwalk, as gun battles often were.

From the corner of his eye, Smoke caught a glimpse of Monte Carson kneeling behind a rain barrel and firing at the outlaws. One of the bank robbers, a tall, lanky man with fair hair under a thumbed-back hat, clutched at his middle and folded up as one of Monte's bullets punched into his belly.

Smoke had two rounds left in his Colt, since he always carried the gun with the hammer resting on an empty chamber unless he knew he was about to encounter trouble. He fired again and saw one of the outlaws go spinning off his feet as the bullet tore through his thigh.

Smoke shifted his aim and fired his last shot. It went into the chest of the man whose shoulder he had broken with a bullet a few seconds earlier. The man dropped his revolver, staggered a few steps to the side, and pitched off the boardwalk to land on his face in the street.

That left two of the outlaws on their feet, including the man with the sawed-off. He had broken the weapon open and was trying frantically to thumb more shells into it.

The remaining outlaw had a canvas bag clutched in his left hand and a Colt in his right. He threw a couple of shots at Smoke and lunged toward the horses, obviously hoping to grab one of them and make a getaway.

Smoke had to dive forward onto his belly to avoid the shots as the slugs whipped through the air above his head. He looked up and saw that the man had gotten hold of a horse and was trying to swing up into the saddle.

Smoke surged up onto his feet and jammed his empty Colt back in its holster as he went after the man trying to escape. With a diving tackle, he crashed into the outlaw and drove him away from the horse and off his feet. Both men sprawled in the dusty street as iron-shod hooves danced perilously close to their heads. Greenbacks flew from the canvas bag as it hit the ground.

The bank robber lashed out in desperation at

Smoke, who avoided the first blow but then caught a knobby fist on the jaw. He threw a punch of his own, hooking his right into the man's belly. The man gasped and tried to lift his knee into Smoke's groin, but Smoke twisted aside and took the blow on his thigh. He swung his left and landed it solidly on the man's nose. Blood spurted hotly across Smoke's knuckles.

The man arched his back and threw Smoke off. As Smoke rolled away, the outlaw grabbed up the gun he had dropped and aimed it at Smoke.

A shot blasted from the boardwalk, and the man crumpled, dropping the gun again. Smoke glanced over and saw Monte Carson lowering his revolver after the shot that had probably saved Smoke's life.

But that still left the shotgunner, who had snapped his weapon closed again and now swung it toward Smoke and Monte. Smoke's Colt was empty, and so was the sheriff's, as became evident when Monte jerked the trigger and the hammer fell with a harmless click. Smoke and Monte were close enough together that the outlaw might be able to cut them both down if he fired both barrels.

"You damn meddlin' sons o' bitches!" the outlaw roared as he brought his sawed-off to bear.

Before he could jerk the triggers, his head seemed to explode in a gory spray of blood, bone fragments, and brain matter. The scattergun fell unfired from his nerveless fingers, and his body dropped to the ground right behind it.

Unsure what had happened, Smoke looked along the street and saw two men sitting on horseback a couple of blocks away. One of them, a lean, white-bearded figure in buckskins and a broad-brimmed felt hat, lowered a Sharps carbine from the barrel of which curled a tendril of powder smoke.

The old-timer hitched his horse forward, rode up to Smoke, and grinned as he said, "You just can't stay outta trouble for any time at all, can you, boy?"

CHAPTER 3

"Preacher!" Smoke exclaimed. "You sure know how to show up at the right time."

"Always have," Preacher said, still grinning. "Might should've showed up a few minutes earlier, though, since you only left one of the varmints for me to kill. Heard the shots as we was ridin' in. Sounded like a right smart fracas. How come you was killin' 'em?"

"They tried to rob the bank," Smoke explained.

Preacher nodded. "Thought it might've been somethin' like that when I saw all them greenbacks scattered around."

Preacher's companion galloped up, threw himself out of the saddle, bounded onto the boardwalk, and swung a fist that crashed into the jaw of the lone surviving outlaw, who had pulled himself up onto his knees and was trying to lift his gun with a trembling hand. The young owlhoot went over backward, knocked cold by the powerful blow.

"While you two were flapping your gums, that varmint was about to shoot Preacher in the back," Matt Jensen said, looking exasperated.

"No, he wasn't," Preacher replied. "I figured you'd take care of him, Matt."

With a shake of his head, Matt asked, "What if I hadn't been paying attention?"

"I knew you would be," Preacher said simply. "Smoke and me taught you well enough."

"Well, I suppose that's true," Matt said with a shrug.

He was the tallest of the three men, a fair-haired, handsome youngster in a black Stetson and a faded-blue bib-front shirt. Most women naturally took a liking to Matt Jensen, and he returned the feeling.

With troublemakers, it was different. Matt carried a holstered Colt .44 double-action revolver on his right hip, and a Bowie knife was sheathed on his left. He didn't hesitate to use the weapons when he needed to, and he was almost as fast and deadly with a gun as his adopted older brother Smoke.

As Smoke thumbed fresh cartridges into his Colt to replace the ones he had fired, he said, "We're much obliged to both of you for your help, aren't we, Monte?"

"We sure are," Big Rock's sheriff agreed. He was reloading, too. As he snapped the cylinder of his gun closed, he went on, "I'd better check on the rest of those varmints and make sure they're all dead.

Gonna be wounded in the bank who need tending to as well, I'll bet."

"Why don't you go see about that?" Smoke suggested. "Preacher and Matt and I will take care of the chores out here."

Monte nodded and said, "Thanks." He hurried into the bank, which was ominously quiet.

Smoke and Matt went quickly from body to body, checking for signs of life. The young outlaw Matt had knocked out was the only one of the bank robbers still alive. He was wounded in the left leg and had lost quite a bit of blood, but Smoke thought he would probably live.

He rolled the unconscious outlaw onto his belly, pulled the man's arms behind his back, and used the outlaw's own belt to lash his wrists together for the time being. That way if he came to, he wouldn't be able to cause a problem.

Dr. Hiram Simpson, the local sawbones, came running from his office and joined several other townspeople in crowding into the bank to see what they could do to help. Monte Carson emerged from the building a few minutes later, his features pale and drawn.

"It's pretty bad in there," he told Smoke, Matt, and Preacher. "Jasper Davenport, who just took over running the bank, is dead. Didn't even make it in the job for a month before those blasted outlaws gunned him down. Mitchell Byrd's dead, too, and Elaine Harris is wounded. Got a dead outlaw in there with most of his face shot off. I reckon that's probably what started the battle. Appears that Mitch got his hands on a gun and shot the desperado."

Smoke trusted Monte's assessment of the situation. He asked, "Does it look like Miz Harris will make it?"

"The doc didn't say," Monte replied with a shake of his head.

Smoke pointed a thumb at the unconscious outlaw. "Well, when he's through in there, this fella's going to need some attention. Matt and I can go ahead and haul him over to the jail for you if you want, though."

Monte nodded and said, "That'd sure be giving me a hand. I'm obliged to you boys."

"Get his feet, Matt," Smoke said.

Smoke and Matt were both very strong, so they didn't have any trouble lifting the bank robber and toting him down the street to the sturdy building that housed Monte Carson's office and Big Rock's jail. All the cells were empty at the moment, so they carried the man into the one nearest the cell block door and placed him on the bunk. As soon as they had stepped out, Monte swung the barred door shut, closing it solidly.

Preacher had followed them into the sheriff's office.

"Beats me why you don't just let the rapscallion bleed to death," he commented when Smoke, Matt, and Monte left the cell block. "Saves the bother and expense of a trial and a hangin'."

"That's not the way the law works, Preacher," Monte said. "It's mighty good to see you again, by the way. You, too, Matt."

"It's good to be here," Matt said. "It's been too long since the three of us have gotten together."

Monte asked, "You fellas want some coffee?"

"I figure we'll go over to the café and have some lunch before we head out to Sugarloaf," Smoke said. "So no thanks to the coffee, but we're obliged for the offer. Were you able to find out what happened inside the bank, Monte?"

The sheriff nodded.

"There were a couple of customers who didn't get hit when the bullets started flying, and the other teller, Fred Reeves, was all right, too. They all hit the dirt, or the floor, rather, when the shooting started. Seems the outlaw who was still inside the bank tried to molest Mrs. Harris. Mitch Byrd had a Colt Lightning on the shelf under his counter. He grabbed it and shot the owlhoot, but that set off the others. I reckon it's only pure luck that it wasn't an even bigger massacre in there."

Smoke shook his head regretfully.

"It's too bad we weren't able to save more of the citizens," he said. "But at least the gang didn't get away."

"Did you recognize any of the bank robbers, Monte?" Matt asked.

"A couple of them looked familiar to me," the lawman said. "I must've seen their pictures on reward dodgers. I've got a big pile of those posters in the desk. I'll go through them later and see if I can match up any names with the faces. Could be you and Preacher have some rewards coming, Smoke."

The old mountain man snorted disdainfully.

"I don't care about no dadblamed ree-ward," he said. "I've had fortunes come an' go through my fingers so many times over the years, money don't mean nothin' to me as long as I've got enough for a meal and a snort o' whiskey now and then."

"And Sugarloaf's doing just fine," Smoke put in, "turning a profit every year, and I expect that to keep up as long as we don't have a bad drought. Maybe Matt should claim the rewards."

"Me?" Matt exclaimed. "I didn't do anything except wallop one of them."

"Those wanted posters all say dead or alive," Monte pointed out. "You ought to at least get paid for the one you laid out, Matt. I'll look into it."

"All right," Matt said, "but I didn't do it for the money. I was just trying to save Preacher's scrawny old hide."

"I told you, I knowed he was back there—"

Smoke cut in on the old-timer's protest.

"Come on, let's get something to eat, and then we'll head for the ranch."

They were about to leave the sheriff's office when the door opened and Dr. Simpson came in.

Smoke paused long enough to ask, "How's Miz Harris doing, Doc?"

"I think there's a good chance she'll pull through," Simpson replied. "She was wounded in the arm and the hip. The arm wound should heal cleanly. The injury to her hip may result in her having a permanent limp. It's too soon to say. She's been taken down to my house, and my nurse is looking after her." The sawbones turned to Monte Carson. "I was told you have a wounded prisoner here, Sheriff."

"Sure do," Monte agreed. "I'll take you back to his cell." He raised a hand in farewell to Smoke, Matt, and Preacher. "See you boys later."

When they were on the boardwalk outside, Matt chuckled and said, "Sheriff Carson must be having trouble with his eyes if he called you a boy, Preacher."

"I reckon so," the old mountain man agreed, "since he didn't notice you was a snot-nosed, wet-behind-the-ears kid, neither."

Smoke grinned and said, "Come on, you two. You can continue this squabble after we've had a surroundin'."

They walked across the street to the café. A crowd was still gathered around the bank. Smoke supposed that the surviving teller was running things for now.

The café was doing a brisk business since it was the middle of the day, and most of the people in there were talking excitedly about the attempted bank robbery and the resulting shoot-out.

Smoke ignored the curious looks the townspeople cast at him and his companions. He had long since gotten used to being gawked at, especially when some trouble had broken out and he'd been in the middle of it.

The three of them sat at a table covered with a blue-checked cloth and ordered meals consisting of roast beef, potatoes, greens, biscuits, and deep dish apple pie.

"And keep the coffee comin'," Preacher told the smiling waitress, who promised to do so.

"How's Sally doing?" Matt asked while they were waiting for their food.

"She's fine," Smoke said. "Anxious to see you fellas again, I expect."

Preacher said, "How about them hands of your'n?"

"Cal and Pearlie?" Smoke grinned. "As quarrelsome as ever. They wouldn't know what to do if they weren't squabbling."

In that respect, Smoke's foreman Pearlie and the young ranch hand Calvin Woods reminded him of a couple of other hombres, namely Preacher and Matt.

"We saw something interesting while we were riding up here," Matt said. "Did you know there's a wagon train headed in this direction, Smoke?"

The grin on Smoke's face was replaced by a puzzled expression.

"This is the first I've heard of it," he said.

"I saw dozens of wagon trains when I was a younger man," Preacher said. "Maybe a hundred or more. Traveled with a few of 'em, too. Them pilgrims wasn't always the smartest folks when it came to gettin' along on the frontier, but they was determined to build new lives for themselves, I'll give 'em that much. Shoot, I guess ever'body was a greenhorn once."

Matt said, "I thought you didn't like all the immigrants who moved west. You said they civilized places too much and changed everything from the way it was back in the Shining Times."

"Well, that's true," Preacher said. "They did, and I ain't overfond of that so-called civilization they brung with 'em. But you can't stop things from changin'. It'll happen while you ain't even lookin'."

Smoke asked, "You didn't talk to the people with the wagon train, did you?"

"Nope," Preacher said. "We just waved at 'em and went on our way."

Matt said, "Why do you ask, Smoke?"

With a shrug, Smoke replied, "I was just curious where they're bound, that's all. I'm not aware of any land around here being opened recently for settlement."

Some of the Sugarloaf stock grazed on open range, but Smoke knew that concept was dying out in the West. More and more land was being claimed officially, instead of just being there for anybody who wanted to use it. The day was coming, he knew, when cattlemen would have to file claims for the range they were using and fence it in. He didn't like the thought of it, but like Preacher said, things changed whether a fella wanted them to or not.

"I wouldn't worry about that wagon train," Matt said. "Chances are it's headed for somewhere north of here. Wyoming, maybe, or even Montana."

"You're probably right," Smoke said. He saw the waitress carrying a tray loaded down with food toward their table and put the subject out of his thoughts with the casual comment, "Anyway, those immigrants don't have anything to do with us."